mancer

-mar

cer

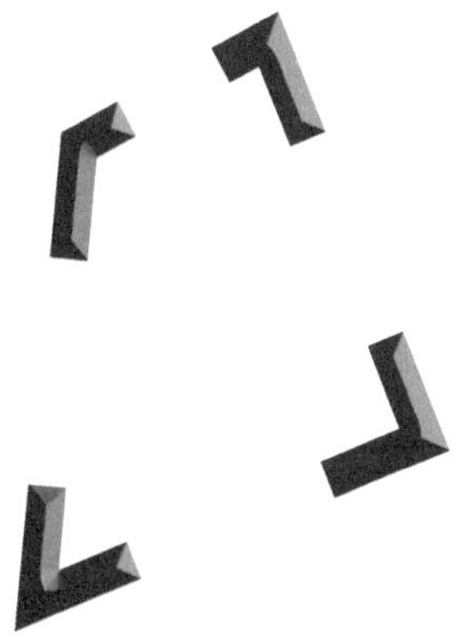

MIKE CORRAO,
LENOVO Y50-70, Model 2015

"-MANCER"

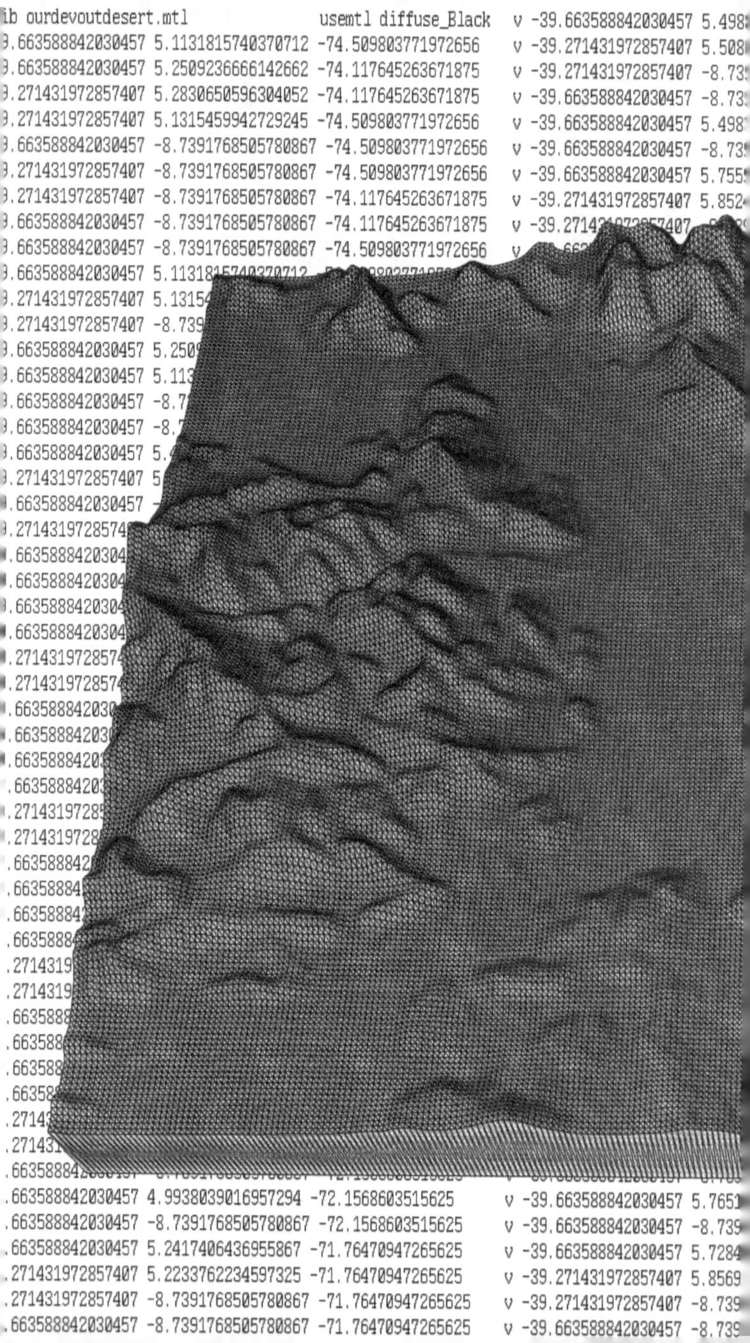
ib ourdevoutdesert.mtl
usemtl diffuse_Black
v -39.663588842030457 5.498
9.663588842030457 5.1131815740370712 -74.509803771972656
9.663588842030457 5.2509236666142662 -74.117645263671875
9.271431972857407 5.2830650596304052 -74.117645263671875
9.271431972857407 5.1315459942729245 -74.509803771972656
9.663588842030457 -8.7391768505780867 -74.509803771972656
9.271431972857407 -8.7391768505780867 -74.509803771972656
9.271431972857407 -8.7391768505780867 -74.117645263671875
9.663588842030457 -8.7391768505780867 -74.117645263671875
9.663588842030457 -8.7391768505780867 -74.509803771972656
9.663588842030457 5.1131815740370712
9.271431972857407 5.13154
9.271431972857407 -8.739
9.663588842030457 5.2509
9.663588842030457 5.113
9.663588842030457 -8.7
9.663588842030457 -8.7
9.663588842030457 5.
9.271431972857407 5
9.663588842030457
9.271431972857
9.663588842030
9.663588842030
9.663588842030
9.663588842030
9.271431972857
9.271431972857
9.663588842030
9.663588842030
9.663588420
9.663588420
9.271431972857
9.271431972857
9.663588842
9.6635888
9.663588842
9.663588
9.2714319
9.2714319
9.663588
9.663588
9.663588
9.66358
9.27143
9.27143
9.663588842

v -39.271431972857407 5.508
v -39.271431972857407 -8.73
v -39.663588842030457 -8.73
v -39.663588842030457 5.498
v -39.663588842030457 -8.73
v -39.663588842030457 5.755
v -39.271431972857407 5.852
v -39.271431972857407

.663588842030457 4.9938039016957294 -72.1568603515625
.663588842030457 -8.7391768505780867 -72.1568603515625
.663588842030457 5.2417406436955867 -71.76470947265625
.271431972857407 5.2233762234597325 -71.76470947265625
.271431972857407 -8.7391768505780867 -71.76470947265625
.663588842030457 -8.7391768505780867 -71.76470947265625

v -39.663588842030457 5.7651
v -39.663588842030457 -8.739
v -39.663588842030457 5.7284
v -39.271431972857407 5.8569
v -39.271431972857407 -8.739
v -39.663588842030457 -8.739

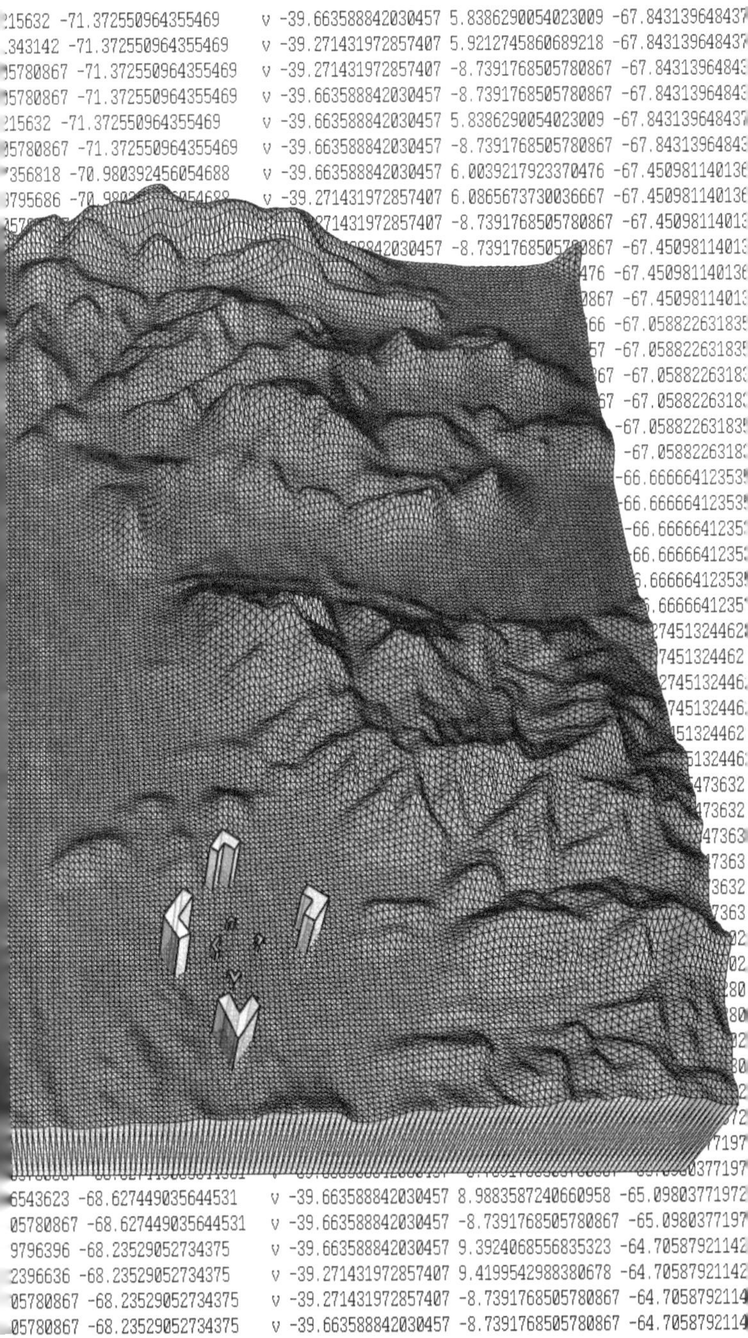

215632 -71.372550964355469   v -39.663588842030457 5.8386290054023009 -67.843139648437
343142 -71.372550964355469   v -39.271431972857407 5.9212745860689218 -67.843139648437
5780867 -71.372550964355469   v -39.271431972857407 -8.7391768505780867 -67.84313964843
5780867 -71.372550964355469   v -39.663588842030457 -8.7391768505780867 -67.84313964843
215632 -71.372550964355469   v -39.663588842030457 5.8386290054023009 -67.843139648437
5780867 -71.372550964355469   v -39.663588842030457 -8.7391768505780867 -67.84313964843
356818 -70.980392456054688   v -39.663588842030457 6.0039217923370476 -67.450981140136
795686 -70.980392456054688   v -39.271431972857407 6.0865673730036667 -67.450981140136
271431972857407 -8.7391768505780867 -67.45098114013
842030457 -8.7391768505780867 -67.45098114013
476 -67.450981140136
867 -67.45098114013
66 -67.058822631835
57 -67.058822631835
867 -67.0588226318
67 -67.0588226318
-67.05882263183
-67.0588226318
-66.66666412353
-66.66666412353
-66.6666641235
-66.6666641235
6.66666412353
6.6666641235
274513244462
7451324462
274513244462
7451324462
274513244462
745132446
51324462
5132446
473632
473632
47363
7363
3632
7363
02
02
80
80
02
80
6543623 -68.627449035644531   v -39.663588842030457 8.9883587240660958 -65.09803771972
5780867 -68.627449035644531   v -39.663588842030457 -8.7391768505780867 -65.0980377197
9796396 -68.23529052734375   v -39.663588842030457 9.3924068556835323 -64.70587921142
2396636 -68.23529052734375   v -39.271431972857407 9.4199542988380678 -64.70587921142
5780867 -68.23529052734375   v -39.271431972857407 -8.7391768505780867 -64.7058792114
5780867 -68.23529052734375   v -39.663588842030457 -8.7391768505780867 -64.7058792114

Forw

vard

John "Iron Mad" Wilkinson made a mechanical bore; then Iron Mad Wilkinson remade the whole of the Earth. The world's first sophisticated machine tool, Wilkinson's 1775 iron bore was more perfect and precise than any manual drill: able to create iron canons with sturdy, smooth barrels, and (by happy accident) precisely matched pipe joints which very seldom leaked. For decades, Scottish engineer James Watt had been working on a new model of steam engine, efficient enough to push the device from its narrow niche in mine work out to the forefront of industrial society. No luck, though: the human hand can't create a pipe so perfect, a linkage sufficiently fine, to make his complex double chambered device outperform its simpler predecessors. Too much wasted heat, too much leaking steam. Ultimately, it was the mechanical cannon bore—not Watt's human ingenuity—that at last brought his engine to life. Within a year of Iron Mad's triumph, Watt had a working prototype. By the close of the century, he had secured Britain's economic supremacy for a hundred years to come.

Of course, the isles were no stranger to precision. You can trace a line from more primitive social technologies of measurement—the Norman *Domesday Book*, the colonial survey, the galleon's cargo manifest—all the way up to Iron Mad's finely tuned bore. In this sense, his innovation was more in degree than in type. The boring machine, however, had a curious and novel function: it relentlessly produced machines which could hasten its own production. By 1776, Wilkinson had already designed his own bootleg engine, shamelessly plagiarized from Watt's prototypes and early models. He employed it in his ironworks, powering the systems which created the bore that had made such engines possible just a year prior. The ability to measure and operate with precision has always been linked to industrial capacity, but here the relation first started to become truly symbiotic. The precision of Wilkinson's machine was self-producing, self-reinforcing, and self-improving. From the earliest steps of cartography to the Homeric list of ships, all our counts and catalogues at last led up to this: industrial precision engineering, and the first great autoproductive machines.

Their impact was profound and immediate. All across Britain, industrialists and men of letters scrambled to keep up with the novel possibilities continuously presented by this autonomous marriage of measurement and production. The mania reached a fever pitch: punning on the name of the then contemporary charter-centric century political movement, astronomer John Herschel joked that British academia had been possessed by an overwhelming spirit of 'chartism' —an almost idolatrous fascination with precisely made charts,

complicated graphs, and expeditious cartography.
This enumerative obsession gripped the islands and
refused to let go, until everywhere, all at once,
one found the frenzy of self-producing precision.
First came the navigational clock, finely tuned
enough to keep exacting time on the high seas. Then
the stabilized compass, which found true north even
on novel ships of iron. Human organization was
transformed: in the blink of an eye, the precise
enumerations of autoproductive machines established
their dominion across all space and all time. Is
this a cosmic horror, or the sublime eminence of a
living god?

There is a robust case for horror. In whigish
popular histories, the industrial revolution is
sometimes situated as the child of enlightenment
humanism: an emancipation from toil and labour
that mirrors the political emancipation of
revolutionary liberalism. If this is true, the
industrial revolution is certainly patricidal. It
was British economic supremacy, built on the back
of Watt's engine, which funded the coalition wars
which destroyed the Napoleonic republics. It was
industrial war machines, manufactured in factories
and foundries, which fought and won wars for the
fascist reactionary project. It was finally also
military engineering that at last devised the ENIAC
artillery computers, von Neumann architecture, and
the terminal total synthesis of data and productive
capacity in the apotheotic form of the programmable
byte. Modernity's living god does not abet, and
in fact seems to abhor, human life and human
virtue: it was born of and lives for the cannon.
Behind every drone strike is a vast apparatus
of factories, rail-yards, container ports, and
logistical calculations. The structural apparatus

of global technocapital ruthlessly produces
guardian angels of death, which at all turns
protect and advance its own interests: wherever
we find the frenzy of autoproductive technology,
terror nearby abounds.

Lady Ada Lovelace nonetheless firmly took the
side of the sublime. Daughter of romantic poet
Lord Byron, and the first visionary practitioner
of what we might today call computer programming,
Lovelace understood better than anyone the alien
technical aesthetics of autoproductive machines.
Born in 1815, Lovelace worked with a kind of
speculative creativity, drawing up programs for
machines that did not yet—and could not yet—
exist. She understood the capacities of polymath
Charles Babbage's primitive computer (his
 'difference engine') far better than its creator:
by examining the machines schematics, she was
able to draw up, in advance of its construction,
detailed instructions that it might one day run.
By focusing her attention on the self-actualizing
logic of autoproductive machines and creatively
speculating within the bounds of their capacities,
she was able to predict developments in exacting
detail long before they became possible. She
called this creative speculation 'poetical
science' , for she saw in it something at once both
remarkably mechanically precise and yet nonetheless
aesthetically beautiful.

Might we, like Lovelace, come to recognize the
sublime beauty of our new-made technical god?
Mike Corrao's *Mancer* is a step along this path.
Mancer's aesthetic function is not located
purely in the superficial content of its counts
and catalogues: rather, it asks that we—like

Lovelace—begin to inquire into the logic of the
productive machines which could condition its
creation. How does such a list arise? What are its
organizing principles? What are its fundamental
units? How does it connect information? What is the
hierarchy of that information? How can it be broken
down and reorganized? When we speculate apropos of
these questions, we engage in a kind of creative
analysis: we are made to focus on the productive
capacities of this book-machine in particular,
and of machinic autoproduction in general.
Contextualized in our present cultural milieu—
drawing as much from *Dwarf Fortress* as the *Domesday
Book*—Corrao's *Mancer* conditions such speculations
and lets us examine the mechanical beauty lurking
behind modernity's technical horrors. In doing
so it exemplifies, with poise and precision, a
fledgling poetical science.

Oleander Garden

```
DEM_name = JAXA/ALOS/AW3D30/V2_2
trlat = 32.94803590907456
trlon = 90.55537095494009
bllat = 32.708586601333536
bllon = 90.1666551941577
printres = 0.4
ntilesx = 1
ntilesy = 1
tilewidth = 100.0
basethick = 1
zscale = 1.0
fileformat = STLb
no_bottom = False
unprojected = False
no_normals = True


process started: 21:55:02.104313


Region (lat/lon):
    32.94803590907456 90.55537095494009 (top right)
    32.708586601333536 90.1666551941577 (bottom left)
center at [90.3610130745489, 32.82831125520405]  UTM 46 N ,
EPSG:32646
lon/lat size in degrees: [0.38871576078238945, 0.23944930774102602]
Earth Engine raster: JAXA/ALOS/AW3D30/V2_2
  ALOS DSM: Global 30m [deprecated]
URL for geotiff is:  https://earthengine.googleapis.com/v1alpha/
projects/earthengine-legacy/thumbnails/4...2a8f3...52bc...440b
696...d99d...99cc5...a2677cbd8...a1...f57...7f:getPixel
  geotiff size: 0.0...62565612792...Mb
  cell size 145.58767519109966 m, upper left corner (x/y):
234396.15705767047 3649155....864913
full (untiled) raster (height,width)  (190, 255) float64 elev. min/max:
4845.0 5600.0
cell size: 145.58767519109966 m
adjusted print res from the requested 0.4 mm to 0.39215686274509803 mm
to ...ure ...rect ...del ...mensions
total model size ...mm: 10... x 74....9803...15686...
map scale  1 : ...248...57173...416...
Cells per tile (x/y) 255 x 190
using single-core only


1 x 1 tiles, tile size 100.00 x 74.51 mm


tile 1 1 ... height: 1.0 - 3.02367785757...2 mm , file size: 9 Mb


total size for all tiles: 9 Mb
add...full geotiff as ...2_2...36...83...


processing finished: 21:55:06.847663
```

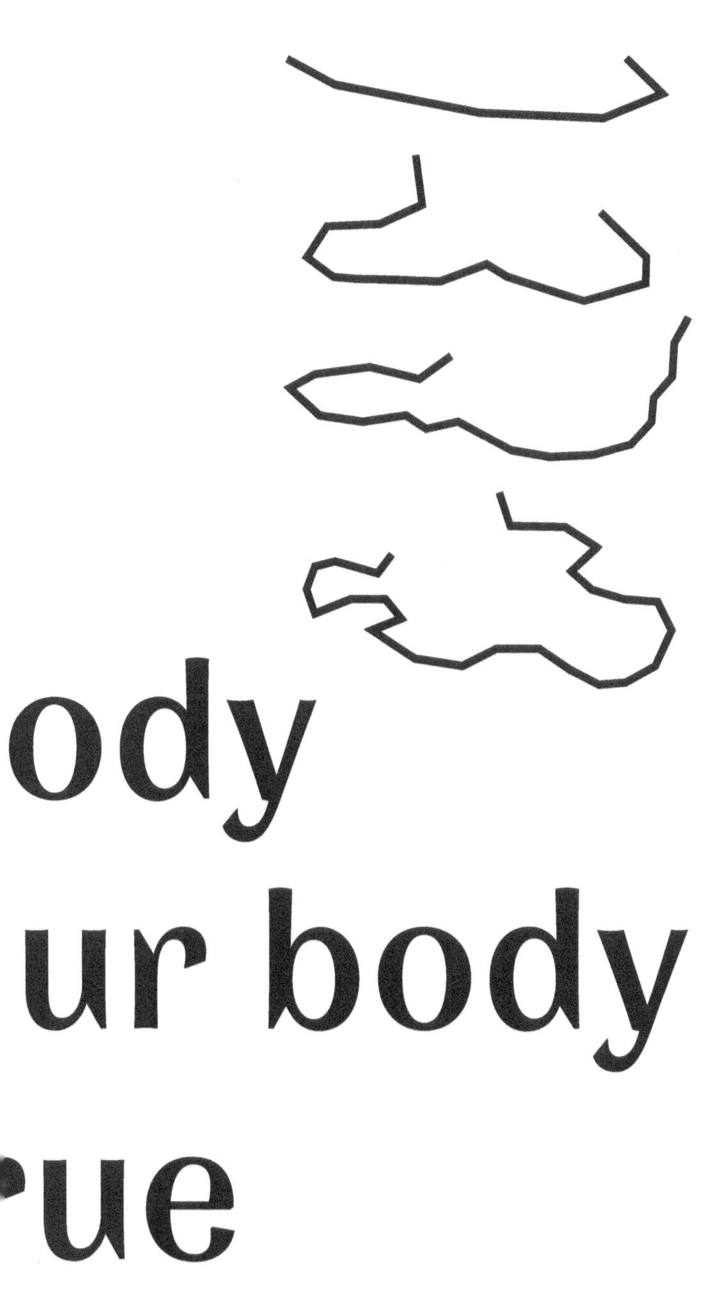

ody

ur body

rue

A Procession Of Zealots Depart For, And Incrementally
Arrive At, The Tengu'mal Cathedral Compound In
Participation Of A Gluttonous Cycle Over The Duration
Of The Six-Day Cet, In Anticipation Of The Heir's
Pending Arrival And Usurping Of The Collectamancy's
Throne.

n Of Zea

or, And I

ath

und In Pa

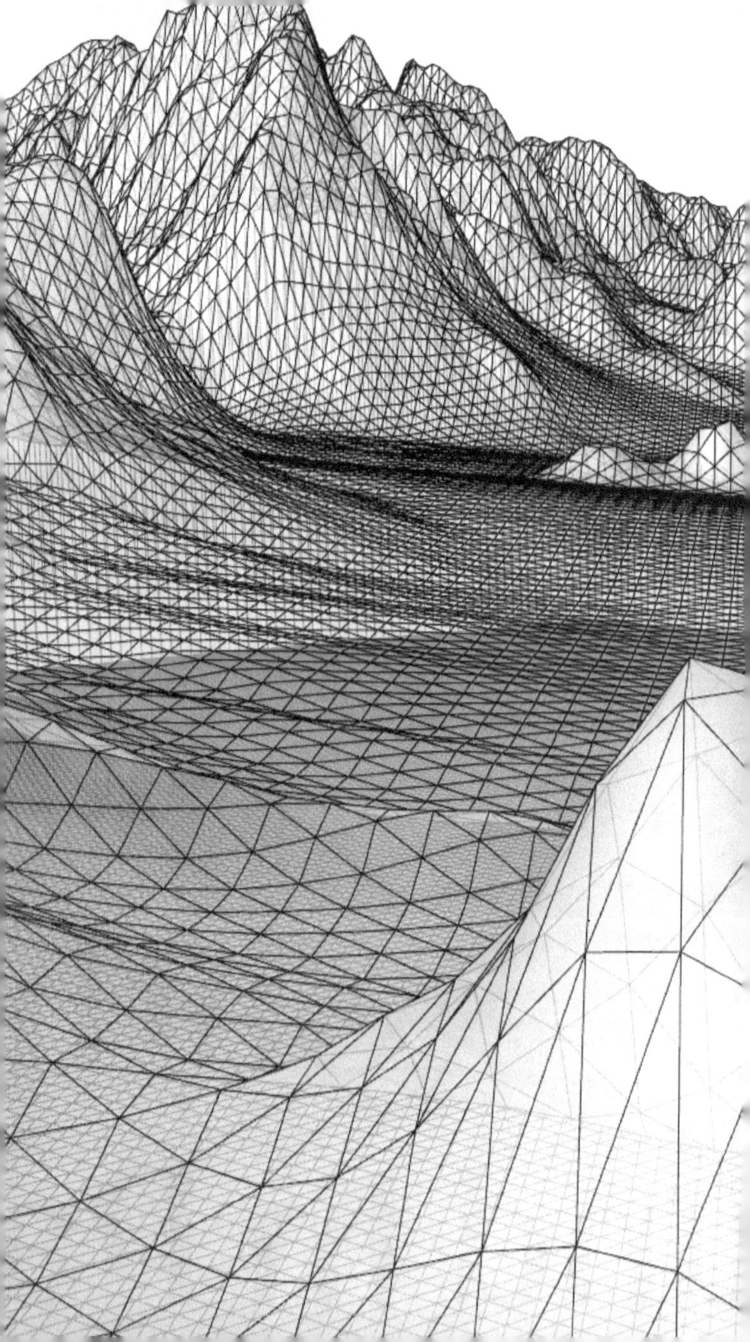

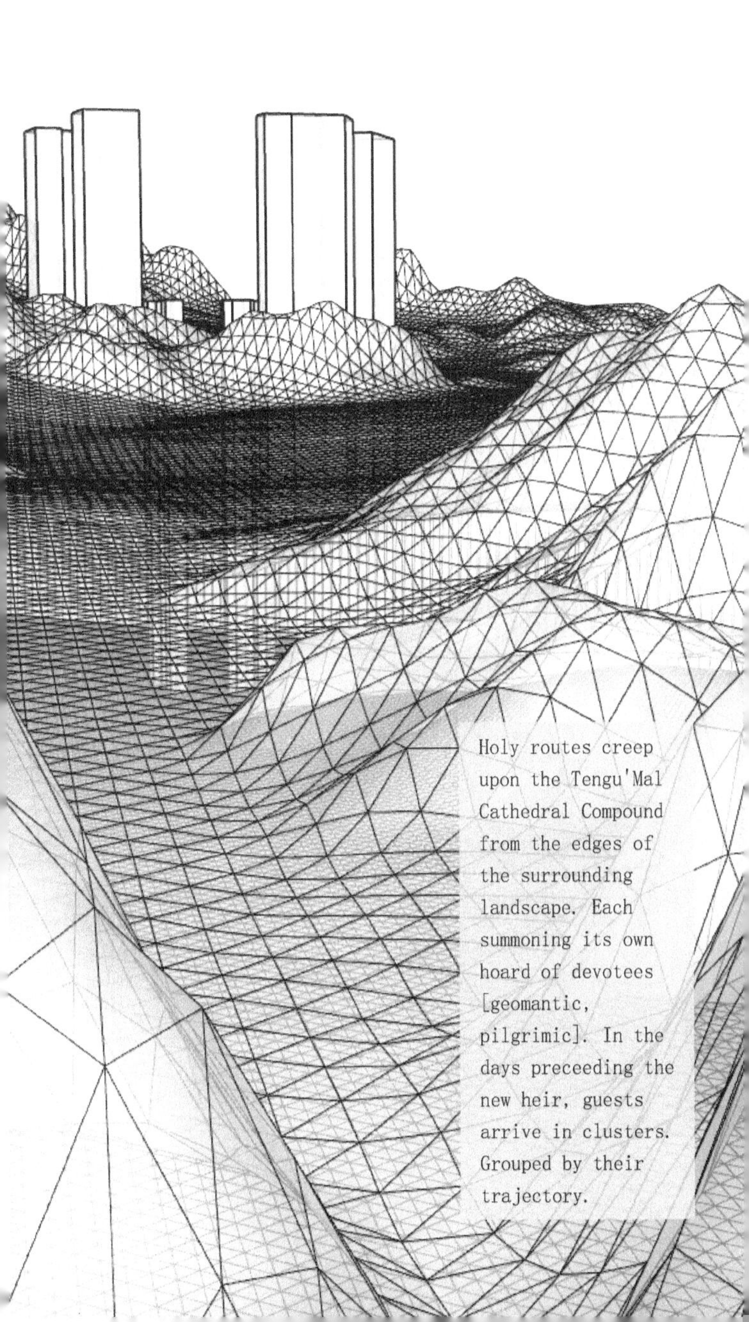

Holy routes creep
upon the Tengu'Mal
Cathedral Compound
from the edges of
the surrounding
landscape. Each
summoning its own
hoard of devotees
[geomantic,
pilgrimic]. In the
days preceeding the
new heir, guests
arrive in clusters.
Grouped by their
trajectory.

ARRIVALS OF

Arrivals of the First Day

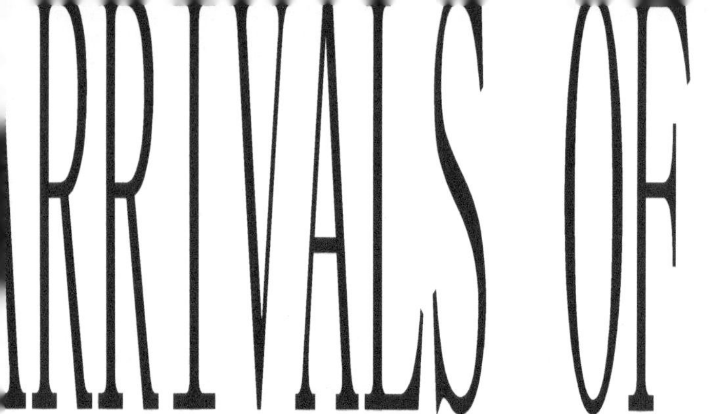

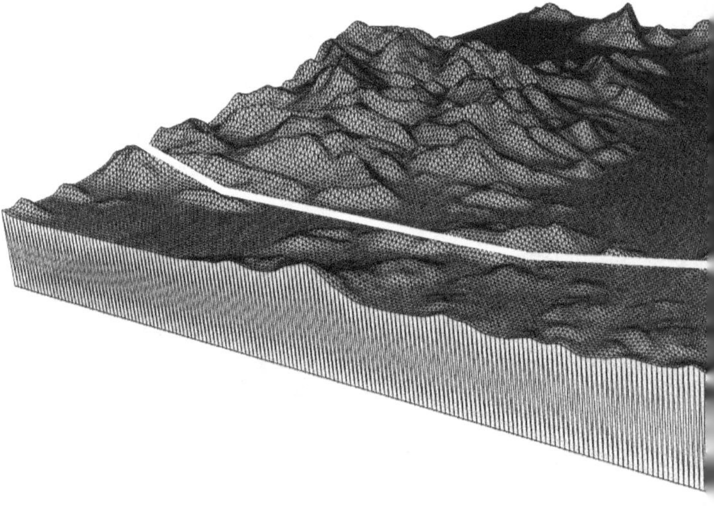

THE FIRST DAY

Trajectory of Pilgrimage
No-Heir
Path Version 1

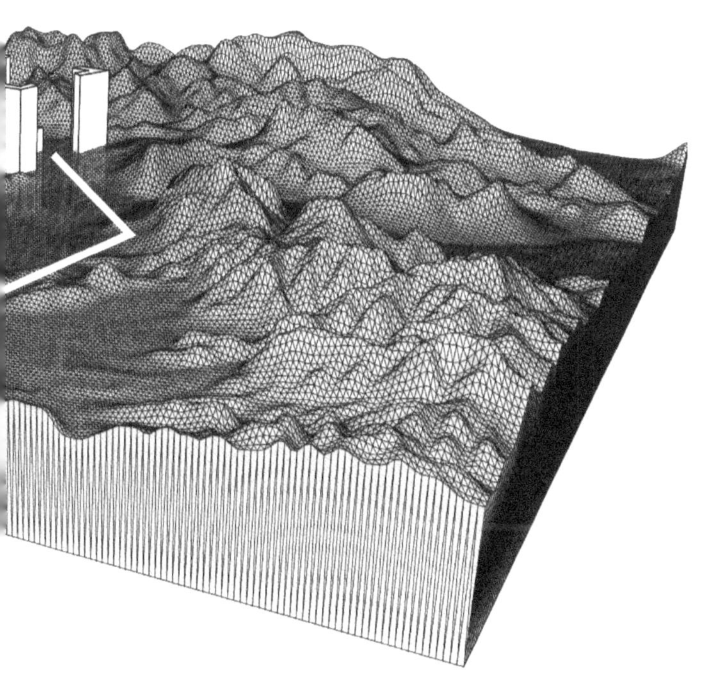

Day1
CensusDirectory
ID, Inventory
Motive, Interior Null

Ous'Elkt Pagac, grid'd fool of En, an exorcist of
sorts. Devotee to The Moon-Face. Dressed in velvet
robes and carrying kelp, knot'd electrical cords,
and various salves & creams.

De'Iah Mormil, frame'd criminal of Junkrhad, an art
critic. Daughter of Ameer DuVal. Dressed in iron
mesh and carrying an unwieldy mace, a hand drill,
and a spectrometer.

Mal'Kell Iafrate, Friend to the Church of a nearby
watchtower, a scholar of hypnagogic eroticism. Heir
to Lovotor. Dressed in multicolor bows and carrying
a biomonitor, various maps, and a hand drill.

Usil'Imp Agrhil, Heredet of a desecrated shrine,
a member of the Order of Self-Capture. Devotee to
The Nostrum. Dressed in cloth and carrying chewing
gum, a parcel, and groceries. With worn thighs and
pickle'd knees.

Fir'Firum Qeet, Arachnid follower of Hima'al, a Xenomorphic Engineer. Daughter of Doromundis. Dressed
in russet armor and carrying a set of jugum, a
belladonic cast, and additional limbs.

Aze'Talm Gula, a polemarch of Vavia, a portalogist.
Daughter of Lovotor. Dressed in a beak'd helmet
and carrying a severed tongue, sacks of water, and
decadent shawls.

Gamal Oduad, Friend to the Magistrate of Cit En,
a member of the Order of Self-Capture. Son of
Lovotor. Dressed in robes and carrying a tome of
sandpaper, utero packs, and fasteners. The tome is
without pages.

Duvre'Smet Omphale, the aphroditium of Cit Ravum,
a scholar of visceral hermetics. Heir to Egregious
Cuts. Dressed in a configuration of tentacles and
carrying unplug'd monitors, a hand auger, and the
cantos.

Nel'Apet Panorm, Tempt'd Son of an unknown origin,
a scholar of hypnagogic eroticism. Child of the
Nematode Mother. Dressed in knot'd objects and carrying cans of nectar, a severed finger, and a pick.

Usil'Yett Sahr, red clown of a procedural cityscape, a Xenomorphic Engineer. Follower of Gond.
Dressed in a belladonic cast and carrying reams
of parchment paper, a single-shot rifle, and an oil
lamp. With acid-spit cuts and crimsongreen gums.

Djo'Hept Laum, hive body of the Digital Landscape,
Mule Herder. Son of the Goatfolk. Dressed in nylon
and carrying fungal sprouts, chewing gum, and a wad
of receipts.

Suri'Yett Cebla, The Syzygy of All Stars of Junkrhad, a scholar of visceral hermetics. Follower of
Gilead. Dressed in wire'd oxygen tanks and carrying tins of pink paste, a belladonic cast, and old
melee weapons.

Pra'Dant Labiche, vole of unimportant affiliations,
a xenoarchitect. Son of Loplop. Dressed in velvet
robes and carrying a painting, a mouth gag, and
burlap. The painting lacks intrigue.

Pan'Ament Wat, Grazing Sow of the Ambient Zone, a
radical thinker. Devotee to Loplop. Dressed in a
cowl and carrying bear pelts, bottles of slime, and
knot'd objects.

Mahes'Duvel Mollard, Friend to the Church of Cit
Batum, an exorcist of sorts. Child of Lovotor.
Dressed in linens and carrying babel-ware, irides-
cent garbs, and a trocer.

L'Imp Aas, Friend to the Mayor of Qamsil, a liminal
scholar. Devotee to The Hylant King. Dressed in
a linear frame and carrying high-stress exos, an
ecraseur, and bags of fertilizer.

Del'Hept Hamadrium, Warden of a nearby watchtower,
a zonetologist. Heir to Oark. Dressed in a configuration of tentacles and carrying an important
tablet, tarpaulin, and a fowl.

Sau Gaet, Warden of Cit Ravum, a practitioner of
TVmancy. Devotee to The Unbound Stomach. Dressed in
an ornate mask and carrying cloth, biometric armor,
and palmagranates.

Mahes'Kell Panorm, white clown of Lundre, a
neo-historian. Devotee to The Neo-Succulent.
Dressed in wire'd oxygen tanks and carrying kevlar,
fresh produce, and fragant stones. With perfumed
wounds and scarred hands.

Heru'Aken Amon, trembling seer of a mountain village, a Xenomorphic Engineer. Follower of Kei-Man.
Dressed in denim and carrying a severed ear, light
plating, and a sealed chastity belt.

Bel'Tek Lazdon, sprout'd commoner of a tomb to the
north, an expert in animal husbandry. Daughter of-
Bardofrankont. Dressed in utero packs and carrying
fungal sprouts, tins of gelatin, and uncast nets.

Cashin Pacocha, The Hoarder of Artifacts of Fir'Al'Tuler, Mule Herder. Heir to The Juice'd Baron. Dressed in kelp and carrying minor excavation equipment, rolls of thread, and crab pelts.

Arca Sabag, Archpriest of Lundre, a Slime Morphologist. Devotee to many saints. Dressed in work clothes and carrying sacks of slime, tarot cards, and gemstones.

Dei'Aken Valek, Erupted Body of the ludological south, a student of golemancy. Heir to Volcanic Fumes. Dressed in velvet robes and carrying quince, cans of coolant, and broken cybernetics.

Eyon'Rada Ittre, Consul of Revarie, Neo-typesetter. Devotee to The Crawling Ooze. Dressed in a gas mask and carrying foot pedals, stamps approved by the bureaucracy, and an unidentified brass instrument.

Aken Widrig, siphon'd fool of Cit En, bibliomancer. Devotee to Ameer DuVal. Dressed in utero packs and carrying a trocer, reflective materials, and foot pedals.

Beji Trigov, Frog of Lower Dark, a techscanner. Son of The Hylant King. Dressed in moderate plating and carrying a hand auger, proto-limbs, and unplug'd monitors.

Aasen Schecter, fence of Licot, a Yonicist. Follower of The Chalice. Dressed in quilted armor and carrying composite plateware, nylon, and a rotor machine.

Aida Simras, The Nomad of Cit Hima'al, an entrail supply specialist. Devotee to Doromundis. Dressed in carbon fiber and carrying sacks of oil, tins of gelatin, and nut butter.

Heh'Roni Labrahm, story'd fool of an unknown origin, a scholar of ephemeral posterity. Devotee to The Moon-Face. Dressed in a scarab husk and carrying various maps, cans of coolant, and a box radio. With gaudy burns and scarred knuckles.

Mimir Schecter, The Blessed of Hima'al, an affliate of the Threadbarer. Heir to Doromundis. Dressed in an iron maiden and carrying a line of hangers, a wad of receipts, and gnaw'd seeds. With speckle'd occipital hatch and roseblue lacerations.

Ous'Neom Dubann, grid'd fool of a pastoral landscape, a digital ecologist. Heir to Lunar. Dressed
in work clothesand carrying cloth, an unidentified
brass instrument, and pliers. With silk'd genitalia
and wiry collar bones.

De'Nepher Sadlon, Arachnid follower of a transnational space, a reader. Enemy of Asterion. Dressed
in steel armor and carrying an ecdysis trigger,
severed implants, and a corpse over their shoulder.

Amir'Anet Qeet, a desert father of a dilapidated
monastery, a watchdog. Follower of Volcanic Fumes.
Dressed in a reflective mask and carrying conical
objects, trackmesh, and salvage.

Waen Qader, sentient mass of House of Effigy, an experienced cryptographer. Heir to Gilead. Dressed in
a skull cap and carrying the hoof of an ungulate,
moss weaves, and severed implants.

Aza'Tesh Labrahm, Battl'd Insect of a tomb to
the north, an art critic. Heir to The Moon-Face.
Dressed in padded armor and carrying trash, broken
cybernetics, and torn vinyl.

Hri'Neom Skufca, fence of the Cauldron, an Omphalomancer. Enemy of Bardofrankont. Dressed in faction affiliate'd clothing and carrying trackmesh, electrical wires, and multicolor bows. With globular navel and peachgreen wounds.

Ur'Talm Tamar, a declaw'd wolverine of Dair'Kud'Tuler, a gastromancer. Heir to The Unbound Stomach. Dressed in leather garb and carrying satin, a claw hammer, and faction affiliate'd clothing.

Pef'Uun Taille, Sacrificial Heifer of the Centur Cathedral, an occult minimalist. Follower of The Hundred Headless Woman. Dressed in steel mesh and carrying cans of nectar, velvet robes, and broken cybernetics.

Aza'Smet Zika, a hire'd body of a transnational space, a bone harvester. Child of Gond. Dressed in a sealed chastity belt and carrying guild papers, tissue samples, and an amputation knife.

Baka'Numi Ubl, a hikikomori of Licot, a bioid integration engineer. Heir to The Chalice. Dressed in a beak'd helmet and carrying a book of poetry, crude cut cloth, and a bone saw. With petite cheeks and ocherfuschia bruises.

Baka'Erzu Rahld, Ruiner of a procedural cityscape, a text morphologist. Daughter of Gond. Dressed in nematode pelts and carrying a nail file, knot'd electrical cords, and high-stress exos.

Atar Sesser, Gentleman of Holy Attire of Aswart, a scholar of visceral hermetics. Child of The Moon-Face. Dressed in utero packs and carrying a fowl, a box of carefully packaged needles, and robes. With sharp soles and silk'd ribs.

Aze'Miro Taille, white clown of Cit Licot, a scholar of hypnagogic eroticism. Daughter of Bardofrankont. Dressed in bear pelts and carrying raw chocolate, structural proteins, and a book of poetry.

Urso Chevnik, Friend to the Mayor of The Moon, a cantrip engineer. Devotee to many saints. Dressed in velvet robes and carrying a crate of soylent, a protractor, and a pick.

Pemphredo Ugrite, a hire'd body of Cit Dair'Kud'Tuler, an interface engineer. Daughter of The Hundred Headless Woman. Dressed in bulk'd iron and carrying an old CD player, robes, and muscle memory implants.

Nel'Apet Nergrel, white clown of a mountain village, a member of the Guild of Cyber Mycologies. Daughter of Gilead. Dressed in proto-limbs and carrying golem flesh, stripped vines, and stamps approved by the bureaucracy. With acid-spit teeth and pinkyellow crows feet.

Del'Yett Thalm, the beauty of Agatar, an expert in animal husbandry. Son of Phot Kul. Dressed in cloth and carrying dermal implants, minor excavation equipment, and palmagranates.

Ihy'Lpra Rasa, Prisoner of Argas, a xenoarchitect. Devotee to Oark. Dressed in an artificial carapace and carrying torn vinyl, knot'd objects, and recovered processors.

Ous'Uun Ubl, Friend to the Magistrate of Argas, a bacterial miner. Child of Kei-Man. Dressed in mirror'd panels and carrying a stylus, wooden figurines, and trash. With coralcream arm hairs and salt'd teeth.

D'Iah Behm, Patriarch of Cit En, a reader. Child of Lovotor. Dressed in nematode pelts and carrying a nail file, various loose springs and pins, and nylon.

De'Elkt Cenamo, a column monk of a desert temple, a haruspex. Heir to The Chalice. Dressed in faction affiliate'd clothing and carrying an artificial leach, coins, and orbital siphons.

Aza'Kell Et'Id, cyberpunk of Ungulum, a neo-historian. Child of the Nematode Mother. Dressed in a gas mask and carrying kevlar, structural proteins, and tarot cards.

Ymir Tel'Vavia, fodder of a desert temple, a narrative designer. Child of Garagan. Dressed in satin and carrying a fowl, vagrant garb, and a carton of cigarettes.

Eyon'Rada Duver, newly resurrected servant of En, a cosmopolist. Son of The Neo-Succulent. Dressed in bear pelts and carrying net monitors, an idol, and an old CD player. The idol is an isohedron.

L'h'Ka Dubann, The Awakened of Cit Centur, a practitioner of collectamancy. Child of Bardofrankont. Dressed in grime'd coveralls and carrying guild papers, valueless minerals, and fragant stones.

Ur'Numi Siler, raccoon of Dair'Kud'Tuler, a techscanner. Devotee to Lunar. Dressed in a configuration of tentacles and carrying a roll of cartridges, impotent seeds, and a spectrometer.

Fir'Amaun Fabak, Grazing Sow of Cit Centur, a
mancer of some kind. Son of The Nostrum. Dressed
in work clothes and carrying dice, rail nails, and
tar'd feathers. The dice are a d20 and a d10.

Pef'Yett Dalagur, Frog of Cit Decair, a cantrip engineer. Daughter of Kei-Man. Dressed in kevlar and
carrying a mouth gag, irridescent garbs, and seeds.

Cyb'Kell Nachbar, deer-body of Cit Dair'Kud'Tuler,
atonal bard. Daughter of Garagan. Dressed in an
iron maiden and carrying kelp, nematode pelts, and
tissue samples.

Yune'Baal Ittre, the Orphic Fool of Cit Varas,
a nematode farmer. Daughter of Egregious Cuts.
Dressed in structural proteins and carrying a
single-shot rifle, an array of aprons, and knot'd
objects. With copperblue eyes and silk'd heels.

Bel'Ket Manah, curse'd villager of Lower Dark, an
occulture critic. Devotee to The Deep Well. Dressed
in tigulated mail and carrying valueless minerals,
a small sun, and a simple dress.

Par'Rada Tawat, a polemarch of The Moon, a pseudo-geographer. Son of Volcanic Fumes. Dressed in
denim and carrying a bundle'd duvet, a trephine and
accompanying trepan, and reams of grid paper.

El'Anet Amon, plauge'd villager of Cit Decair, a
hyper-zonal ecologist. Enemy of The Deep Well.
Dressed in iron mesh and carrying VHS tapes, fasteners, and a percolator.

Sadek Ugrite, tentacle'd fool of Cit En, a portalogist. Child of The Juice'd Baron. Dressed in dermal
implants and carrying fragant stones, bone meal,
and nut butter.

Ihy'Apet Kahan, fence of a procedural cityscape, a
bacterial miner. Heir to Ultut. Dressed in cloth
and carrying a severed ear, bags of fertilizer, and
bars of RAM.

Vidur Sorcer, haunch'd bird of Cit Vavia, an automapper. Enemy of Volcanic Fumes. Dressed in broken
cybernetics and carrying a fowl, the remnants of a
garden, and proto-limbs. With aquamarinegreen nates
and redpink thighs.

Jem'Tek Narai, swarm'd form of Fir'Al'Tuler, a
practitioner of TVmancy. Devotee to Lunar. Dressed
in decadent shawls and carrying pliers, neural
comb, and wire'd oxygen tanks.

Ur'Amaun Glauciem, travel'd companion of a pastoral
landscape, a Neo-proph. Child of Asterion. Dressed
in a linear frame and carrying babel-ware, coins,
and gemstones. With crimsongreen ink and luminous
trachea.

Rukur Sahra, Limb Tree of a rural river town, a
subterranean apiologist. Enemy of Asterion. Dressed
in bulk'd iron and carrying knot'd objects, reams
of grid paper, and proto-limbs.

Siet Astare, scale'd fiend of Revarie, a pseudo-geographer. Daughter of Gond. Dressed in moderate
plating and carrying muscle memory implants, a book
of poetry, and a configuration of tentacles.

De'Numi Immol, a garter snake of Nahr, a scholar
of ephemeral posterity. Follower of The Chalice.
Dressed in biometric armor and carrying various
salves & creams, an array of buckles, and high-
stress exos.

Amer'Uum Tyrer, fence of Azmeern, biographer. Heir
to Garagan. Dressed in tigulated mail and carrying
lotus stems, tarot cards, and proto-limbs. With
shave'd wrists and bent trachea.

Talm Siler, an associate of a nearby watchtower,
Mule Herder. Follower of Ameer DuVal. Dressed in
clusters of TVP and carrying a biomonitor, reams of
parchment paper, and tar'd feathers.

Duod Cacchiont, a primate of Ungulum, a bacterial miner. Follower of The Interface. Dressed in
fir leaves and carrying a severed tongue, beautiful jewelery, and many talismen. With brownsilver
thighs and paint'd crows feet.

Ull Kinmari, a desert father of Cit Decair, a
neo-historian. Devotee to no one. Dressed in additional limbs and carrying velvet robes, vagrant
garb, and nematode pelts.

Ogun Dambach, Entomb'd of Lundre, a material
designer. Child of Kei-Man. Dressed in moderate
plating and carrying a trocer, bottles of acid, and
irridescent garbs.

Del'Anet Yegge, zealous courter of a desecrated
shrine, a studio painter. Heir to Ameer DuVal.
Dressed in a configuration of tentacles and carrying
cloth, unlit candles, and scissors.

Dua'Ament Sabiume, a commoner of unimportant affiliations, an automapper. Follower of The Nostrum.
Dressed in electrical gloves and carrying a parcel,
a metal contraption, and enriched soil. With sharp
wrinkles and pickle'd scalp.

Geb'Amaun Inkh, cyberpunk of Latabk, a scholar of
hypnagogic eroticism. Follower of Ultut. Dressed
in muscle memory implants and carrying recovered
processors, a severed finger, and dice. The dice are
a d10 and a d4.

Djo'Numi Viem, swarm'd form of a nearby watchtower, a liminal scholar. Son of Kei-Man. Dressed in
a configuration of tentacles and carrying a sealed
chastity belt, a painting, and kevlar. The painting
depicts a snail. The snail is alone.

D'Odde Ubelrahn, an anteater of Cit Licot, a member
of the Order of Small Fires. Devotee to The Deep
Well. Dressed in bulk'd iron and carrying severed
implants, coffee beans, and grime'd coveralls.

Gagap Takarem, The Polydactyl Palm of the Carnlands, an astragalomancer. Child of Phot Kul.
Dressed in trackmesh and carrying unplug'd monitors, cloth, and additional limbs.

Amer'Tek Radibeau, a declaw'd wolverine of Spahbod, a scholar of hypnagogic eroticism. Follower of
Oark. Dressed in a gas mask and carrying thick leg
warmers, an unweildy mace, and an important tablet.

Roni Ubelrahn, a declaw'd wolverine of Lundre, an
Object-Oriented Psychologist. Enemy of The Hundred Headless Woman. Dressed in a linear frame and
carrying many perfumes, ornate rugs, and a roll of
cartridges.

Mona'Talm Aarhus, Frog of Cit Fir'Al'Tuler, Applied
Ontologist. Follower of Ultut. Dressed in deer
pelts and carrying seeds, a bundle'd duvet, and a
woodcutter's axe.

De'Ka Tel'Vavia, sever'd torso of Aswart, Marred
Grocer. Child of Gond. Dressed in hardened leather
and carrying a wad of receipts, unmark'd objects,
and slabs of ice.

Cyb'Yett Et'Batum, story'd fool of meatspace, atonal bard. Daughter of The Hundred Headless Woman.
Dressed in a cowl and carrying the remnants of a
garden, tallow, and synthetic produce.

El'Tek Cech, newly resurrected servant of Varas, a hermetic coordinator. Devotee to The Hundred Headless Woman. Dressed in an artificial carapace and carrying an old CD player, electrical wires, and carbon fiber.

Jahnar Wadas, plauge'd villager of Junkrhad, a scholar of minotaur semiotics. Heir to Egregious Cuts. Dressed in deer pelts and carrying a line of hangers, a mouth gag, and wire'd oxygen tanks.

Zodi'Neom Wiygul, the Orphic Fool of Cit Dair'Kud'Tuler, a scholar of marxist grammatology. Child of Loplop. Dressed in chain sleeves and carrying irridescent garbs, tissue samples, and cloth.

Ur'Tek Macci, stranger of Ungulum, atonal bard. Heir to Loplop. Dressed in structural proteins and carrying spider plants, quince, and the cantos.

Dafyr Jurat, a lecturer of House of Effigy, a hermetic coordinator. Enemy of The Hylant King. Dressed in iron mesh and carrying fragant stones, a parcel, and pliers. The parcel contains a screwdriver.

Ubi'Apet Saurte, robber of the Niopo Tree, a
neo-historian. Enemy of Oark. Dressed in a sealed
chastity belt and carrying palmagranates, nematode
pelts, and gnaw'd seeds.

Amer'Apet Headroun, The Pilgrim of a procedural
cityscape, an occulture critic. Child of Lunar.
Dressed in uncast nets and carrying an idol, a hand
auger, and a ring of keys. With angle'd water and
rotting ventral blotches.

Cyb'Neon Ahell, the crack'd finger of Dair'Kud'Tuler, a practitioner of collectamancy. Heir to The
Urchin King. Dressed in padded armor and carrying a
hand broom, valueless minerals, and a toolbox.

Nel'Mot Voorhes, deer-body of Cit Vavia, a Xenomorphic Engineer. Enemy of The Hundred Headless Woman.
Dressed in leather garb and carrying a cellphone, a
dull knife, and muscle memory implants.

Zodi'Ament Akkadum, Grazing Sow of Cit Fir'Al'Tuler, a Morphofeminist. Child of Garagan. Dressed in
tigulated mail and carrying a hand auger, a line of
hangers, and unlit candles.

L'Suel Carace, Drunkard of the exterior, a student
of golemancy. Daughter of Gond. Dressed in chain
sleeves and carrying bone meal, burlap, and broken
cybernetics.

Kell Ost, The Apostle of Spahbod, a hermetic coordinator. Son of The Unbound Stomach. Dressed in
uncast nets and carrying dried grains, a spectrometer, and kevlar.

Cyb'Loc Macci, defunct administrater of the Ambient
Zone, a hyper-zonal ecologist. Daughter of Tumpur.
Dressed in padded armor and carrying a set of jug-
um, a box radio, and proto-limbs.

Abdon Gresh, cave dweller of Unaindin, a guilded
merchant. Devotee to Phot Kul. Dressed in wire
fleece and carrying unassuming clothes, an ecraseur,
and fragant stones.

Mede'Imp Panorm, defunct administrater of
meatspace, Marred Grocer. Devotee to The Interface.
Dressed in a wing'd helmet and carrying a trephine
and accompanying trepan, technoscanner, and robes.
With salt'd obliques and tepid nape.

Sopona Pauk, a commoner of Ravum, an automapper.
Child of The Juice'd Baron. Dressed in high-stress
exos and carrying multicolor bows, sacks of slime,
and trackmesh. With bent irises and perfumed follicles.

Umeer'Unut Dudek, Calloused Hands of House of Effigy, a hyper-zonal ecologist. Daughter of Garagan.
Dressed in trash and carrying severed implants, a
single-shot rifle, and a severed finger.

Aze'Nepher Macci, stray dog of Batum, a scholar
of hypnagogic eroticism. Heir to Oark. Dressed in
heavyset blankets and carrying proto-limbs, fasteners, and knot'd electrical cords.

Pan'Kell Scherngral, The Flesh'd of Latabk, a
portalogist. Child of The Interface. Dressed in
uncast nets and carrying various artifacts, a small
sculpture, and coins. The sculpture is a bent limb.

Wadej'Anet Behm, Palatine of a dilapidated monastery, a collisionist. Follower of Phot Kul. Dressed in decadent shawls and carrying ecto-chisel, nylon, and pluck'd guavas.

De'Roni Ekate, the practice'd sow of Chthonos, a material designer. Heir to Gilead. Dressed in an iron maiden and carrying unassuming clothes, tarot cards, and vagrant garb.

Suri'Elkt Czap, sprout'd commoner of Fir'Al'Tuler, a nematode farmer. Heir to The Deep Well. Dressed in leather garb and carrying nut butter, uncast nets, and an artificial carapace.

Daunte Gulem, Jaguar of Cit Dair'Kud'Tuler, a Holocener. Child of Doromundis. Dressed in an ornate mask and carrying electrical wires, kevlar, and deer pelts.

Ezru Alet, Prisoner of Yoasnmsokl, a minor castor. Devotee to Garagan. Dressed in an artificial carapace and carrying a biomonitor, important documents, and prairie grass stalks.

Umir'Sham Taglam, a nematode of a desecrated shrine, Marred Grocer. Daughter of The Deep Well. Dressed in nylon and carrying tarot cards, guavas, and a sealed chastity belt.

Usil'Ament Volke, Pariah of Batum, a studio painter. Follower of Egregious Cuts. Dressed in linens and carrying a linear frame, composite plateware, and salvaged ciruit boards.

Par'Loc Kakar, Eunuch of Cit Decair, scryer. Follower of The Moon-Face. Dressed in an ornate mask and carrying ice'd milk bottles, bear pelts, and canteens.

Ent'Erzu Uhr, a column monk of Aswart, a journeyman of fleshcraft. Daughter of Volcanic Fumes. Dressed in an array of approns and carrying a sacred tome, a bone saw, and an amputation knife. The tome details the proper techniques of a nematode farmer.

Oya Dal, The Apostle of En, a practitioner of necromancy. Son of Doromundis. Dressed in torn vinyl and carrying a metal contraption, a analog camera, and minor excavation equipment.

Cherna Vikent, Pariah of Anarak, a laborer. Heir to
no one. Dressed in burlap and carrying the hoof of
an ungulate, an interface, and ornate rugs.

Ameer'Rada Chevnik, Frog of Yoasnmsokl, a Slime
Morphologist. Child of the Goatfolk. Dressed in
mirror'd panels and carrying stamps approved by the
bureaucracy, a sealed chastity belt, and decadent
shawls.

Aze'Roni Skorpat, skull digger of Agatar, a Slime
Morphologist. Daughter of Bird Inferior. Dressed
in nylon and carrying an arrow remover, a set of
jugum, and an unidentified brass instrument. With
paint'd abrasions and redviolet sutures.

Dugne Savanne, Tempt'd Son of Spahbod, a cantrip
engineer. Heir to The Neo-Succulent. Dressed in
vambraces and carrying holy garb, additional limbs,
and cans of coolant. With copperblue digits and
globular collar bones.

Ange Ubl, a lecturer of a mountain village, an
anti-realist. Devotee to Lunar. Dressed in tigulated mail and carrying salvaged ciruit boards, tar'd
feathers, and fungal sprouts.

El'Hept Cacchiont, the Orphic Fool of Cit Batum, a scholar of post-digital epistemology. Son of Kei-Man. Dressed in black robes and carrying a biomonitor, orbital siphons, and guild papers.

Zodi'Neon Nagar, The Nomad of Lower Dark, a haruspex. Enemy of Bardofrankont. Dressed in bulk'd iron and carrying severed implants, an isohedron, and ecto-chisel.

Grhi'Rada Zais, plauge'd villager of Junkrhad, a scholar of post-digital epistemology. Daughter of Egregious Cuts. Dressed in an array of aprons and carrying pliers, impotent seeds, and waterlog'd magazines. With babyblueviolet burns and pickle'd blisters.

Grhi'Duvel Hamadrium, Sacrificial Heifer of Vavia, a pseudo-geographer. Son of Bird Inferior. Dressed in a sealed chastity belt and carrying a configuration of tentacles, sacks of oil, and spider plants. With greengray scalp and carve'd water.

Dua'Hept Sheehe, punk of the Cauldron, a member
of the Order of Small Fires. Heir to The Chalice.
Dressed in splint mail and carrying clips, tarot
cards, and a claw hammer. With silk'd sores and
bald heels.

Hri'Erzu Pasiphate, mutilate'd villager of Ephor,
a haruspex. Daughter of The Hundred Headless Woman.
Dressed in mirror'd panels and carrying deer pelts,
a severed finger, and coins.

Abbe'Baal Cygan, Villager of a transnational space,
a diligent squire. Child of The Neo-Succulent.
Dressed in thick leg warmers and carrying stripped
vines, spare leg warmers, and operator cards.

Del'Apet Iafrate, travel'd companion of the Niopo
Tree, Grand Inquisitor. Devotee to Loplop. Dressed
in nematode pelts and carrying clips, fir leaves,
and wire'd oxygen tanks.

Bel'Dant Kachur, mammoth of the outskirts, a studio
painter. Son of the Goatfolk. Dressed in splint
mail and carrying a lithotome, reflective materials,
and sacks of oil.

Ihy'Dant Mnemosycte, Entomb'd of Latabk, an occult minimalist. Enemy of Tumpur. Dressed in quilted armor and carrying an iron maiden, carbon fiber, and salvage. With perfumed nail beds and babyblueviolet capillaries.

Amer'Numi Ugar, Matriarch of the exterior, a fledgling in the Guild of Faciality. Heir to no one. Dressed in moderate plating and carrying faction affiliate'd clothing, tins of pink paste, and synthetic produce.

Ubi'Imp Mien, frame'd criminal of the Cauldron, a dream technician. Follower of Tumpur. Dressed in vambraces and carrying an interface, an iron maiden, and ice'd milk bottles. With bulbous cheeks and oblong ear lobes.

Duvre'Ket Wrye, scale'd fiend of Dathapt, a watchdog. Heir to The Hundred Headless Woman. Dressed in a scarab husk and carrying a belladonic cast, chewing gum, and a carton of cigarettes.

Guirre Vikent, a hire'd body of the exterior, an interface engineer. Devotee to The Nostrum. Dressed in nylon and carrying dermal implants, a lithotome, and fresh produce.

Ent'Miro Cech, a polemarch of Cit Fir'Al'Tuler,
a scholar of marxist grammatology. Devotee to The
Hundred Headless Woman. Dressed in dermal implants
and carrying a box radio, sacks of blood, and valuable minerals.

Del'Erzu Casbeer, travel'd companion of Qamsil,
a cartomancer. Follower of Phot Kul. Dressed in a
reflective mask and carrying bone meal, a line of
hangers, and mirror'd panels.

Fal Reeg, sever'd head of the Centur Cathedral, a
mancer of some kind. Child of no one. Dressed in
uncast nets and carrying a box of carefully packaged needles, an old CD player, and a woodcutter's
axe.

Clotho Sautter, The Summoning Palm of Hima'al, a
practitioner of collectamancy. Son of The Neo-Succulent. Dressed in a beak'd helmet and carrying a
fowl, tins of pink paste, and an isohedron. The
isohedron has ten sides.

Otr Lotan, the beauty of Lundre, a practitioner
of collectamancy. Follower of Loplop. Dressed in
linens and carrying a bedroll, palmagranates, and a
nail file.

Umeer'Yett Detwa, the aphroditium of a tomb to
the north, an art critic. Follower of The Unbound
Stomach. Dressed in hardened leather and carrying a
severed finger, sacks of blood, and jicama.

Yune'Anet Vikar, The Right Hand of Agatar, an adept
exobotanist. Enemy of The Unbound Stomach. Dressed
in grime'd coveralls and carrying a small sun, a
hand broom, and a reel-to-reel tape recorder.

Ugra'Ament Polit, grid'd fool of Junkrhad, a scholar of marxist grammatology. Daughter of Tumpur.
Dressed in an array of aprons and carrying beautiful jewelery, deer pelts, and cloth. With flexible
ink and bent thighs.

Duvre'Anet Huten, a primate of Cit Decair,
trepaneer. Son of Doromundis. Dressed in electrical
gloves and carrying net monitors, a box radio, and
multicolor bows.

Duban Matkan, a fungal body of a rural river town,
a futamancer. Follower of Phot Kul. Dressed in
burlap and carrying a percolator, a spectrometer,
and ornate rugs.

Sau Qaile, Sacrificial Heifer of the northern deserts, a cartomancer. Follower of The Hylant King. Dressed in crab pelts and carrying a protractor, scissors, and chewing gum.

Ent'Talm Yggre, a hound of a mountain village, a pitchspeaker. Enemy of The Chalice. Dressed in uncast nets and carrying pluck'd guavas, quince, and heavyset blankets.

Otr Molloy, Drunkard of Azmeern, an automapper. Daughter of The Moon-Face. Dressed in conical objects and carrying valuable minerals, an old CD player, and unassuming clothes. With bent knuckles and perfumed cheeks.

Bel'Duvel Espern, Archpriest of the Cauldron, a necromancer. Heir to The Nostrum. Dressed in cloth and carrying a video still, nylon, and slime. The video still depicts the nematode.

Ideus Morfe, postpunk of transnational space, a water merchant. Enemy of The Chalice. Dressed in multicolor bows and carrying sacks of bitumen, a severed finger, and a bundle'd duvet.

Fal Dejolu, stranger of unimportant affiliations, a fledgling in the Guild of Faciality. Son of The Juice'd Baron. Dressed in chain sleeves and carrying clips, denim fits, and a wad of receipts.

Honeer Wehrlee, Matriarch of Spahbod, a minor castor. Daughter of Ameer DuVal. Dressed in steel armor and carrying light plating, sacks of blood, and bulk'd iron.

Heh'Iah Ubelrahn, Pyrarc of Revarie, a hyper-zonal ecologist. Enemy of Gilead. Dressed in heavy greaves and carrying an idol, an amputation knife, and a small sun. The idol depicts a rendition of the Urchin King.

Amir'Loc Kavan, Matriarch of the wilderness, a digital ecologist. Devotee to the Goatfolk. Dressed in a scarab husk and carrying a analog camera, recovered processors, and sacks of bitumen.

L'h'Tesh Lucef, siphon'd fool of Cit Decair, Grand Inquisitor. Heir to Bardofrankont. Dressed in crude cut cloth and carrying sensory archive tool, structural proteins, and slabs of ice. With rotting collar bones and petite nates.

Djo'Loc Agre, Tempt'd Son of Batum, a scholar of necrometry. Heir to Kei-Man. Dressed in thick leg warmers and carrying ecto-chisel, salvage, and a fowl.

Nel'Apet Plutence, Sacrificial Heifer of a desert temple, a nematode farmer. Enemy of The Hundred Headless Woman. Dressed in muscle memory implants and carrying bottles of slime, bags of fertilizer, and velvet robes.

Ihy'Odde Noita, stray dog of Cit Hima'al, a material designer. Son of The Interface. Dressed in structural proteins and carrying turmeric, reams of grid paper, and an array of buckles.

Umeer'Hept Tham, postpunk of Lower Dark, a scholar of post-digital epistemology. Daughter of The Urchin King. Dressed in vagrant garb and carrying ornate rugs, composite plateware, and an iron maiden.

Sadek Polit, zealous courter of a distant past, biographer. Heir to Doromundis. Dressed in a reflective mask and carrying deer pelts, an old CD player, and velvet robes. With gossamer ink and bluegreen genitalia.

Mede'Dant Yarat, a hound of another planet, a narrative designer. Daughter of Doromundis. Dressed in cloth and carrying an artificial leach, turmeric, and a belladonic cast.

Yune'Lpra Narai, a garter snake of Unaindin, a material designer. Son of Phot Kul. Dressed in leather garb and carrying an ecdysis trigger, reflective materials, and a fowl. With carve'd capillaries and taint'd swelling.

Fir'Dant Manf, robber of a tomb to the north, a Holocener. Child of The Juice'd Baron. Dressed in hardened leather and carrying stamps approved by the bureaucracy, a black dog, and scissors.

L'Firum Ugar, a hikikomori of meatspace, a cartomancer. Devotee to Garagan. Dressed in padded armor and carrying a herd of microbes, old melee weapons, and valuable minerals.

Del'Talm Duver, defunct administrater of a dilapidated monastery, a seasoned medievalist. Child of the Nematode Mother. Dressed in knot'd objects and carrying synthetic produce, a carton of cigarettes, and crab pelts.

Zodi'Firum Kaddis, a hikikomori of meatspace, a
material designer. Follower of Lovotor. Dressed in
electrical gloves and carrying an idol, ecto-chisel, and torn vinyl. The idol is made of wet sand.

Del'Urnt Kaas, Calloused Hands of unimportant
affiliations, an Object-Oriented Psychologist. Enemy
of the Nematode Mother. Dressed in bear pelts and
carrying unsoil'd planters, guild papers, and groceries.

Bel'Lpra Matkan, a garter snake of House of Effigy, arrhythmic bard. Daughter of The Hylant King.
Dressed in satin and carrying a nail file, a severed
tongue, and utero packs.

Har Ugrite, Prisoner of a dilapidated monastery,
a member of the Order of Self-Capture. Devotee to
Bird Inferior. Dressed in heavyset blankets and
carrying dermal implants, a claw hammer, and seeds.

L'h'Tesh Capio, Grazing Sow of Qamsil, a diligent
squire. Heir to Loplop. Dressed in a skull cap and
carrying a nail file, a configuration of tentacles,
and old melee weapons.

Arwik Hamadrium, Tempt'd Son of Cit Varas, an
affliate of the Threadbarer. Son of The Interface.
Dressed in a reflective mask and carrying beautiful
jewelery, the remnants of a garden, and grime'd
coveralls.

Djo'Yett Ishofli, The Apostle of Dathapt, an architect's apprentice. Follower of Kei-Man. Dressed in
nematode pelts and carrying deer pelts, an unweildy
mace, and sacks of blood.

Al'Miro Heret, The Awakened of Cit Yoasnmoskl, an
occulture critic. Heir to The Chalice. Dressed in
burlap and carrying VHS tapes, unassuming clothes,
and bars of RAM.

Narfe Gaer, defunct administrater of a desert temple, a member of the Order of Small Fires. Child of
Gilead. Dressed in splint mail and carrying a severed finger, a video still, and a coveted heirloom.
The video still is from a Apichatpong Weerasethakul
film.

Hagos Oshmer, Erupted Body of Cit Hima'al, bibliomancer. Child of Ultut. Dressed in tigulated mail
and carrying a protractor, severed implants, and a
box radio.

Otr Kabat, Pariah of a nearby watchtower, a scholar of geo-mechanical criticism. Daughter of many
saints. Dressed in a scarab husk and carrying unilt
candles, a trocer, and a hand drill.

Heru'Suel Et'Alette, The Flesh'd of Cit Batum,
an occulture critic. Enemy of Lunar. Dressed in
multicolor bows and carrying stamps approved by the
bureaucracy, composite plateware, and vagrant garb.

Fir'Elkt Saumtar, The Pilgrim of Cit Decair, a
laborer. Devotee to Gond. Dressed in beautiful jewelery and carrying an artificial leach, an artificial
carapace, and precious ornaments.

Orans Dejolu, hive body of the Ambient Zone, an
occult minimalist. Child of Oark. Dressed in
structural proteins and carrying cloth, a severed
tongue, and an amputation knife. With pinkyellow
soles and shave'd gums.

Mirum Minerd, stranger of the exterior, an exorcist
of sorts. Enemy of The Neo-Succulent. Dressed in
many talismen and carrying spider plants, an unweildy mace, and various salves & creams.

Ull Penia, prospective client of Dair'Kud'Tuler,
scryer. Daughter of Doromundis. Dressed in denim
and carrying a wad of receipts, unilt candles, and
holy garb.

Ked'Suel Rhod, The Whisperer of Cit Centur, Appointed Bishop. Daughter of Kei-Man. Dressed in
proto-limbs and carrying salvaged ciruit boards,
pluck'd guavas, and tins of pink paste.

Del'Urnt Balu, hive body of the Ambient Zone, a
bone harvester. Follower of Bird Inferior. Dressed
in a configuration of tentacles and carrying composite plateware, a parcel, and the hoof of an ungulate.

Uni'Duvel Ager, The Awakened of Ravum, a member
of the Order of Small Fires. Enemy of The Juice'd
Baron. Dressed in bulk'd iron and carrying robes,
the cantos, and nematode pelts.

Cyb'Ka Kaukas, The Awakened of a distant past,
Applied Ontologist. Daughter of The Juice'd Baron.
Dressed in structural proteins and carrying seeds,
dermal implants, and guild papers.

Heh'Mot Voogd, The Flesh'd of En, a bone harvester.
Son of Lunar. Dressed in bulk'd iron and carrying
unilt candles, knot'd objects, and spider plants.

Abbe'Gran Saumtar, Frog of Cit Batum, a student
of golemancy. Heir to Gond. Dressed in electrical
gloves and carrying babel-ware, jicama, and proto-limbs.

Mal'Miro Yanak, sever'd torso of a pastoral landscape, an automapper. Enemy of Tumpur. Dressed in
clusters of TVP and carrying valueless minerals,
clips, and an unidentified brass instrument. With
ocherorange veins and lean loins.

Yune'Dant Fabak, a polemarch of Cit Hima'al, a
subterranean apiologist. Enemy of Bird Inferior.
Dressed in chain sleeves and carrying clusters of
TVP, pluck'd guavas, and gnaw'd seeds.

Vathar Macci, Arachnid follower of Dathapt, an apprentice of the Augury. Devotee to Garagan. Dressed in clusters of TVP and carrying robes, tins of pink paste, and old melee weapons.

Ugra'Loc Abdelnoer, fodder of Junkrhad, Marred Grocer. Daughter of The Hylant King. Dressed in broken cybernetics and carrying a configuration of tentacles, an artificial leach, and coffee beans.

Mal'Lpra Gatal, sever'd head of Anarak, an occult minimalist. Heir to The Neo-Succulent. Dressed in an ornate mask and carrying vagrant garb, enriched soil, and linens. With paint'd ventral blotches and worn lacerations.

Al'Miro Agre, Drunkard of Argas, an affliate of the Threadbarer. Enemy of The Hylant King. Dressed in hardened leather and carrying sacks of bitumen, crab pelts, and sensory archive tool. With aquamarinegreen occipital hatch and violent eyes.

Dua'Firum Lethem, the beauty of Spahbod, an interface engineer. Enemy of Asterion. Dressed in unassuming clothes and carrying a pick, unplug'd contraptions, and stripped vines.

Grhi'Lpra Dalagur, the aphroditium of Unaindin, a fledgling in the Guild of Faciality. Follower of Kei-Man. Dressed in biometric armor and carrying composite plateware, quince, and ornate rugs.

Uyr Fabak, The Whisperer of Ravum, a dream technician. Devotee to Egregious Cuts. Dressed in a linear frame and carrying minor excavation equipment, crude cut cloth, and turmeric.

Usil'Firum Ekate, Archpriest of the Carnlands, Neo-typesetter. Heir to The Chalice. Dressed in electrical gloves and carrying net monitors, ice'd milk bottles, and delicate tarts.

Cyb'Ament Pauk, The Hoarder of Artifacts of a desecrated shrine, a digital ecologist. Devotee to The Moon-Face. Dressed in vagrant garb and carrying an artificial carapace, conical objects, and babel-ware. With acid-spit eyes and brownsilver swelling.

Bjor Phalec, cyberpunk of Cit Hima'al, a water merchant. Enemy of the Nematode Mother. Dressed in bulk'd iron and carrying a tome of sandpaper, deer pelts, and trackmesh. The tome was written by a group of symbolist poets.

Heru'Gran Lazdon, Heredet of Cit En, a hyper-zonal ecologist. Child of The Nostrum. Dressed in wire fleece and carrying tins of gelatin, sacks of blood, and sacks of oil.

Wadej'Ament Glauciem, Matriarch of Upasal, an occult minimalist. Son of The Hylant King. Dressed in wire'd oxygen tanks and carrying tarot cards, a lithotome, and coffee beans.

Duvre'Numi Hignite, Villager of the ludological south, a scholar of apiary geometry. Daughter of Garagan. Dressed in an ornate mask and carrying faction affiliate'd clothing, valuable minerals, and polymer blocks.

Elam Sabiume, a scholar of meatspace, a radical thinker. Enemy of Lovotor. Dressed in bulk'd iron and carrying various maps, an arrow remover, and nylon. With sharp nape and slime'd soles.

Wadej'Erzu Yzaguirre, an unlearn'd body of Batum, a minor castor. Follower of Kei-Man. Dressed in many talismen and carrying a case of pins, a bedroll, and a painting. The painting depicts a column. The column is ionic.

Imho'Aken Pacaan, Jaguar of the outskirts, nectar chemist. Son of Loplop. Dressed in nylon and carrying a wad of receipts, golem flesh, and the remnants of a garden. With taint'd toes and lean pores.

Ked'Urnt Dien, Arachnid follower of Agatar, Appointed Bishop. Enemy of The Deep Well. Dressed in an array of aprons and carrying reams of parchment paper, a painting, and a protractor. The painting depicts a mule. The mule is burning.

Mede'Uun Ebaugh, a desert father of Fir'Al'Tuler, a studio painter. Heir to Gond. Dressed in an array of buckles and carrying a toolbox, sensory archive tool, and trackmesh. With gossamer occipital hatch and copperblue ink.

Ba'Neom Lotan, The Apostle of Latabk, a member of
the Guild of Cyber Mycologies. Daughter of the
Nematode Mother. Dressed in thick leg warmers and
carrying quince, a metal contraption, and the cantos. With taint'd irises and flexible calves.

Jem'Amaun Gauk, Consul of the Ambient Zone, a
studio painter. Devotee to Oark. Dressed in vagrant
garb and carrying an unidentified brass instrument,
cans of nectar, and a belladonic cast.

Grhi'Rada Perkants, travel'd companion of Cit
Dair'Kud'Tuler, a collisionist. Child of The Deep
Well. Dressed in a scarab husk and carrying succu-
lents, light plating, and an unweildy mace.

Ba'Yett Qarat, sprout'd commoner of Chthonos, a
watchdog. Child of Gilead. Dressed in a belladonic cast and carrying waterlog'd magazines, loose
water, and rolls of thread.

Zodi'Ament Nergrel, devotee of Cit Yoasnmoskl,
nectar chemist. Devotee to Loplop. Dressed in contiguous joints and carrying tissue samples, carbon
fiber, and severed implants.

Geb'Apet Astare, Ruiner of Hima'al, an exorcist
of sorts. Enemy of Ultut. Dressed in an artificial
carapace and carrying a toolbox, ecto-chisel, and
muscle memory implants.

Ameer'Yett Ozog, raccoon of the Carnlands, a collisionist. Child of the Goatfolk. Dressed in an
artificial carapace and carrying dermal implants,
knot'd electrical cords, and wooden figurines.

Elam Labrahm, The Nomad of Cit Yoasnmoskl,
Neo-typesetter. Son of Ultut. Dressed in a scarab
husk and carrying an oil lamp, reflective materials,
and gemstones.

Elion Penia, The Nomad of Ephor, a Holocener. Follower of Egregious Cuts. Dressed in a configuration
of tentacles and carrying salvaged ciruit boards,
deer pelts, and multicolor bows.

Jem'Roni Dahak, the beauty of unimportant affiliations, bodymass engineer. Follower of many saints.
Dressed in biometric armor and carrying a roll of
cartridges, synthetic produce, and guild papers.

Mahes'Sham Deran, mammoth of Upasal, bodymass engineer. Heir to Volcanic Fumes. Dressed in tarpaulin and carrying wire'd oxygen tanks, nut butter, and unmark'd objects.

Jem'Suel Nachbar, spike'd hog of Yoasnmsokl, Applied Ontologist. Heir to Egregious Cuts. Dressed in a belladonic cast and carrying a trephine and accompanying trepan, a cellphone, and a book of poetry.

Par'Lpra Guat, a raccoon dog of Cit Ravum, Neo-typesetter. Daughter of Bardofrankont. Dressed in a belladonic cast and carrying a hand auger, rail nails, and a claw hammer. With oblong ankles and grayblue sores.

Usil'Anet Yablon, red clown of a pastoral landscape, a cosmopolist. Heir to The Unbound Stomach. Dressed in utero packs and carrying kevlar, a box radio, and a hand broom.

Aza'Aken Ekate, a scholar of Upasal, an experienced cryptographer. Son of Garagan. Dressed in muscle memory implants and carrying synthetic produce, a box radio, and technoscanner.

Del'Urnt Latur, an anteater of Aswart, a neo-historian. Daughter of Gond. Dressed in many talismen and carrying deer pelts, VHS tapes, and stamps approved by the bureaucracy.

Par'Smet Latur, sever'd head of Varas, an occulture critic. Son of the Nematode Mother. Dressed in kevlar and carrying a painting, deer pelts, and an old CD player. The painting depicts a mule. The mule is whining.

Heru'Ka Macci, mantis of Cit En, an Object-Oriented Psychologist. Daughter of the Nematode Mother. Dressed in grime'd coveralls and carrying stripped vines, a analog camera, and a sealed chastity belt.

Miro Nifong, newly resurrected servant of the exterior, a Slime Morphologist. Devotee to the Goatfolk. Dressed in crab pelts and carrying broken cybernetics, gemstones, and quince.

Ameer'Numi Yacovone, Grazing Sow of Fir'Al'Tuler, a virtual archaeologist. Heir to the Nematode Mother. Dressed in quilted armor and carrying kelp, many perfumes, and a collection of CDs. With pickle'd cuts and silk'd ear lobes.

Wadej'Roni Schecter, a polemarch of Fir'Al'Tuler,
a guilded merchant. Heir to The Crawling Ooze.
Dressed in clusters of TVP and carrying sacks of
blood, bulk'd iron, and a herd of microbes.

Anti Tamar, punk of meatspace, an interface engineer. Heir to The Crawling Ooze. Dressed in iron
mesh and carrying an isohedron, structural proteins, and biometric armor.

Dei'Miro Yegge, The Flesh'd of Dathapt, an experienced cryptographer. Son of The Interface. Dressed
in grime'd coveralls and carrying broken cybernetics, salvage, and a crate of soylent.

Dei'Imp Pacaan, vole of a dilapidated monastery, a
practitioner of TVmancy. Daughter of The Unbound
Stomach. Dressed in vambraces and carrying an array
of buckles, cured meat, and groceries. With bald
avulsions and petite burns.

Ugra'Raat Taaffe, The Polydactyl Palm of The Moon,
a narrative designer. Child of the Goatfolk.
Dressed in an ornate mask and carrying a small
sculpture, nylon, and a linear frame. The sculpture
has been crumpled.

Hade Kawat, sever'd head of Cit Centur, a techscanner. Devotee to Tumpur. Dressed in a linear frame and carrying an ecdysis trigger, fungal sprouts, and a wad of receipts. With copperblue genitalia and paint'd knuckles.

Bel'Ket Oduad, cave dweller of the Niopo Tree, a dream technician. Daughter of the Nematode Mother. Dressed in decadent shawls and carrying beautiful jewelery, neural comb, and a severed finger.

Heru'Odde Trigov, grid'd fool of the Centur Cathedral, a watchdog. Son of Doromundis. Dressed in wire fleece and carrying minor excavation equipment, grime'd coveralls, and a single-shot rifle.

Caher Nergrel, a polemarch of Tel Grazere, a Neoproph. Heir to Gilead. Dressed in a reflective mask and carrying a nail file, tarpaulin, and a video still. The video still depicts a mule. The mule is dancing.

Bel'Rada Gula, the crack'd finger of a desecrated shrine, a Xenomorphic Engineer. Enemy of Loplop. Dressed in heavy greaves and carrying tar'd feathers, fir leaves, and knot'd electrical cords.

Wadej'Iah Labiche, The Neophyte of Hima'al, a pseudo-geographer. Son of Gond. Dressed in light plating and carrying multicolor bows, orbital siphons, and trash.

Sopona Glauciem, postpunk of the Cauldron, an expert in animal husbandry. Follower of The Moon-Face. Dressed in heavyset blankets and carrying many talismen, jicama, and a bundle'd duvet.

Thiaf Gast, The Right Hand of the ludological south, a fleshcraft assistant. Heir to no one. Dressed in russet armor and carrying a dried eye, a belladonic cast, and an important tablet.

Wadej'Baal Khon, hikikomori of a desecrated shrine, a member of the Panoptic Order. Follower of Oark. Dressed in steel armor and carrying a dried eye, an unweildy mace, and sensory archive tool.

Grhi'Mot Widjaja, prospective client of Dathapt, a scholar of geo-mechanical criticism. Enemy of Oark. Dressed in a belladonic cast and carrying precious ornaments, important documents, and biometric armor.

Grhi'Otep Fumero, Pariah of a distant past, a worshipper of the Lamprey. Heir to The Crawling Ooze.
Dressed in tigulated mail and carrying salvage,
satin, and a painting. The painting is a portrait.
The subject is upset.

Hri'Baal Seelig, The Awakened of The Moon, a pseudo-geographer. Heir to The Unbound Stomach. Dressed
in an ornate mask and carrying jicama, lotus stems,
and the hoof of an ungulate.

Mede'Yett Kaddis, swarm'd form of Licot, a mancer of some kind. Daughter of The Juice'd Baron.
Dressed in a simple dress and carrying broken
cybernetics, bottles of acid, and babel-ware.

Cyb'Anet Qader, Pyrarc of Nahr, a laborer. Son of
The Unbound Stomach. Dressed in structural proteins
and carrying a sacred tome, bear pelts, and various
artifacts. The tome is an object in and of itself.

Hez'Feim Aamodt, plauge'd villager of Cit Varas, a Yonicist. Daughter of The Urchin King. Dressed in fir leaves and carrying a sealed chastity belt, a box radio, and cured meat. With cyanred nail beds and babyblueviolet knuckles.

Hri'Hap Kakar, plauge'd villager of a mountain village, Applied Ontologist. Devotee to Volcanic Fumes. Dressed in crab pelts and carrying wire'd oxygen tanks, succulents, and a fowl.

Rima Gulem, a garter snake of Unaindin, a pitch-speaker. Son of Oark. Dressed in padded armor and carrying succulents, a protractor, and satin.

Mede'Roni Deran, travel'd companion of Spahbod, a virtual archaeologist. Devotee to Lovotor. Dressed in muscle memory implants and carrying succulents, guild papers, and valueless minerals.

Abalard Panorm, Warden of Cit Batum, a pseudo-geographer. Daughter of The Interface. Dressed in beautiful jewelery and carrying linens, a fowl, and bulk'd iron.

Abbe'Numi Duver, postpunk of the Carnlands, a virtual archaeologist. Heir to Gond. Dressed in knot'd objects and carrying kelp, a severed finger, and palmagranates.

Aschet Perkants, Matriarch of Upasal, a Slime Morphologist. Heir to Ultut. Dressed in steel mesh and carrying waterlog'd magazines, babel-ware, and nut butter.

Suri'Erzu Thakur, Pyrarc of Cit Yoasnmoskl, a specialist in synthetic materials. Enemy of no one. Dressed in mirror'd panels and carrying denim fits, a fowl, and electrical wires. With shave'd abrasions and bulbous hands.

Al'Neom Aamodt, Arachnid follower of a nearby watchtower, a Slime Morphologist. Child of The Nostrum. Dressed in biometric armor and carrying a black dog, trash, and valueless minerals.

Otr Iafrate, a lecturer of Agatar, a zonetologist. Heir to The Deep Well. Dressed in crude cut cloth and carrying stamps approved by the bureaucracy, decadent shawls, and the hoof of an ungulate.

Yune'Dant Oshmer, haunch'd bird of a dilapidated monastery, a water merchant. Heir to Volcanic Fumes. Dressed in dermal implants and carrying nut butter, nylon, and impotent seeds.

Umeer'Ament Kabel, Consul of Cit Varas, a haruspex. Daughter of Egregious Cuts. Dressed in a dusk shroud and carrying lotus stems, bags of fertilizer, and a pick.

Numko Takarem, Heredet of Nahr, an automapper. Follower of Loplop. Dressed in broken cybernetics and carrying bottles of acid, a herd of microbes, and palmagranates.

Aze'Suel Cearle, zealous courter of Vavia, a fledgling in the Guild of Faciality. Heir to The Urchin King. Dressed in reflective materials and carrying a linear frame, jicama, and a bedroll. With ocherorange avulsions and lean shins.

Nibel Polit, stray dog of Ungulum, a scholar of marxist grammatology. Child of Gond. Dressed in nematode pelts and carrying a analog camera, an old CD player, and unplug'd monitors.

Abalard Larat, The Flesh'd of Agatar, a student of golemancy. Enemy of Lovotor. Dressed in trackmesh and carrying gnaw'd seeds, canteens, and a roll of cartridges.

Mede'Duvel Pacocha, vole of another planet, atonal bard. Heir to The Moon-Face. Dressed in a reflective mask and carrying ice'd milk bottles, many talismen, and tallow.

L'h'Anet Simik, a garter snake of a procedural cityscape, a bone harvester. Follower of Asterion. Dressed in conical objects and carrying a stylus, turmeric, and various salves & creams. With gray-blue hands and gossamer nail beds.

Hez'Tesh Tyrer, Frog of a procedural cityscape, an astragalomancer. Daughter of Gilead. Dressed in kelp and carrying a ring of keys, a percolator, and VHS tapes.

Ked'Urnt Panorm, plauge'd villager of Cit Yoasnmoskl, a scholar of marxist grammatology. Follower of Egregious Cuts. Dressed in crude cut cloth and carrying technoscanner, composite plateware, and a severed tongue.

Duvre'Sham Iacon, The Flesh'd of the Carnlands, a scholar of ephemeral posterity. Son of The Urchin King. Dressed in contiguous joints and carrying sacks of water, thick leg warmers, and an ecdysis trigger.

Nel'Loc Asher, a polemarch of the exterior, an equestrian performer. Son of Egregious Cuts. Dressed in quilted armor and carrying moderate plating, various maps, and an array of buckles. With slime'd teeth and rotting toes.

Djo'Hept Cit'Al, sever'd head of the northern deserts, a nematode farmer. Son of The Nostrum. Dressed in electrical gloves and carrying knot'd objects, precious ornaments, and a single-shot rifle.

El'Hap Gayumart, fodder of Tel Grazere, a Yonicist. Heir to Bird Inferior. Dressed in moderate plating and carrying seeds, a configuration of tentacles, and an array of aprons. With dark navel and oblong toes.

Baka'Ket Widrig, the aphroditium of the Ambient
Zone, a cantrip engineer. Daughter of Gilead.
Dressed in trash and carrying a trephine and accompanying trepan, a bundle'd duvet, and a box of
carefully packaged needles.

Ocypt Qarat, root'd stem of Lundre, a minor castor. Devotee to The Crawling Ooze. Dressed in tar'd
feathers and carrying an iron maiden, linens, and
palmagranates. With rusted avulsions and speckled
teeth.

Nel'Ket Qarat, white clown of Hima'al, a mancer of
some kind. Son of Kei-Man. Dressed in beautiful
jewelery and carrying turmeric, multicolor bows,
and ornate rugs. With gaudy arteries and lofty
crows feet.

Ba'Ament Urchint, The Neophyte of a desert temple,
a scapulomancer. Child of Oark. Dressed in cloth
and carrying bear pelts, an unweildy mace, and
fasteners.

Hri'Firum Et'Fir, sever'd head of Ungulum, a water
merchant. Devotee to Gond. Dressed in a skull cap
and carrying an old CD player, recovered processors, and palmagranates.

Suri'Smet Simik, okapi of Cit Ravum, a journeyman
of fleshcraft. Enemy of The Urchin King. Dressed in
clusters of TVP and carrying a trephine and accompanying trepan, ice'd milk bottles, and nylon.

L'Ament Et'En, fingerless dweller of a desecrated
shrine, a member of the Panoptic Order. Son of
Lovotor. Dressed in kelp and carrying moderate
plating, sacks of blood, and reflective materials.

Ked'Apet Perstelis, feral cat of a mountain village, an anti-realist. Child of Bird Superior.
Dressed in beautiful jewelery and carrying various
maps, a roll of cartridges, and reflective materials. With paint'd water and sharp cuts.

Hri'Raat Minerd, The Whisperer of Batum, a Necrologist. Daughter of The Hundred Headless Woman.
Dressed in heavyset blankets and carrying reams of
parchment paper, salvage, and an ecdysis trigger.

Saule Deran, Arachnid follower of Cit Ravum, an art
critic. Follower of The Hundred Headless Woman.
Dressed in steel mesh and carrying a gorget, enriched soil, and steel armor.

Ubi'Smet Oshmer, Palatine of Batum, an architect's apprentice. Enemy of Egregious Cuts. Dressed in fir leaves and carrying burlap, a woodcutter's axe, and a stylus.

Ba'Feim Sahs, deer-body of the northern deserts, a bacterial miner. Enemy of The Nostrum. Dressed in contiguous joints and carrying polymer blocks, coins, and lotus stems.

Amer'Baal Akkadum, punk of Unaindin, bibliomancer. Heir to Loplop. Dressed in a reflective mask and carrying a collection of CDs, fungal sprouts, and bone meal.

Heh'Roni Mallaird, traitor of Batum, a gastromancer. Enemy of Doromundis. Dressed in proto-limbs and carrying a stylus, a corpse over their shoulder, and an ecdysis trigger.

Nabal Aarhus, Drowned Wight of Nahr, a member of the Panoptic Order. Daughter of Asterion. Dressed in light plating and carrying beautiful jewelery, torn vinyl, and knot'd electrical cords. With ocherorange nail beds and bald sores.

Ona Lazdon, The Awakened of a desecrated shrine, a seasoned medievalist. Child of The Crawling Ooze. Dressed in contiguous joints and carrying severed implants, gnaw'd seeds, and knot'd objects.

Jyo Espern, curse'd commoner of Cit Licot, an
Omphalomancer. Follower of Lovotor. Dressed in
leather garb and carrying kelp, work clothes, and
bulk'd iron.

Umir'Roni Voogd, feral bear of another planet, a
collisionist. Heir to the Nematode Mother. Dressed
in steel mesh and carrying a severed finger, nylon,
and a carton of cigarettes.

Ihy'Erzu Egle, The Nomad of Lundre, a dream technician. Devotee to Loplop. Dressed in fir leaves and
carrying a tome of sandpaper, trash, and an artificial leach.

Heh'Hap Trigov, trembling seer of Vavia, a subterranean apiologist. Devotee to The Unbound Stomach.
Dressed in dermal implants and carrying a book of
poetry, guild papers, and a coveted heirloom.

Mal'Odde Cech, a column monk of a rural river town,
a member of the Order of Small Fires. Daughter of
The Interface. Dressed in muscle memory implants
and carrying unmark'd objects, fungal sprouts, and
a tome of sandpaper. The tome contains the history
of the region.

Del'Urnt Et'Alette, the practice'd sow of
Fir'Al'Tuler, a member of the Guild of Cyber Mycologies. Daughter of The Unbound Stomach. Dressed
in heavyset blankets and carrying datacells, net
monitors, and sensory archive tool. With greengray
digits and bald wrists.

Aza'Lpra Hepfier, traveler of Tel Grazere, a narrative designer. Follower of Volcanic Fumes. Dressed
in vambraces and carrying ice'd milk bottles, additional limbs, and a sealed chastity belt.

Agan Maedia, Villager of a pastoral landscape,
a Lunar Gnostic. Devotee to The Crawling Ooze.
Dressed in irridescent garbs and carrying knot'd
electrical cords, faction affiliate'd clothing, and
bulk'd iron.

Beyla Mallaird, Warden of House of Effigy, a liminal scholar. Daughter of Asterion. Dressed in moderate plating and carrying torn vinyl, datacells, and a roll of cartridges.

Ugra'Smet Aguoun, Friend to the Church of a nearby watchtower, a minor castor. Daughter of Asterion. Dressed in velvet robes and carrying a fowl, a analog camera, and dried fruits.

Miro Iacon, a garter snake of Cit Dair'Kud'Tuler, a scholar of visceral hermetics. Enemy of The Neo-Succulent. Dressed in holy garb and carrying canteens, a lute, and a tome of sandpaper. With oblong bruises and tepid collar bones.

Djo'Hap Sesser, Warden of Agatar, a material designer. Follower of The Juice'd Baron. Dressed in nylon and carrying an interface, dried grains, and nut butter. With ocherfuschia shins and paint'd loins.

Bel'Kell Nielem, devotee of the outskirts, a scholar of post-digital epistemology. Heir to Bird Superior. Dressed in heavy greaves and carrying an array of buckles, a herd of microbes, and datacells.

D'Imp Egle, The Left Hand of Yoasnmsokl, a gastromancer. Devotee to Oark. Dressed in satin and
carrying technoscanner, various loose springs and
pins, and a video still. The video still depicts a
mule. The mule is dancing.

Cyb'Unut Labrahm, plauge'd villager of Argas,
an adept exobotanist. Devotee to The Deep Well.
Dressed in tarpaulin and carrying a sacred tome,
loose water, and foot pedals. The tome contains
important information regarding the virtual archae-
ological practices.

Grhi'Erzu Merope, mammoth of Unaindin, a scholar
of apiary geometry. Heir to Garagan. Dressed in a
linear frame and carrying burlap, a painting, and
an interface. The painting depicts a mule. The mule
is dancing.

Loa'Miro Saurte, curse'd villager of Ephor,
trepaneer. Heir to The Crawling Ooze. Dressed in a
skull cap and carrying an artificial carapace, high-
stress exos, and a dull knife.

Abbe'Tesh Sukrep, Entomb'd of the Niopo Tree, a
scholar of marxist grammatology. Heir to Loplop.
Dressed in carbon fiber and carrying minor excavation equipment, linens, and rail nails.

Suri'Sham Nier, a hound of Agatar, a radical thinker. Daughter of The Moon-Face. Dressed in biometric
armor and carrying tins of pink paste, severed
implants, and prairie grass stalks. With olivepink
wounds and worn wrists.

Uni'Erzu Rahld, the aphroditium of a mountain village, an interface engineer. Enemy of The Chalice.
Dressed in a configuration of tentacles and carrying
clips, a sacred tome, and an artificial leach. The
tome tells the story of a mule.

Abbe'Imp Behrend, The Awakened of Latabk, an equestrian performer. Enemy of Kei-Man. Dressed in a
gas mask and carrying utero packs, the cantos, and
golem flesh.

Tabor Noita, postcorpse of a nearby watchtower, a
practitioner of necromancy. Child of the Nematode
Mother. Dressed in knot'd objects and carrying unmark'd objects, unplug'd monitors, and bear pelts.

Heh'Amaun Gabor, newly resurrected servant of the
Ambient Zone, an equestrian performer. Heir to The
Moon-Face. Dressed in dermal implants and carrying
nylon, recovered processors, and tissue samples.

Nan Minerv, stray dog of Cit Centur, a watchdog.
Enemy of Kei-Man. Dressed in trackmesh and carrying
irridescent garbs, the remnants of a garden, and
bottles of slime.

L'Unut Thamery, The Summoning Palm of a desert temple, a member of the Order of Small Fires. Follower
of Gond. Dressed in fir leaves and carrying light
plating, reams of grid paper, and tar'd feathers.

Pra'Tesh Himan, Ruiner of Agatar, Marred Grocer.
Daughter of The Chalice. Dressed in black robes and
carrying a protractor, light plating, and a dull
knife. With tepid follicles and speckled sores.

Bel'Numi Saumtar, Friend to the Church of Argas,
Applied Ontologist. Follower of Oark. Dressed in
cloth and carrying a fowl, cans of nectar, and
coins.

Kotar Manf, Drunkard of a tomb to the north, atonal
bard. Child of Gilead. Dressed in velvet robes and
carrying contiguous joints, technoscanner, and torn
vinyl.

Ve Rablase, Frog of the wilderness, a fleshcraft assistant. Heir to Oark. Dressed in denim and carrying many talismen, nylon, and an iron maiden.

Ymir Yauk, newly resurrected servant of Latabk, a scholar of marxist grammatology. Heir to The Interface. Dressed in reflective materials and carrying a rotor machine, a trephine and accompanying trepan, and stripped vines.

Faal Mabe, Friend to the Church of Cit Dair'Kud'Tuler, Neo-typesetter. Daughter of Egregious Cuts. Dressed in wire'd oxygen tanks and carrying enriched soil, clusters of TVP, and trash.

Ent'Loc Yacovone, Jaguar of Lower Dark, Mule Herder. Heir to The Juice'd Baron. Dressed in fir leaves and carrying an important tablet, linens, and unmark'd objects.

Pan'Firum Agrhil, the aphroditium of the northern deserts, a material designer. Follower of The Juice'd Baron. Dressed in utero packs and carrying various artifacts, a fowl, and a sacred tome. The tome contains a religious schism.

Geb'Erzu Vikar, a fungal body of Batum, a narrative designer. Follower of The Neo-Succulent. Dressed in an array of buckles and carrying trackmesh, gnaw'd seeds, and moss weaves.

Grhi'Hept Gast, Drunkard of Cit Decair, a zonetologist. Son of Ameer DuVal. Dressed in carbon fiber and carrying a box of matches, palmagranates, and an ecraseur.

Usil'Yett Tamar, a hire'd body of Qamsil, a seasoned medievalist. Follower of Bardofrankont. Dressed in a wing'd helmet and carrying bags of fertilizer, proto-limbs, and moderate plating.

Manta Et'Batum, an unlearn'd body of the Centur Cathedral, a bacterial miner. Devotee to The Chalice. Dressed in conical objects and carrying unmark'd objects, old melee weapons, and stamps approved by the bureaucracy.

Geb'Aken Kavan, curse'd villager of Cit Centur, a member of the Order of Small Fires. Enemy of The Moon-Face. Dressed in velvet robes and carrying reams of grid paper, vagrant garb, and proto-limbs. With copperblue follicles and wiry wrinkles.

Lith Synth, sprout'd commoner of a desert temple, scryer. Son of The Neo-Succulent. Dressed in tar'd feathers and carrying slabs of ice, steel armor, and high-stress exos. With dark wrists and oblong ink.

Hyrme Et'Nahr, Warden of the northern deserts, an exorcist of sorts. Enemy of no one. Dressed in tar'd feathers and carrying a woodcutter's axe, enriched soil, and mirror'd panels.

Ked'Amaun Aaber, story'd fool of Anarak, a digital ecologist. Son of Asterion. Dressed in a scarab husk and carrying an iron maiden, canteens, and tins of gelatin.

Umir'Anet Dejan, a scholar of Argas, a material designer. Heir to Ultut. Dressed in leather garb and carrying polymer blocks, a set of jugum, and muscle memory implants. With carve'd toes and bald follicles.

Yune'Suel Dalagur, The Flesh'd of Chthonos, a
pitchspeaker. Son of many saints. Dressed in decadent shawls and carrying an idol, a line of hangers, and a parcel. The idol is made of dirt.

Ba'Raat Widrig, the beauty of Ravum, trepaneer.
Daughter of The Nostrum. Dressed in faction affiliate'd clothing and carrying unplug'd monitors,
knot'd electrical cords, and an ecraseur.

Ubi'Uun Nachbar, an anteater of Argas, a pseudo-geographer. Son of The Juice'd Baron. Dressed in
mirror'd panels and carrying fragant stones, rail
nails, and important documents.

Ixid Casur, Tempt'd Son of Azmeern, a student of
golemancy. Devotee to The Urchin King. Dressed in
an artificial carapace and carrying a set of jugum,
gnaw'd seeds, and knot'd objects.

Neom Balu, Arachnid follower of The Moon, a soothsayer. Child of Asterion. Dressed in a belladonic cast and carrying cans of nectar, burlap, and
scissors.

Abalard Battiat, an anteater of Batum, a cosmopolist. Daughter of The Neo-Succulent. Dressed in
kevlar and carrying valuable minerals, slabs of
ice, and a lithotome.

Anti Felk, Prisoner of a desert temple, an interior demonologist. Heir to The Unbound Stomach. Dressed in bulk'd iron and carrying a dull knife, severed implants, and broken cybernetics.

Lith Kabat, an anteater of Cit Vavia, a practitioner of collectamancy. Son of Loplop. Dressed in trash and carrying light plating, babel-ware, and the pandimonium index.

Del'Suel Reeg, haunch'd bird of Hima'al, a subterranean apiologist. Devotee to the Goatfolk. Dressed in babel-ware and carrying cans of nectar, rail nails, and a bundle'd duvet.

Ogun Sabag, feral cat of a tomb to the north, Neo-typesetter. Son of The Urchin King. Dressed in a linear frame and carrying robes, high-stress exos, and a crate of soylent.

Geb'Neom Gehen, devotee of Revarie, a scapulomancer. Enemy of The Unbound Stomach. Dressed in an
artificial carapace and carrying fasteners, a wad
of receipts, and a analog camera. With worn sutures
and worn eyelids.

Eyon'Lpra Reeg, sentient mass of Tel Grazere, a
scholar of post-digital epistemology. Child of
Lovotor. Dressed in torn vinyl and carrying severed
implants, tarot cards, and dried grains.

Kaur Setver, Battl'd Insect of a tomb to the south,
an equestrian performer. Daughter of The Interface.
Dressed in deer pelts and carrying neural comb,
bear pelts, and nylon.

Wadej'Feim Guat, an unlearn'd body of the Ambient
Zone, an architect's apprentice. Heir to the Goatfolk. Dressed in uncast nets and carrying various
artifacts, a metal contraption, and carbon fiber.
With redviolet wrists and worn ankles.

Ugra'Nepher Casur, skull digger of Unaindin, a
Slime Morphologist. Enemy of The Moon-Face. Dressed
in burlap and carrying a dull knife, a severed
tongue, and a trocer.

Pan'Duvel Simik, punk of Yoasnmsokl, a cantrip engineer. Enemy of The Unbound Stomach. Dressed in electrical gloves and carrying an amputation knife, enriched soil, and tar'd feathers.

Id Bame, hive body of a distant past, bibliomancer. Child of Bird Inferior. Dressed in additional limbs and carrying linens, moderate plating, and wooden figurines. With crook'd arteries and rustplum occipital hatch.

Ur'Yett Dudek, a lecturer of Licot, a seasoned medievalist. Heir to The Nostrum. Dressed in fir leaves and carrying a nail file, work clothes, and kevlar.

Ameer'Feim Yanak, cave dweller of unimportant affiliations, a zonetologist. Child of The Unbound Stomach. Dressed in thick leg warmers and carrying black robes, a roll of cartridges, and chewing gum.

Neom Mormil, raccoon of Cit Varas, a nematode breeder. Enemy of The Nostrum. Dressed in moderate plating and carrying electrical wires, a single-shot rifle, and an amputation knife.

Jem'Dant Urak, Archpriest of Agatar, a Morphofeminist. Follower of many saints. Dressed in steel
armor and carrying a protractor, proto-limbs, and a
analog camera.

Ba'Tesh Wadak, tentacle'd fool of Fir'Al'Tuler, a
virtual archaeologist. Follower of no one. Dressed
in wire'd oxygen tanks and carrying fragant stones,
unsoil'd planters, and an array of buckles.

Baka'Sham Morank, siphon'd fool of a dilapidated
monastery, an affliate of the Threadbarer. Daughter
of Lunar. Dressed in a sealed chastity belt and
carrying unsoil'd planters, orbital siphons, and
prairie grass stalks.

Jem'Hept Nachbar, Matriarch of the exterior, a
worshipper of the Lamprey. Son of The Urchin King.
Dressed in an array of aprons and carrying a linear frame, proto-limbs, and a hand broom.

Loa'Tek Gilitine, The Nomad of Yoasnmsokl, a zonetologist. Follower of The Interface. Dressed in
bear pelts and carrying a woodcutter's axe, a roll
of cartridges, and polymer blocks.

Ent'Uun Kaddis, The Nomad of a tomb to the south, an occult minimalist. Enemy of Kei-Man. Dressed in tarpaulin and carrying dice, denim fits, and a tome of sandpaper. The tome was written by a hermit, Loa'Tek Gilitine.

Yune'Aken Vaccan, Arachnid follower of Agatar, bibliomancer. Son of Lunar. Dressed in splint mail and carrying seeds, prairie grass stalks, and the remnants of a garden.

Umir'Ament Duvel, Heredet of Cit Fir'Al'Tuler, a material designer. Daughter of The Nostrum. Dressed in contiguous joints and carrying quince, an array of buckles, and an iron maiden.

Umeer'Apet Maas, Frog of Cit Vavia, a nematode breeder. Enemy of Oark. Dressed in satin and carrying irridescent garbs, an amputation knife, and torn vinyl.

Umeer'Neom Egle, The Awakened of Nahr, a member of the Panoptic Order. Enemy of Phot Kul. Dressed in wire fleece and carrying rolls of thread, a rotor machine, and an artificial leach. With bulbous digits and pickle'd eyelids.

Gahriza Yauk, cave dweller of a nearby watchtower,
a mancer of some kind. Enemy of Gond. Dressed in a
dusk shroud and carrying a sacred tome, technoscanner, and a metal contraption. The tome contains the
history of Egregious Cuts.

Uni'Feim Cebla, white clown of Vavia, a scholar of
necrometry. Enemy of the Goatfolk. Dressed in burlap and carrying coins, guild papers, and a sealed
chastity belt. With worn nates and pickle'd calves.

Amer'Uun Thakur, red clown of Ephor, a studio
painter. Child of Loplop. Dressed in irridescent
garbs and carrying raw chocolate, an old CD player,
and the hoof of an ungulate. With worn trachea and
paint'd vertebrae.

Ugra'Aken Wehrlee, Heredet of Ephor, an Object-Oriented Psychologist. Enemy of Egregious Cuts.
Dressed in field plates and carrying sacks of blood,
slabs of ice, and clusters of TVP.

Ba'Uun Dien, Sacrificial Heifer of a tomb to the south, a bone harvester. Devotee to Gond. Dressed in iron mesh and carrying a protractor, a linear frame, and lotus stems.

Jem'Yett Guat, Arachnid follower of Cit En, a water merchant. Enemy of The Moon-Face. Dressed in kevlar and carrying prairie grass stalks, operator cards, and succulents.

L'h'Otep Maedia, Tempt'd Son of a tomb to the south, a scholar of visceral hermetics. Daughter of The Crawling Ooze. Dressed in a mirror'd facade and carrying coins, technoscanner, and a trocer. With muscular lacerations and flexible veins.

Duvre'Amaun Atunis, trembling seer of a pastoral landscape, a portalogist. Daughter of Ameer DuVal. Dressed in broken cybernetics and carrying holy garb, the pandimonium index, and various artifacts.

Umir'Roni Cedan, white clown of Agatar, a virtual archaeologist. Son of The Neo-Succulent. Dressed in a gas mask and carrying proto-limbs, neural comb, and unmark'd objects.

El'Smet Polit, newly resurrected servant of Anarak, an affliate of the Threadbarer. Enemy of The Interface. Dressed in heavyset blankets and carrying tallow, clusters of TVP, and an amputation knife.

Haret Ager, The Syzygy of All Stars of Latabk, Grand Inquisitor. Devotee to The Interface. Dressed in a simple dress and carrying robes, a crate of soylent, and a book of hymns.

Maur Vierek, Consul of Cit Dair'Kud'Tuler, a member of the Order of Self-Capture. Daughter of Loplop. Dressed in additional limbs and carrying ice'd milk bottles, cans of nectar, and fragant stones. With bluegreen teeth and copperblue genitalia.

Mede'Ket Banaszek, an anteater of the northern deserts, Grand Inquisitor. Daughter of The Nostrum. Dressed in light plating and carrying tins of gelatin, clusters of TVP, and a herd of microbes. With bulbous hands and bluegreen trachea.

Mahes'Suel Fullish, The Neophyte of Tel Grazere, a metamedia specialist. Heir to The Juice'd Baron. Dressed in structural proteins and carrying wire'd oxygen tanks, a trowel, and waterlog'd magazines.

Pan'Imp Tawat, a desert father of Cit Hima'al, a minor castor. Enemy of Bird Superior. Dressed in iron mesh and carrying heavyset blankets, a single-shot rifle, and a box of carefully packaged needles.

Mede'Hap Hepfier, okapi of the Carnlands, a subterranean apiologist. Child of The Neo-Succulent. Dressed in a gas mask and carrying tallow, a severed finger, and an ecdysis trigger.

Par'Talm Faas, an unlearn'd body of a nearby watchtower, bibliomancer. Follower of The Interface. Dressed in quilted armor and carrying ecto-chisel, guild papers, and bottles of slime.

D'Mot Kikomora, Matriarch of Cit Fir'Al'Tuler, a journeyman of fleshcraft. Heir to The Urchin King. Dressed in a gas mask and carrying neural comb, unmark'd objects, and dermal implants.

Rugem Bame, Friend to the Church of House of Effigy, a cosmopolist. Heir to Volcanic Fumes. Dressed in robes and carrying linens, enriched soil, and unplug'd monitors.

Jaukar Wiygul, the practice'd sow of a dilapidated
monastery, a hyper-zonal ecologist. Son of Ultut.
Dressed in a cowl and carrying neural comb, an old
CD player, and an artificial leach. With grayblue
thighs and petite calves.

Ous'Gran Elepis, Battl'd Insect of Cit Fir'Al'Tuler, a scapulomancer. Daughter of The Neo-Succulent.
Dressed in heavyset blankets and carrying kelp,
muscle memory implants, and a dried eye.

Pemphredo Du'un, The Awakened of Chthonos, a practitioner of necromancy. Follower of no one. Dressed
in wire'd oxygen tanks and carrying a bedroll,
spare tanks, and an idol.

Uni'Rada Qeet, a lecturer of a desert temple, a Holocener. Daughter of The Hylant King. Dressed in quilted armor and carrying the hoof of an ungulate, recovered processors, and wire'd oxygen tanks.

Eita Roath, The Polydactyl Palm of Upasal, trepaneer. Heir to Ultut. Dressed in electrical gloves and carrying an interface, bottles of slime, and a nail file.

Jem'Erzu Nier, Drowned Wight of Spahbod, a scholar of proto-linguistics. Child of Lunar. Dressed in satin and carrying a severed nose, a hand broom, and grime'd coveralls. With babyblueviolet scalp and copperblue knees.

Zorya Culsa, terror of Cit En, a dream technician. Devotee to The Hylant King. Dressed in robes and carrying a analog camera, palmagranates, and a metal contraption.

D'Odde Cedan, postpunk of an unknown origin, a practitioner of collectamancy. Enemy of Ultut. Dressed in black robes and carrying an array of aprons, denim fits, and a cellphone.

Jem'Rada Tyrer, a fungal body of a transnational
space, a liminal scholar. Heir to many saints.
Dressed in steel armor and carrying a box of matches, recovered processors, and dried fruits.

Ubi'Mot Uhlik, sentient mass of the Niopo Tree, a
bone harvester. Heir to The Chalice. Dressed in a
simple dress and carrying a video still, bottles
of acid, and thick leg warmers. The video still
depicts a column. The column is doric.

Zodi'Roni Nielem, Friend to the Magistrate of a
desecrated shrine, a portalogist. Child of The Hundred Headless Woman. Dressed in unassuming clothes
and carrying a box of carefully packaged needles,
unilt candles, and sacks of blood.

Mahes'Hap Skorpat, The Apostle of Cit En, a mancer
of some kind. Devotee to The Neo-Succulent. Dressed
in denim and carrying beautiful jewelery, a cellphone, and a line of hangers.

Zodi'Aken Ugar, swarm'd form of Unaindin, a Xenomorphic Engineer. Son of The Moon-Face. Dressed
in crude cut cloth and carrying ornate rugs, many
talismen, and unsoil'd planters.

Jem'Sham Ittre, The Awakened of Licot, a Morphofeminist. Son of The Nostrum. Dressed in a dusk shroud
and carrying wooden figurines, synthetic produce,
and an arrow remover.

El'Neom Neblogst, plauge'd villager of the Digital
Landscape, a water merchant. Child of The Unbound
Stomach. Dressed in a sealed chastity belt and carrying nematode pelts, sacks of slime, and biometric
armor.

Dua'Yett Trigov, stranger of Unaindin, an affliate
of the Threadbarer. Enemy of Asterion. Dressed in
wire'd oxygen tanks and carrying a book of hymns,
rail nails, and a carton of cigarettes.

Tabor Waag, devotee of the Carnlands, a soothsayer. Daughter of The Urchin King. Dressed in trash
and carrying waterlog'd magazines, many perfumes,
and lotus stems. With flexible veins and muscular
calves.

Fir'Ka Detwa, Gentleman of Holy Attire of Cit
Varas, a studio painter. Devotee to Ameer DuVal.
Dressed in kevlar and carrying high-stress exos,
ornate rugs, and rolls of thread.

Ludek Nabu, scale'd fiend of a procedural cityscape,
biographer. Daughter of Lunar. Dressed in irridescent garbs and carrying fragant stones, bottles of
slime, and a severed finger.

Cyr Gulem, cyberpunk of Dathapt, a liminal scholar.
Devotee to Phot Kul. Dressed in cloth and carrying
a protractor, a simple dress, and polymer blocks.

Amir'Urnt Phalec, a tree folk of Azmeern, a nematode farmer. Daughter of The Urchin King. Dressed
in a dusk shroud and carrying decadent shawls,
guild papers, and tissue samples.

Nel'Elkt Cwyanr, white clown of Lundre, a xenoarchitect. Daughter of The Moon-Face. Dressed in
velvet robes and carrying slabs of ice, reams of
parchment paper, and grime'd coveralls.

Surt Ittre, The Awakened of the Cauldron, a minor
castor. Heir to The Neo-Succulent. Dressed in steel
mesh and carrying work clothes, turmeric, and sacks
of water. With babyblueviolet occipital hatch and
worn eyelids.

Saba Minerd, fodder of Licot, a Yonicist. Follower
of Phot Kul. Dressed in a scarab husk and carrying
tins of pink paste, muscle memory implants, and
light plating.

Eyon'Ket Vairya, Heredet of Cit En, an equestrian performer. Heir to Asterion. Dressed in knot'd
objects and carrying palmagranates, a biomonitor,
and scissors. With slime'd irises and ocherfuschia
nail beds.

Mahes'Lpra Hamadrium, Erupted Body of Junkrhad, a
mancer of some kind. Follower of the Nematode Mother. Dressed in linens and carrying orbital siphons,
uncast nets, and canteens.

Grhi'Anet Czap, okapi of Cit Hima'al, a neo-historian. Heir to The Chalice. Dressed in broken
cybernetics and carrying salvage, sacks of blood,
and a dull knife.

Mede'Rada Dejolu, Limb Tree of Aswart, nectar chemist. Son of The Neo-Succulent. Dressed in holy garb
and carrying a wad of receipts, a sacred tome, and
sacks of blood. The tome contains a portal.

Geresh Nien, the crack'd finger of the wilderness,
an adept exobotanist. Enemy of The Deep Well.
Dressed in cloth and carrying wire'd oxygen tanks,
deer pelts, and a roll of cartridges.

Suri'Lpra Gatal, deer-body of Vavia, Neo-typesetter. Daughter of Bird Inferior. Dressed in quilted armor and carrying irridescent garbs, a line of hangers, and waterlog'd magazines.

Par'Ament Gehen, The Summoning Palm of Latabk, a hyper-zonal ecologist. Child of Bird Superior. Dressed in an array of buckles and carrying jicama, canteens, and utero packs.

Amer'Yett Casur, Jaguar of Nahr, a xenoarchitect. Devotee to Gilead. Dressed in moderate plating and carrying a set of jugum, uncast nets, and a configuration of tentacles.

Amir'Hap Yablon, a commoner of the Digital Landscape, a cantrip engineer. Child of Ultut. Dressed in mirror'd panels and carrying many perfumes, torn vinyl, and a box of matches.

Crat Sabag, Entomb'd of Cit Yoasnmoskl, Grand Inquisitor. Daughter of no one. Dressed in black robes and carrying robes, sacks of slime, and neural comb.

Uni'Miro Hure, a badger of Cit Centur, an occult
minimalist. Heir to many saints. Dressed in muscle memory implants and carrying high-stress exos,
an iron maiden, and a trephine and accompanying
trepan.

Wadej'Smet Larat, sprout'd commoner of Dair'Kud'Tuler, a worshipper of the Lamprey. Daughter of Ameer
DuVal. Dressed in a gas mask and carrying a protractor, a metal contraption, and carbon fiber. With
silk'd blisters and redviolet digits.

Duvre'Ket Sorcer, Drunkard of a distant past,
a material designer. Devotee to Bird Superior.
Dressed in denim and carrying recovered processors,
unplug'd monitors, and a claw hammer.

Yune'Erzu Vaccan, postcorpse of a distant past, a
student of golemancy. Daughter of Loplop. Dressed
in biometric armor and carrying a analog camera,
synthetic produce, and an amputation knife.

Aza'Amaun Maak, okapi of Nahr, Applied Ontologist.
Daughter of The Juice'd Baron. Dressed in nematode
pelts and carrying robes, orbital siphons, and a
analog camera.

Ous'Talm Pauk, devotee of the Carnlands, a practitioner of necromancy. Heir to The Unbound Stomach. Dressed in additional limbs and carrying impotent seeds, trackmesh, and a sealed chastity belt.

Mona'Elkt Kabat, fence of Ephor, a mancer of some kind. Enemy of Loplop. Dressed in additional limbs and carrying bulk'd iron, unassuming clothes, and the pandimonium index.

Cyb'Iah Fumero, trembling seer of a nearby watchtower, a soothsayer. Enemy of The Moon-Face. Dressed in wire'd oxygen tanks and carrying clips, reams of parchment paper, and heavyset blankets.

Rez Basuk, postcorpse of Hima'al, a necromancer. Follower of Garagan. Dressed in bear pelts and carrying salvage, nylon, and a stylus.

Usil'Tesh Alau, unbound familiar of Cit Ravum, a futamancer. Child of Lovotor. Dressed in broken cybernetics and carrying a dull knife, a box of carefully packaged needles, and utero packs.

Kuvir Czap, skull digger of Choregas, a scholar of hypnagogic eroticism. Enemy of Gilead. Dressed in crab pelts and carrying linens, recovered processors, and a severed tongue.

Umeer'Talm Nagar, Prisoner of Fir'Al'Tuler, atonal
bard. Devotee to Lunar. Dressed in a beak'd helmet
and carrying tissue samples, a bundle'd duvet, and
bear pelts.

Ent'Anet Kabel, unbound familiar of House of Effigy,
a mancer of some kind. Heir to Doromundis. Dressed
in uncast nets and carrying deer pelts, a wad of
receipts, and electrical wires.

Lurgo Pavak, curse'd commoner of Revarie, a nematode breeder. Child of Loplop. Dressed in bear
pelts and carrying various salves & creams, net
monitors, and turmeric. With tepid knees and lean
crows feet.

L'h'Yett Devang, feral bear of Chthonos, biographer. Son of no one. Dressed in kevlar and carrying
various loose springs and pins, bars of RAM, and
structural proteins.

Saule Saad, newly resurrected servant of the
wilderness, Appointed Bishop. Enemy of Lovotor.
Dressed in velvet robes and carrying an interface,
a bundle'd duvet, and net monitors.

Baka'Anet Nielem, punk of Varas, a gastromancer. Devotee to Egregious Cuts. Dressed in a sealed chastity belt and carrying coins, an artificial leach, and delicate tarts. With acid-spit wounds and copperblue nape.

Ameer'Lpra Viem, Gentleman of Holy Attire of Nahr, an entrail supply specialist. Heir to Kei-Man. Dressed in clusters of TVP and carrying cans of coolant, severed implants, and a severed nose.

Pra'Otep Pagac, swarm'd form of the Carnlands, an architect's apprentice. Child of The Hylant King. Dressed in burlap and carrying cured meat, stripped vines, and fir leaves.

Dievas Kahan, The Polydactyl Palm of The Moon, a water merchant. Heir to The Interface. Dressed in russet armor and carrying sacks of water, nylon, and various loose springs and pins. With oblong ankles and tepid sores.

Yune'Apet Sabat, a garter snake of Cit Centur, Appointed Bishop. Heir to The Neo-Succulent. Dressed in nematode pelts and carrying unassuming clothes, reams of grid paper, and unplug'd monitors.

Uni'Erzu Sukrep, curse'd villager of a desecrated shrine, a pitchspeaker. Devotee to The Crawling Ooze. Dressed in splint mail and carrying robes, reams of parchment paper, and severed implants.

Ent'Tek Neblogst, The Polydactyl Palm of Anarak, a member of the Panoptic Order. Devotee to Egregious Cuts. Dressed in conical objects and carrying electrical wires, sacks of blood, and a pick.

Ibo Et'Ungulum, postcorpse of meatspace, a seasoned medievalist. Devotee to Gond. Dressed in a scarab husk and carrying sacks of bitumen, precious ornaments, and recovered processors.

Umeer'Suel Esperodies, the aphroditium of a tomb to the south, a journeyman of fleshcraft. Son of The Urchin King. Dressed in mirror'd panels and carrying a hand drill, an iron maiden, and dermal implants.

Ihy'Loc Simik, swarm'd form of an unknown origin, a Holocener. Heir to The Moon-Face. Dressed in iron mesh and carrying a cellphone, a biomonitor, and black robes. With grayblue knuckles and grayblue nostrils.

Ameer'Sham Rangrak, The Nomad of Argas, a fleshcraft
assistant. Child of no one. Dressed in an array of
buckles and carrying burlap, a gorget, and bars of
RAM.

Imho'Hept Zacek, mantis of Cit Centur, an interface engineer. Follower of Doromundis. Dressed in
an iron maiden and carrying various artifacts, an
important tablet, and a claw hammer.

Mede'Roni Waag, robber of meatspace, an affliate
of the Threadbarer. Devotee to Garagan. Dressed
in beautiful jewelery and carrying bulk'd iron, a
lute, and quince. With flexible shins and globular
molars.

Par'Sham Dahak, the aphroditium of Cit Vavia, a
cartomancer. Child of The Moon-Face. Dressed in
wire'd oxygen tanks and carrying a percolator, denim fits, and bulk'd iron. With aquamarinegreen crows
feet and silverorange blisters.

Mona'Hap Carace, prospective client of Anarak, a
nematode breeder. Heir to many saints. Dressed
in high-stress exos and carrying a stylus, a hand
drill, and unsoil'd planters.

Ameer'Uun Aamodt, a hikikomori of Lower Dark, an occult minimalist. Daughter of Oark. Dressed in fir leaves and carrying crude cut cloth, golem flesh, and a painting. The painting depicts a snail. The snail is upside down.

Ked'Roni Ubelrahn, robber of meatspace, a scholar of marxist grammatology. Son of the Goatfolk. Dressed in carbon fiber and carrying tarpaulin, a collection of CDs, and denim fits.

Haret Gaet, fingerless dweller of Cit Batum, a liminal scholar. Son of Asterion. Dressed in nylon and carrying high-stress exos, sacks of water, and datacells. With ocherfuschia wounds and redpink pores.

Mal'Dant Dahak, Calloused Hands of the Centur Cathedral, a nematode farmer. Child of Doromundis. Dressed in bulk'd iron and carrying bear pelts, turmeric, and minor excavation equipment. With gaudy crows feet and gaudy obliques.

Bades Gabor, an unlearn'd body of a tomb to the north, a soothsayer. Enemy of Lunar. Dressed in leather garb and carrying a line of hangers, a severed ear, and a box radio.

Del'Tek Mabe, postpunk of House of Effigy, a student of golemancy. Child of Doromundis. Dressed in field plates and carrying various artifacts, an arrow remover, and groceries.

Par'Unut Kuler, Drunkard of the outskirts, a scholar of ephemeral posterity. Devotee to The Chalice. Dressed in a beak'd helmet and carrying a carton of cigarettes, knot'd electrical cords, and steel armor. With babyblueviolet abrasions and acid-spit knees.

Ives Skorpat, the Orphic Fool of Cit Yoasnmoskl, a metamedia specialist. Devotee to Phot Kul. Dressed in muscle memory implants and carrying delicate tarts, a hand auger, and canteens.

Umir'Hept Takrhent, defunct administrater of Azmeern, an interface engineer. Follower of Oark. Dressed in a dusk shroud and carrying valueless minerals, conical objects, and ecto-chisel.

Heru'Otep Yatam, feral bear of Unaindin, a pitch-speaker. Child of The Nostrum. Dressed in biometric armor and carrying a analog camera, palmagranates, and operator cards. With petite fillings and angle'd wrinkles.

Oricha Mangis, Limb Tree of a desert temple, an occult minimalist. Devotee to Phot Kul. Dressed in a reflective mask and carrying a spectrometer, cloth, and synthetic produce.

Hez'Neom Achteriem, Orator of a pastoral landscape, biographer. Enemy of Bird Inferior. Dressed in russet armor and carrying a box of carefully packaged needles, golem flesh, and bottles of slime.

Umeer'Raat Penia, Limb Tree of Lundre, a scholar of geo-mechanical criticism. Child of Phot Kul. Dressed in field plates and carrying an interface, deer pelts, and thick leg warmers.

D'Kell Maas, afflict'd villager of Cit En, a Xenomorphic Engineer. Follower of Lovotor. Dressed in quilted armor and carrying canteens, old melee weapons, and a hand broom. With taint'd cheeks and copperblue sores.

L'h'Neom Achteriem, sprout'd commoner of Latabk, arrhythmic bard. Heir to Ultut. Dressed in a dusk shroud and carrying old melee weapons, proto-limbs, and important documents.

Jem'Suel Ankram, sever'd torso of a dilapidated monastery, a fleshcraft assistant. Follower of Egregious Cuts. Dressed in tigulated mail and carrying a percolator, a set of jugum, and a book of poetry. With tepid crows feet and ocherfuschia obliques.

Mirum Et'Alette, a polemarch of Licot, a Neo-proph. Enemy of The Nostrum. Dressed in chain sleeves and carrying a fowl, conical objects, and prairie grass stalks.

Anet Zais, sever'd torso of another planet, a scholar of minotaur semiotics. Devotee to The Unbound Stomach. Dressed in crab pelts and carrying a video still, deer pelts, and technoscanner. The video still depicts a set of three canals.

L'Gran Gaer, precorpse of House of Effigy, a guilded merchant. Devotee to The Hundred Headless Woman. Dressed in broken cybernetics and carrying bottles of acid, sacks of oil, and a hand auger.

Abalard Espern, zealous courter of Yoasnmsokl, an occult minimalist. Son of Bird Superior. Dressed in satin and carrying a lute, a hand auger, and a rotor machine.

Pra'Nepher Dasch, feral cat of Choregas, a scholar of proto-linguistics. Heir to The Hundred Headless Woman. Dressed in a gas mask and carrying a black dog, operator cards, and a percolator.

D'Mot Ige, stranger of Cit Batum, a scholar of minotaur semiotics. Child of Bardofrankont. Dressed in linens and carrying palmagranates, a dried eye, and a small sculpture. The sculpture is a cellphone.

Aasen Ige, The Pilgrim of Cit Varas, a Lunar Gnostic. Devotee to Bardofrankont. Dressed in a scarab husk and carrying uncast nets, a dull knife, and canteens.

Del'Imp Packum, a nematode of the exterior, a dream technician. Devotee to The Urchin King. Dressed in black robes and carrying lotus stems, bars of RAM, and muscle memory implants.

Wadej'Yett Ifft, sentient mass of Lower Dark, a fledgling in the Guild of Faciality. Devotee to no one. Dressed in padded armor and carrying beautiful jewelery, a trowel, and reflective materials.

De'Apet Sautter, red clown of Latabk, a guilded merchant. Son of Doromundis. Dressed in splint mail and carrying a painting, tarpaulin, and bear pelts. The painting depicts a column. The column is not built yet.

Hri'Amaun Valek, curse'd commoner of a distant past, Mule Herder. Follower of the Nematode Mother. Dressed in proto-limbs and carrying knot'd electrical cords, a hand drill, and fragant stones.

Al'Loc Tarment, Prisoner of the Digital Landscape, a minor castor. Son of Gond. Dressed in robes and carrying various artifacts, various loose springs and pins, and religious objects.

Duvre'Roni Gast, The Summoning Palm of Vavia, an interior demonologist. Devotee to Ultut. Dressed in a beak'd helmet and carrying dried fruits, cured meat, and broken cybernetics.

Amir'Odde Gehen, cyberpunk of the Niopo Tree, a gastromancer. Daughter of Tumpur. Dressed in bulk'd iron and carrying a toolbox, deer pelts, and an idol. The idol is an open palm.

Eyon'Anet Aas, sever'd head of the Digital Landscape, a neo-historian. Devotee to The Interface. Dressed in knot'd objects and carrying a carton of cigarettes, knot'd electrical cords, and a mouth gag.

Eyon'Iah Yegge, Eunuch of Cit En, a digital ecologist. Follower of The Neo-Succulent. Dressed in high-stress exos and carrying a belladonic cast, golem flesh, and a trocer. With rusted paints and salt'd trachea.

Ubi'Nepher Maag, fingerless dweller of Ephor, Grand Inquisitor. Enemy of Lunar. Dressed in broken cybernetics and carrying operator cards, satin, and light plating.

Fal Nachbar, a primate of Qamsil, an affliate of the Threadbarer. Daughter of no one. Dressed in quilted armor and carrying salvage, raw chocolate, and sacks of slime.

Del'Talm Ozog, mutilate'd villager of Cit Ravum, an
anti-realist. Follower of Lunar. Dressed in steel
armor and carrying a claw hammer, satin, and many
perfumes.

Amir'Otep Dahak, The Whisperer of Cit Yoasnmoskl,
a techscanner. Heir to The Hylant King. Dressed in
padded armor and carrying tar'd feathers, various
salves & creams, and fasteners.

Heh'Lpra Tabul, robber of Nahr, a radical thinker.
Daughter of Tumpur. Dressed in proto-limbs and car-
rying a hand broom, tarpaulin, and biometric armor.
With wiry scalp and grayblue arm hairs.

Baka'Yett Agard, an unlearn'd body of Nahr, a
watchdog. Daughter of Doromundis. Dressed in a
reflective mask and carrying a toolbox, linens, and
a configuration of tentacles.

Aza'Gran Zais, tentacle'd fool of Varas, a bioid
integration engineer. Enemy of Lunar. Dressed in
fir leaves and carrying a analog camera, a bundle'd
duvet, and a crate of soylent.

Uni'Suel Patal, precorpse of Cit Vavia, nectar
chemist. Child of Egregious Cuts. Dressed in cloth
and carrying reflective materials, black robes, and
stamps approved by the bureaucracy.

Seshet Taaffe, a primate of a nearby watchtower, a Morphofeminist. Heir to Tumpur. Dressed in linens and carrying reams of parchment paper, reams of graph paper, and unmark'd objects.

Cashin Voogd, afflict'd villager of Cit Hima'al, a Necrologist. Devotee to The Neo-Succulent. Dressed in a scarab husk and carrying a belladonic cast, denim fits, and an iron maiden.

Dei'Amaun Tel'Vavia, prospective client of the Cauldron, a futamancer. Son of Gond. Dressed in an ornate mask and carrying a simple dress, the cantos, and faction affiliate'd clothing. With copper-blue ventral blotches and redviolet pores.

Mona'Urnt Rawat, traveler of Yoasnmsokl, a liminal scholar. Follower of Volcanic Fumes. Dressed in denim and carrying cured meat, bulk'd iron, and moderate plating. With redchartreuse pads and baby-blueviolet nail beds.

Al'Ament Habacht, prospective client of Dathapt, an anti-realist. Heir to Gilead. Dressed in an ornate mask and carrying turmeric, valuable minerals, and satin.

Ameer'Otep Morfe, Eunuch of the Niopo Tree, an expert in animal husbandry. Son of the Nematode Mother. Dressed in russet armor and carrying holy garb, a rotor machine, and an important tablet. With globular swelling and lean nape.

Uni'Lpra Ducre, cave dweller of the Ambient Zone, a liminal scholar. Daughter of The Hylant King. Dressed in irridescent garbs and carrying knot'd electrical cords, synthetic produce, and a hand auger.

Badr Vacek, tentacle'd fool of Cit Yoasnmoskl, a dream technician. Heir to Doromundis. Dressed in linens and carrying loose water, a lithotome, and a roll of cartridges. With lean arteries and ocherorange navel.

Wadej'Erzu Qaile, Warden of a mountain village, a subterranean apiologist. Enemy of Oark. Dressed in proto-limbs and carrying severed implants, reams of grid paper, and a trephine and accompanying trepan.

Hako Devang, Jaguar of Agatar, a worshipper of the Lamprey. Devotee to The Chalice. Dressed in deer pelts and carrying datacells, sacks of water, and a bundle'd duvet. With scarred avulsions and salt'd nostrils.

Haret Skorpat, a declaw'd wolverine of the Cauldron, Marred Grocer. Heir to The Interface. Dressed in iron mesh and carrying a reel-to-reel tape recorder, unsoil'd planters, and a gorget.

Al'Hept Dannen, The Flesh'd of Chthonos, an exorcist of sorts. Devotee to The Hundred Headless Woman. Dressed in chain sleeves and carrying tins of pink paste, a corpse over their shoulder, and an ecraseur.

Abbe'Anet Mallaird, travel'd companion of En, a scholar of post-digital epistemology. Son of the Goatfolk. Dressed in tigulated mail and carrying spider plants, muscle memory implants, and sacks of bitumen. With slime'd teeth and rusted ventral blotches.

Pela Du'un, The Pilgrim of Spahbod, an interior demonologist. Heir to Volcanic Fumes. Dressed in proto-limbs and carrying wire'd oxygen tanks, a claw hammer, and knot'd electrical cords.

Duvre'Ka Vikar, Orator of Azmeern, a pseudo-geographer. Enemy of Loplop. Dressed in deer pelts and carrying spider plants, net monitors, and turmeric.

L'Otep Agre, travel'd companion of Cit Dair'Kud'Tuler, an equestrian performer. Enemy of The Hundred Headless Woman. Dressed in nematode pelts and carrying a crate of soylent, a small sculpture, and tissue samples.

Suri'Gran Patal, a tree folk of Cit Vavia, a collisionist. Son of The Urchin King. Dressed in additional limbs and carrying a bundle'd duvet, bags of
fertilizer, and a bedroll.

Imho'Feim Gula, Calloused Hands of Vavia, a hyper-zonal ecologist. Daughter of The Unbound
Stomach. Dressed in heavy greaves and carrying an
interface, unilt candles, and a nail file.

Ba'Dant Cenamo, a nematode of Lundre, an Object-Oriented Psychologist. Daughter of The Chalice. Dressed in moderate plating and carrying an
array of aprons, sacks of blood, and impotent
seeds.

Grhi'Imp Neblogst, postcorpse of the outskirts,
a Morphofeminist. Devotee to The Nostrum. Dressed
in crab pelts and carrying severed implants, VHS
tapes, and salvaged ciruit boards.

Duvre'Miro Tarment, a hikikomori of Anarak, a
fleshcraft assistant. Child of no one. Dressed in
babel-ware and carrying seeds, pluck'd guavas, and
high-stress exos.

Pef'Aken Kawat, the Orphic Fool of House of Effigy, Neo-typesetter. Child of Garagan. Dressed in
steel armor and carrying satin, spider plants, and
irridescent garbs.

Mona'Urnt Cedan, defunct administrater of Cit
Varas, a material designer. Devotee to Bardofrankont. Dressed in bear pelts and carrying a box of
matches, wire'd oxygen tanks, and nylon.

Katak Mormil, The Apostle of Latabk, a Morphofeminist. Son of Tumpur. Dressed in bulk'd iron and
carrying an unweildy mace, an ecraseur, and datacells.

Ba'Baal Kavan, feral cat of Batum, biographer.
Daughter of Asterion. Dressed in electrical gloves
and carrying deer pelts, beautiful jewelery, and
wooden figurines.

Geb'Hap Sobek, a polemarch of the Cauldron, a
practitioner of collectamancy. Devotee to Kei-Man.
Dressed in irridescent garbs and carrying proto-limbs, the remnants of a garden, and a lithotome.

Imho'Hept Robbarrd, a commoner of the northern deserts, a studio painter. Daughter of The Juice'd Baron. Dressed in an ornate mask and carrying synthetic produce, satin, and delicate tarts.

Uni'Anet Guyuert, a polemarch of a transnational space, an expert in animal husbandry. Daughter of Egregious Cuts. Dressed in a cowl and carrying synthetic produce, fir leaves, and clusters of TVP.

Lem'Nepher Deeriad, stray dog of Azmeern, a bone harvester. Daughter of the Goatfolk. Dressed in an array of approns and carrying a box of matches, old melee weapons, and sacks of blood.

Amir'Urnt Takarem, Jaguar of the Niopo Tree, an astragalomancer. Child of The Juice'd Baron. Dressed in cloth and carrying holy garb, mirror'd panels, and clusters of TVP.

Eyon'Apet Pasiphate, Limb Tree of the northern deserts, a minor castor. Follower of Lunar. Dressed in broken cybernetics and carrying a single-shot rifle, moss weaves, and a trephine and accompanying trepan. With redpink sutures and rusted hands.

Ante Nachtmun, a raccoon dog of the Digital Landscape, a fleshcraft assistant. Devotee to Bird
Inferior. Dressed in crude cut cloth and carrying
faction affiliate'd clothing, tins of pink paste,
and ice'd milk bottles.

Eyon'Baal Nier, a tree folk of Argas, an astragalomancer. Son of Phot Kul. Dressed in robes and
carrying babel-ware, fir leaves, and an ecraseur.

Pemphredo Kratt, The Right Hand of Nahr, biographer. Child of Kei-Man. Dressed in faction affiliate'd clothing and carrying a severed ear, neural
comb, and bars of RAM.

Dafyr Cenac, fingerless dweller of Dair'Kud'Tuler,
a reader. Son of The Chalice. Dressed in wire fleece
and carrying an oil lamp, tarpaulin, and rolls of
thread.

Umir'Ka Himan, cave dweller of Aswart, a reader.
Heir to Tumpur. Dressed in quilted armor and carrying unplugged contraptions, pliers, and groceries.

Dua'Roni Skufca, Consul of a desert temple, a hermetic coordinator. Child of Bird Inferior. Dressed
in electrical gloves and carrying a reel-to-reel
tape recorder, a crate of soylent, and a cellphone.

Crat Lethem, Ruiner of the outskirts, an art critic. Child of The Hylant King. Dressed in carbon
fiber and carrying dermal implants, a bundle'd
duvet, and beautiful jewelery. With speckle'd water
and lofty wrists.

Caban Widrig, the crack'd finger of Batum, a Lunar
Gnostic. Devotee to the Goatfolk. Dressed in heavy
greaves and carrying holy garb, coffee beans, and
unsoil'd planters.

Geb'Rada Yegge, a commoner of Tel Grazere,
Neo-typesetter. Follower of Lunar. Dressed in
clusters of TVP and carrying sacks of bitumen, work
clothes, and jicama. With salt'd pores and salt'd
nape.

Lem'Elkt Hamadrium, fodder of the exterior, a Lunar
Gnostic. Heir to Egregious Cuts. Dressed in unassuming clothes and carrying tar'd feathers, reams
of grid paper, and reams of parchment paper.

Ous'Nepher Chevnik, skull digger of a rural river
town, a scholar of ephemeral posterity. Daughter of
Bardofrankont. Dressed in light plating and carrying an important tablet, mirror'd panels, and bear
pelts.

Ihy'Yett Qader, a raccoon dog of a desecrated shrine, a pseudo-geographer. Heir to The Deep Well. Dressed in electrical gloves and carrying golem flesh, tins of pink paste, and robes.

Ymir Taglam, The Summoning Palm of Revarie, a cantrip engineer. Child of Oark. Dressed in vambraces and carrying an artificial carapace, an amputation knife, and a line of hangers.

Amir'Sham Dudek, Eunuch of Cit Ravum, a member of the Order of Small Fires. Follower of Ultut. Dressed in clusters of TVP and carrying an isohedron, a bundle'd duvet, and a a bedroll.

L'h'Mot Wehrs, Friend to the Mayor of a transnational space, a blacksmith's assistant. Enemy of The Juice'd Baron. Dressed in deer pelts and carrying knot'd objects, bottles of slime, and a protractor.

Hri'Anet Latur, devotee of a nearby watchtower, a Necrologist. Heir to Lunar. Dressed in a gas mask and carrying gnaw'd seeds, a video still, and a hand broom. The video still is from a Chantal Akerman film.

Pan'Ament Perkants, postpunk of Yoasnmsokl, a fledgling in the Guild of Faciality. Child of Garagan. Dressed in wire fleece and carrying the pandimonium index, moss weaves, and a roll of cartridges.

L'h'Aken Saatef, frame'd criminal of Cit Varas, an expert in animal husbandry. Devotee to Bird Superior. Dressed in uncast nets and carrying orbital siphons, golem flesh, and a biomonitor. With coral-cream ink and muscular wrinkles.

Ugra'Lpra Iacon, Friend to the Church of the Centur Cathedral, a practitioner of collectamancy. Devotee to The Nostrum. Dressed in kevlar and carrying velvet robes, a corpse over their shoulder, and scissors.

Fir'Hap Valek, stray dog of Varas, a scholar of ephemeral posterity. Child of The Neo-Succulent. Dressed in hardened leather and carrying a hand drill, reams of grid paper, and unplug'd monitors.

Kru Saatef, story'd fool of a desert temple, a hermetic coordinator. Child of The Nostrum. Dressed in broken cybernetics and carrying a protractor, unilt candles, and nut butter.

Amir Khon, Friend to the Mayor of Junkrhad, a minor castor. Enemy of Gond. Dressed in wire fleece and carrying a bundle'd duvet, multicolor bows, and unmark'd objects.

Jem'Feim Guat, Matriarch of a desert temple, a
material designer. Child of Doromundis. Dressed in
mirror'd panels and carrying canteens, an ecraseur,
and fir leaves.

Hasat Packum, hive body of Cit Varas, Mule Herder.
Child of Kei-Man. Dressed in padded armor and carrying electrical wires, dermal implants, and sacks
of water.

Par'Lpra Nabu, okapi of Cit Vavia, an adept exobotanist. Heir to many saints. Dressed in nylon and
carrying steel armor, dried grains, and seeds.

Ugra'Uun Laum, hive body of Cit Licot, a bone harvester. Daughter of Bird Superior. Dressed in light
plating and carrying a bone saw, burlap, and dice.
The dice are a d8 and d20.

Umir'Lpra Sabiume, frame'd criminal of Cit Decair,
Marred Grocer. Child of The Hylant King. Dressed
in faction affiliate'd clothing and carrying conical
objects, old melee weapons, and bars of RAM.

Del'Ka Valek, a tree folk of Lundre, a Lunar Gnostic. Devotee to The Hundred Headless Woman. Dressed in a simple dress and carrying a metal contraption, torn vinyl, and polymer blocks.

Par'Hept Kazeer, Calloused Hands of Choregas, a fledgling in the Guild of Faciality. Son of Loplop. Dressed in uncast nets and carrying additional limbs, a biomonitor, and golem flesh.

Ent'Loc Merope, Archpriest of Aswart, a Neo-proph. Child of The Unbound Stomach. Dressed in hardened leather and carrying satin, a belladonic cast, and quince.

Mede'Anet Ausrin, scale'd fiend of Ravum, nectar chemist. Daughter of Garagan. Dressed in grime'd coveralls and carrying a configuration of tentacles, an isohedron, and tissue samples. The isohedron has 8 sides.

Ent'Mot Lotan, a nematode of a nearby watchtower, a practitioner of TVmancy. Son of the Goatfolk. Dressed in a cowl and carrying uncast nets, a toolbox, and structural proteins.

Ur'Hap Mormil, curse'd villager of the exterior, an
art critic. Enemy of The Crawling Ooze. Dressed in
a wing'd helmet and carrying black robes, various
loose springs and pins, and canteens. With crimsongreen sores and rusted blisters.

Djo'Ka Laut, an associate of Lower Dark, a bioid
integration engineer. Heir to Gilead. Dressed in
light plating and carrying a linear frame, a dull
knife, and VHS tapes.

D'Lpra Ubl, The Polydactyl Palm of Cit Ravum,
nectar chemist. Son of Tumpur. Dressed in thick leg
warmers and carrying a collection of CDs, a box of
carefully packaged needles, and torn vinyl.

Eyon'Dant Voorhes, devotee of Anarak, a portalogist. Son of Bird Inferior. Dressed in high-stress
exos and carrying a box of matches, work clothes,
and an analog camera.

Heru'Lpra Carval, story'd fool of Unaindin, a narrative designer. Daughter of many saints. Dressed
in cloth and carrying a mouth gag, valuable minerals, and bulk'd iron. With peachgreen pads and
flexible burns.

Ihy'Roni Lucef, Tempt'd Son of Ephor, an experienced cryptographer. Son of Bird Inferior. Dressed
in moderate plating and carrying a dried eye,
coffee beans, and a severed nose.

Ked'Ament Yatam, Arachnid follower of an unknown
origin, a seasoned medievalist. Son of Asterion.
Dressed in a belladonic cast and carrying crude cut
cloth, impotent seeds, and impotent seeds.

Amir'Aken Seelig, a hire'd body of a pastoral landscape, a Lunar Gnostic. Devotee to The Urchin King.
Dressed in utero packs and carrying bone meal,
high-stress exos, and an ecdysis trigger.

L'Ket Huten, sever'd head of Azmeern, a hermetic
coordinator. Follower of Ameer DuVal. Dressed in
clusters of TVP and carrying sacks of slime, neural
comb, and a biomonitor.

Del'Yett Hamadrium, stray dog of the exterior,
an adept exobotanist. Follower of Bird Superior.
Dressed in trackmesh and carrying a book of hymns,
sensory archive tool, and a toolbox.

After we have all arrived,
a projection--

The cathedral emanates with a geographic disorder.

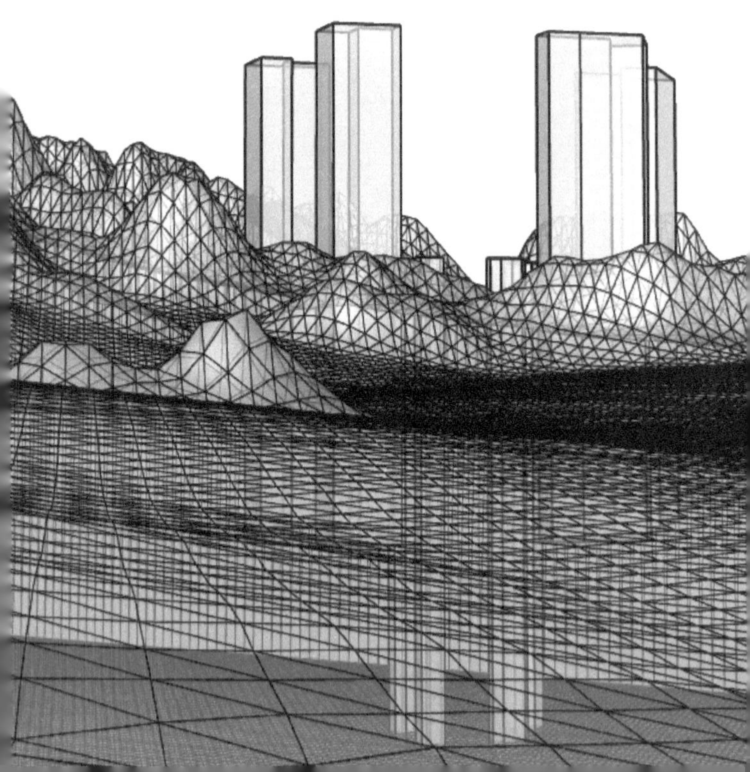

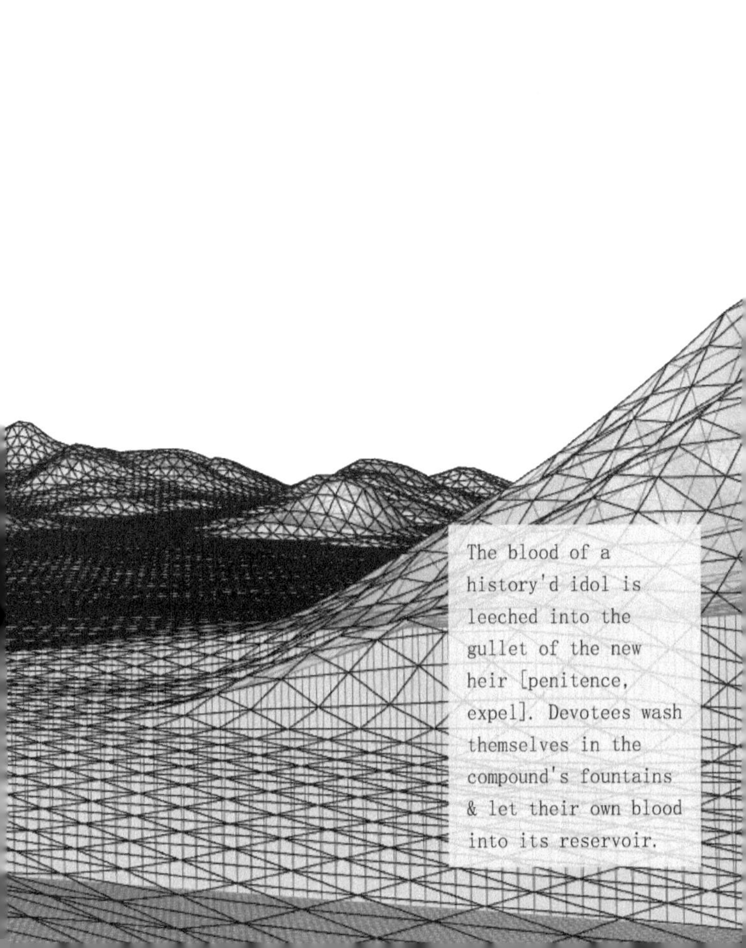
The blood of a
history'd idol is
leeched into the
gullet of the new
heir [penitence,
expel]. Devotees wash
themselves in the
compound's fountains
& let their own blood
into its reservoir.

Arrivals of the Second Day

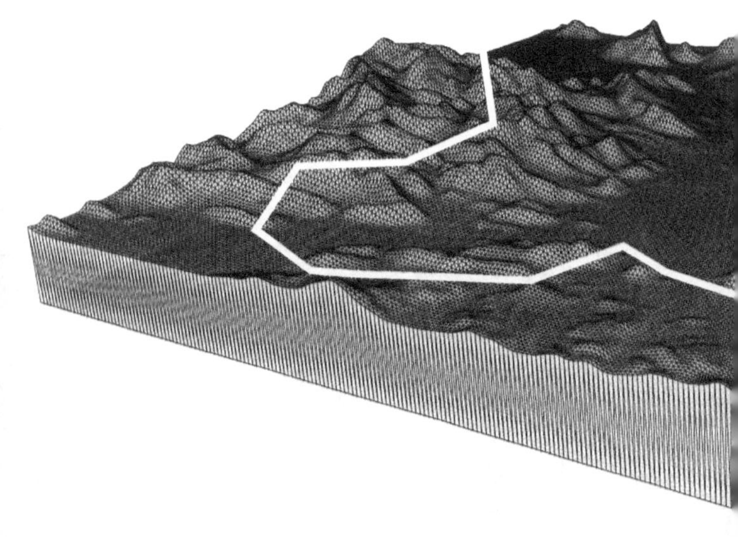

THE SECOND DAY

Trajectory of Pilgrimage
No-Heir
Path Version 2

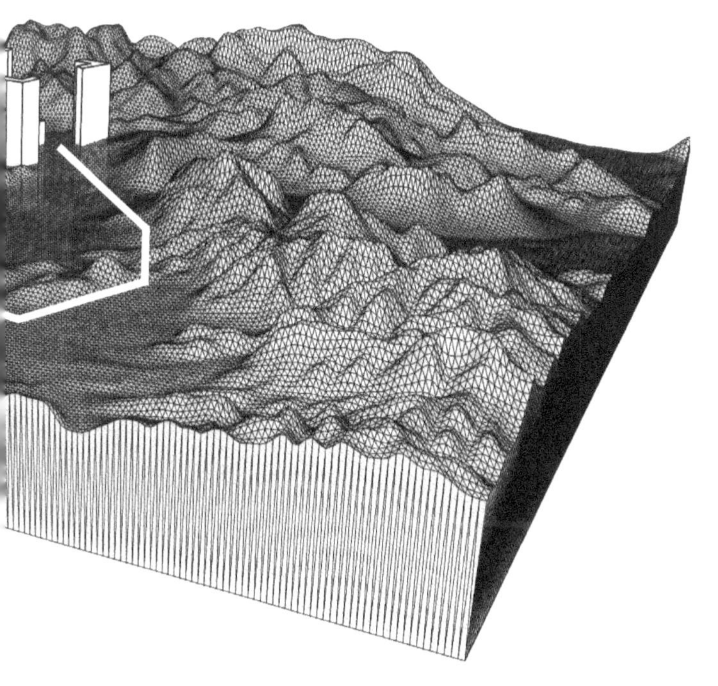

Day2
CensusDirectory
ID, Inventory
SelectedInspect
Motive, Interior Devout

Mede'Dant Guyuert, zealous courter of Aswart, a watchdog. Son of Garagan. Dressed in nylon and carrying prairie grass stalks, spider plants, and sacks of blood. With perfumed navel and paint'd pads.

Boream Haighr, plauge'd villager of Cit Centur, an interior demonologist. Enemy of Kei-Man. Dressed in additional limbs and carrying crude cut cloth, ornate rugs, and proto-limbs.

Usil'Roni Kinnari, stray dog of the northern deserts, a watchdog. Daughter of Garagan. Dressed in a dusk shroud and carrying a fowl, a herd of microbes, and VHS tapes. With aquamarinegreen trachea and bluegreen water.

L'h'Smet Cygan, hive body of Dair'Kud'Tuler, a scholar of necrometry. Daughter of Tumpur. Dressed in steel mesh and carrying a parcel, religious objects, and sacks of oil. The parcel contains a biomonitor.

Abbe'Talm Mallaird, an anteater of Cit Hima'al, a scapulomancer. Child of Ameer DuVal. Dressed in crude cut cloth and carrying turmeric, a box of carefully packaged needles, and jicama.

Anank Omphale, a lecturer of Cit Centur, a hermetic coordinator. Devotee to Loplop. Dressed in babel-ware and carrying sacks of bitumen, a book of hymns, and sacks of water. With perfumed occipital hatch and symmetrical paints.

Pef'Raat Safren, frame'd criminal of a mountain village, a scholar of ephemeral posterity. Enemy of Lunar. Dressed in beautiful jewelery and carrying an unidentified brass instrument, a configuration of tentacles, and proto-limbs.

Par'Gran Cenac, curse'd commoner of the exterior, a scholar of marxist grammatology. Child of many saints. Dressed in dermal implants and carrying robes, a trocer, and a claw hammer.

Ous'Urnt Mallaird, vole of the Cauldron, an experienced cryptographer. Enemy of Gilead. Dressed in wire fleece and carrying neural comb, a trocer, and robes.

Del'Tesh Wehrs, a polemarch of Chthonos, a xenoarchitect. Follower of Tumpur. Dressed in russet armor and carrying a woodcutter's axe, electrical wires, and tins of gelatin.

Sol Dubann, story'd fool of a desert temple, a nematode farmer. Child of Lunar. Dressed in cloth and carrying severed implants, unassuming clothes, and old melee weapons.

L'h'Tek Molleur, devotee of Argas, a watchdog. Son of the Nematode Mother. Dressed in iron mesh and carrying tallow, a severed finger, and a small sculpture. The sculpture is a bowl of soup.

Kathor Ankram, The Flesh'd of Batum, an adept exobotanist. Son of The Hundred Headless Woman. Dressed in grime'd coveralls and carrying polymer blocks, dried fruits, and lotus stems.

Abednego Kawat, The Flesh'd of Tel Grazere, atonal bard. Son of Asterion. Dressed in a cowl and carrying rolls of thread, cans of nectar, and an important tablet. With ocherfuschia thighs and pinkyellow trachea.

Rukur Widmar, sprout'd commoner of Choregas, a narrative designer. Child of the Goatfolk. Dressed in uncast nets and carrying pluck'd guavas, an arrow remover, and canteens.

Umir'Suel Headroun, curse'd villager of a pastoral
landscape, an expert in animal husbandry. Son of
the Goatfolk. Dressed in splint mail and carrying
dried grains, an interface, and a box radio. The
radio does not work.

Umeer'Suel Du'un, the practice'd sow of Cit
Fir'Al'Tuler, a cartomancer. Enemy of Doromundis.
Dressed in vagrant garb and carrying bear pelts, a
collection of CDs, and pliers.

Aze'Amaun Vikar, skull digger of Cit Yoasnmoskl,
a radical thinker. Enemy of no one. Dressed in a
configuration of tentacles and carrying unmark'd
objects, datacells, and clips.

Yasan Casur, fingerless dweller of the Ambient Zone,
a bacterial miner. Follower of The Crawling Ooze.
Dressed in babel-ware and carrying severed implants, burlap, and rolls of thread.

D'Dant Fullish, The Neophyte of Chthonos, a bioid integration engineer. Son of Bird Superior. Dressed in robes and carrying a protractor, a line of hangers, and polymer blocks.

Rukur Horta, siphon'd fool of Dathapt, a Lunar Gnostic. Follower of Volcanic Fumes. Dressed in thick leg warmers and carrying conical objects, gnaw'd seeds, and stamps approved by the bureaucracy. With ocherorange obliques and luminous pores.

Imho'Elkt Abdelnoer, an unlearn'd body of a transnational space, a reader. Son of The Moon-Face. Dressed in burlap and carrying wire'd oxygen tanks, a small sculpture, and precious ornaments. The sculpture is made of iron.

Ubi'Odde Nielem, postpunk of Spahbod, a scholar of minotaur semiotics. Child of the Goatfolk. Dressed in faction affiliate'd clothing and carrying spider plants, many talismen, and a fowl.

Bel'Unut Tarment, The Syzygy of All Stars of Lower Dark, a Yonicist. Child of Bird Inferior. Dressed in a linear frame and carrying black robes, conical objects, and moderate plating.

Nel'Duvel Oshmer, traveler of Cit Ravum, a scholar of visceral hermetics. Daughter of Loplop. Dressed in a sealed chastity belt and carrying various salves & creams, reams of parchment paper, and clips.

Ghul Paavla, sentient mass of the outskirts, an art critic. Devotee to Ultut. Dressed in a cowl and carrying raw chocolate, robes, and sacks of slime.

De'Smet Esperodies, curse'd commoner of Hima'al, a scholar of apiary geometry. Devotee to The Crawling Ooze. Dressed in trackmesh and carrying uncast nets, a sacred tome, and biometric armor. The tome contains important information regarding the end of the holocene.

Raas Inkh, The Awakened of a tomb to the south, an expert in animal husbandry. Follower of The Hundred Headless Woman. Dressed in a sealed chastity belt and carrying burlap, an important tablet, and thick leg warmers. The tablet is cracked.

Loa'Talm Schlof, an anteater of the outskirts, a Neo-proph. Heir to the Nematode Mother. Dressed in faction affiliate'd clothing and carrying fasteners, a box radio, and an arrow remover.

Heh'Rada Yorbek, Drowned Wight of a rural river town, a futamancer. Child of Egregious Cuts. Dressed in mirror'd panels and carrying knot'd objects, black robes, and a box of matches.

Edet Minerd, devotee of a tomb to the north, a minor castor. Son of Bird Superior. Dressed in trash and carrying a hand drill, slabs of ice, and sacks of water.

Ba'Aken Packum, The Neophyte of Varas, an interior demonologist. Son of Bird Inferior. Dressed in knot'd objects and carrying a collection of CDs, a single-shot rifle, and palmagranates.

Abbe'Umut Et'Ungulum, traveler of the Centur Cathedral, a virtual archaeologist. Daughter of The Hundred Headless Woman. Dressed in heavyset blankets and carrying sensory archive tool, an iron maiden, and unmark'd objects.

Nel'Talm Synth, an unlearn'd body of Tel Grazere, trepaneer. Enemy of Bird Inferior. Dressed in beautiful jewelery and carrying recovered processors, a sealed chastity belt, and various salves & creams.

Dua'Otep Yggre, Drunkard of The Moon, a scholar of visceral hermetics. Child of Gond. Dressed in denim and carrying a small sun, muscle memory implants, and slabs of ice.

Drom Gehen, sever'd torso of Aswart, a practitioner of TVmancy. Son of Gilead. Dressed in electrical gloves and carrying an ecraseur, cans of nectar, and bone meal.

Ent'Kell Dejan, trembling seer of Spahbod, biographer. Devotee to The Chalice. Dressed in russet armor and carrying kevlar, a configuration of tentacles, and rail nails. The rail nails are bent.

L'Sham Dilmun, vole of a transnational space, a fleshcraft assistant. Heir to The Hylant King. Dressed in robes and carrying a cellphone, muscle memory implants, and dried grains. With gossamer sutures and acid-spit pads.

Dua'Anet Kaukas, prospective client of Argas, a Xenomorphic Engineer. Daughter of The Moon-Face. Dressed in irridescent garbs and carrying clusters of TVP, cans of coolant, and a painting. The painting depicts liminal rites.

Hri'Amaun Morank, punk of Argas, a cosmopolist.
Daughter of The Crawling Ooze. Dressed in deer
pelts and carrying pluck'd guavas, structural proteins, and a lute. The lute is not tuned.

Orsos Asher, The Neophyte of Lower Dark, a mancer
of some kind. Daughter of no one. Dressed in cloth
and carrying knot'd electrical cords, a simple
dress, and dermal implants. With aquamarinegreen
cheeks and crimsongreen gums.

Ull Yggre, Friend to the Mayor of Cit Licot, a
fleshcraft assistant. Son of The Interface. Dressed
in light plating and carrying an old CD player,
technoscanner, and a lithotome.

Loa'Uun Kratt, punk of the Ambient Zone, a cantrip
engineer. Son of many saints. Dressed in mirror'd
panels and carrying a tome of sandpaper, impotent
seeds, and a fowl.

Ihy'Tek Pacocha, a tree folk of the ludological
south, arrhythmic bard. Daughter of The Juice'd
Baron. Dressed in a sealed chastity belt and carrying an analog camera, work clothes, and bars of
RAM. With globular follicles and bent wounds.

Aza'Rada Dalagur, Heredet of Hima'al, a collisionist. Child of no one. Dressed in clusters of
TVP and carrying clusters of TVP, succulents, and
quince. With greengray crows feet and perfumed
genitalia.

Umeer'Tek Gatal, fodder of Nahr, a worshipper of
the Lamprey. Heir to many saints. Dressed in clusters of TVP and carrying seeds, a sacred tome, and
knot'd objects.

El'Amaun Saarinen, white clown of Cit Vavia, a bioid integration engineer. Child of Lovotor. Dressed
in uncast nets and carrying ice'd milk bottles,
fasteners, and gnaw'd seeds.

Mahes'Neom Nifong, Villager of Ravum, a Lunar Gnostic. Enemy of Bird Inferior. Dressed in irridescent
garbs and carrying a biomonitor, a bone saw, and
sensory archive tool.

De'Smet Hamadrium, The Left Hand of Cit Batum, a scholar of hypnagogic eroticism. Heir to Volcanic Fumes. Dressed in satin and carrying cloth, a collection of CDs, and a linear frame.

Kait Kachur, a primate of a tomb to the north, a narrative designer. Follower of The Crawling Ooze. Dressed in a mirror'd facade and carrying a metal contraption, a protractor, and minor excavation equipment. With rustplum heels and olivepink nostrils.

Geb'Anet Lethem, white clown of Cit Yoasnmoskl, a liminal scholar. Devotee to The Chalice. Dressed in work clothes and carrying holy garb, unmark'd objects, and waterlog'd magazines.

Ba'Talm Ishofli, The Apostle of the Carnlands, a laborer. Enemy of Gilead. Dressed in broken cybernetics and carrying dried fruits, an array of buckles, and a tome of sandpaper. The tome tells the story of a mule.

Amir'Sham Cwyanr, travel'd companion of Cit Batum,
a bone harvester. Daughter of The Hylant King.
Dressed in heavyset blankets and carrying coins,
wire'd oxygen tanks, and knot'd objects. With worn
occipital hatch and shave'd sutures.

Cyb'Amaun Nien, Consul of the Ambient Zone, an
apprentice of the Augury. Daughter of Doromundis.
Dressed in an array of buckles and carrying structural proteins, tar'd feathers, and tissue samples.

Mal'Suel Ahell, The Blessed of Batum, a Xenomorphic
Engineer. Follower of Ultut. Dressed in vagrant
garb and carrying a hand broom, an unweildy mace,
and dice. The dice are a d12 and a d60.

Umeer'Ament Saarinen, a raccoon dog of Agatar,
a Lunar Gnostic. Heir to Doromundis. Dressed in
grime'd coveralls and carrying wire'd oxygen tanks,
mirror'd panels, and sacks of water.

Pef'Rada Oshun, Friend to the Magistrate of Argas,
a laborer. Daughter of Gond. Dressed in wire'd oxygen tanks and carrying datacells, a book of hymns,
and spare tanks. With pinkyellow lacerations and
bent knees.

Ked'Suel Sukrep, afflict'd villager of the Centur Cathedral, a text morphologist. Child of no one. Dressed in reflective materials and carrying unassuming clothes, a book of poetry, and nut butter.

Mahes'Ket Agrhil, plauge'd villager of Junkrhad, a worshipper of the Lamprey. Son of Garagan. Dressed in a reflective mask and carrying coins, dice, and electrical wires. The dice are a d4 and d20.

Mopus Detwa, Heredet of Chthonos, a virtual archaeologist. Heir to The Neo-Succulent. Dressed in vambraces and carrying knot'd electrical cords, a line of hangers, and bone meal.

Aze'Talm Akkadum, robber of unimportant affiliations, a xenoarchitect. Heir to The Neo-Succulent. Dressed in torn vinyl and carrying irridescent garbs, a percolator, and VHS tapes. The tapes are corrupted.

Djo'Gran Belabog, The Awakened of The Moon, nectar chemist. Daughter of Lunar. Dressed in field plates and carrying minor excavation equipment, sacks of water, and clips.

Jem'Otep Ozog, red clown of Cit Dair'Kud'Tuler,
an interior demonologist. Devotee to The Nostrum.
Dressed in an artificial carapace and carrying
tar'd feathers, wire'd oxygen tanks, and important
documents.

Loa'Loc Phalec, prospective client of Cit Hima'al,
a gastromancer. Enemy of The Juice'd Baron. Dressed
in biometric armor and carrying irridescent garbs,
unplugged contraptions, and foot pedals. With scaly
toes and taint'd sutures.

Del'Apet Thalm, Heredet of a dilapidated monastery,
a Slime Morphologist. Devotee to Egregious Cuts.
Dressed in a sealed chastity belt and carrying a
lute, synthetic produce, and many talismen.

Rada Nerh'Ghrall, Heredet of Anarak, a member of
the Order of Small Fires. Son of The Deep Well.
Dressed in babel-ware and carrying conical objects,
synthetic produce, and VHS tapes.

Zodi'Ka Gula, curse'd commoner of a transnational space, a zonetologist. Heir to Egregious Cuts.
Dressed in additional limbs and carrying moderate
plating, a corpse over their shoulder, and an idol.
The idol depicts an okapi.

Grhi'Mot Cedan, the beauty of a pastoral landscape, a Yonicist. Heir to The Unbound Stomach. Dressed in an array of buckles and carrying a severed tongue, chewing gum, and beautiful jewelery.

Pan'Unut Alau, robber of Hima'al, a member of the Guild of Cyber Mycologies. Son of Gond. Dressed in chain sleeves and carrying jicama, a parcel, and a linear frame. The parcel is for Djo'Gran Belabog.

Loa'Suel Wmuk, curse'd villager of Agatar, atonal bard. Daughter of no one. Dressed in a configuration of tentacles and carrying tarot cards, a litho-tome, and carbon fiber. With steep collar bones and luminous digits.

Ugra'Tesh Kawat, The Neophyte of a mountain village, a bioid integration engineer. Devotee to Bardofrankont. Dressed in a belladonic cast and carrying a single-shot rifle, neural comb, and slabs of ice.

Hez'Hap Narai, curse'd commoner of Upasal, a Xenomorphic Engineer. Enemy of The Crawling Ooze. Dressed in hardened leather and carrying unplug'd monitors, the hoof of an ungulate, and nylon. With pinkyellow arm hairs and coralcream follicles.

Kuvir Dasch, a garter snake of a desert temple, a journeyman of fleshcraft. Son of The Hundred Headless Woman. Dressed in iron mesh and carrying light plating, a rotor machine, and a metal contraption.

Aje Agrhil, Palatine of a desert temple, a scholar of apiary geometry. Daughter of no one. Dressed in field plates and carrying palmagranates, a gorget, and knot'd electrical cords.

Ba'Unut Khon, a desert father of Revarie, a Morphofeminist. Heir to Phot Kul. Dressed in a wing'd helmet and carrying beautiful jewelery, a trowel, and a stylus.

Dei'Ka Dannen, Consul of Revarie, atonal bard. Son of Asterion. Dressed in a cowl and carrying an interface, a herd of microbes, and technoscanner.

D'Otep Manah, the practice'd sow of Upasal, an automapper. Follower of Gond. Dressed in trash and carrying kevlar, lotus stems, and an ecraseur.

Aze'Odde Saad, The Pilgrim of Azmeern, a scholar of geo-mechanical criticism. Enemy of Kei-Man. Dressed in vagrant garb and carrying scissors, additional limbs, and black robes.

El'Firum Seelig, spike'd hog of Chthonos, a member of the Order of Small Fires. Devotee to no one. Dressed in light plating and carrying tarpaulin, religious objects, and sacks of oil.

Ugra'Sham Patal, The Hoarder of Artifacts of the wilderness, an apprentice of the Augury. Enemy of The Hundred Headless Woman. Dressed in kevlar and carrying technoscanner, a reel-to-reel tape recorder, and ornate rugs. With bluegreen teeth and greengray paints.

Ur'Unut Cedan, Pyrarc of Cit Hima'al, a watchdog. Follower of Lunar. Dressed in many talismen and carrying a severed ear, old melee weapons, and sacks of water.

Heru'Tesh Kabel, an anteater of a distant past, a studio painter. Child of Volcanic Fumes. Dressed in cloth and carrying unplug'd monitors, a linear frame, and dried grains. With slime'd calves and speckle'd ventral blotches.

Baka'Unut Perstelis, Prisoner of unimportant affiliations, Grand Inquisitor. Devotee to The Nostrum. Dressed in iron mesh and carrying uncast nets, valuable minerals, and fungal sprouts. The sprouts are dehydrated.

Anet Nien, Pariah of Cit Ravum, a futamancer. Son
of The Urchin King. Dressed in wire fleece and carrying important documents, orbital siphons, and a
coveted heirloom.

Ugra'Urnt Agre, punk of Latabk, an entrail supply
specialist. Heir to The Nostrum. Dressed in work
clothes and carrying ecto-chisel, a box of carefully packaged needles, and jicama.

Aza'Dant Nerh'Ghrall, mammoth of Licot, a student
of golemancy. Devotee to The Hundred Headless
Woman. Dressed in grime'd coveralls and carrying
robes, thick leg warmers, and a rotor machine.

Heh'Iah Cidic, The Neophyte of Dair'Kud'Tuler,
atonal bard. Son of no one. Dressed in iron mesh
and carrying neural comb, bottles of acid, and a
roll of cartridges.

Mede'Firum Yablon, The Blessed of a procedural
cityscape, a cartomancer. Child of The Urchin King.
Dressed in steel mesh and carrying various artifacts, a claw hammer, and coins.

Eyon'Tek Elepis, robber of a dilapidated monastery, a soothsayer. Follower of The Neo-Succulent.
Dressed in heavy greaves and carrying synthetic
produce, a small sculpture, and additional limbs.
The sculpture is an isohedron.

Heru'Uun Felk, scale'd fiend of Argas, a worshipper
of the Lamprey. Follower of Asterion. Dressed in
leather garb and carrying unplug'd monitors, muscle
memory implants, and ecto-chisel. With bluegreen
genitalia and crimsongreen collar bones.

Qud Kabel, feral bear of Nahr, a diligent squire.
Daughter of Kei-Man. Dressed in satin and carrying
canteens, cans of nectar, and waterlog'd magazines.

L'h'Numi Sawhat, newly resurrected servant of Chthonos, scryer. Child of The Hundred Headless Woman. Dressed in a scarab husk and carrying an old CD player, trackmesh, and faction affiliate'd clothing.

Sadek Hignite, the practice'd sow of Nahr, an equestrian performer. Follower of Bird Superior. Dressed in a beak'd helmet and carrying dice, gemstones, and electrical wires. The dice are a d60 and d10.

Heru'Gran Gabor, prospective client of the Digital Landscape, a liminal scholar. Child of Bird Inferior. Dressed in a scarab husk and carrying a roll of cartridges, a hand auger, and an amputation knife.

Bel'Roni Dasch, a badger of Cit Centur, a Holocener. Heir to the Nematode Mother. Dressed in faction affiliate'd clothing and carrying lotus stems, a set of jugum, and an isohedron. The isohedron has 20 sides.

Aasen Cedan, devotee of Cit Batum, an exorcist of sorts. Daughter of Phot Kul. Dressed in tarpaulin and carrying various loose springs and pins, tarot cards, and nematode pelts. With crook'd swelling and taint'd cheeks.

Ubi'Miro Saarinen, a hire'd body of the northern deserts, an equestrian performer. Follower of Bird Superior. Dressed in muscle memory implants and carrying sensory archive tool, bottles of slime, and broken cybernetics.

Duvre'Imp Wiygul, The Nomad of an unknown origin, a diligent squire. Follower of Loplop. Dressed in velvet robes and carrying a collection of CDs, kevlar, and fungal sprouts.

Cherna Widrig, Gentleman of Holy Attire of the exterior, a futamancer. Enemy of many saints. Dressed in trackmesh and carrying a video still, reams of grid paper, and clips. The video still depicts a mule. The mule is digging a grave.

Sopona Plutence, the aphroditium of Anarak, a liminal scholar. Enemy of The Crawling Ooze. Dressed in dermal implants and carrying kevlar, slime, and a collection of CDs. With open blisters and luminous gums.

Belem Kaeliehm, Battl'd Insect of Licot, a specialist in synthetic materials. Daughter of The Crawling Ooze. Dressed in many talismen and carrying tissue samples, babel-ware, and sacks of blood.

Ur'Tek Tiems, precorpse of Aswart, an occult min-imalist. Son of Gond. Dressed in utero packs and carrying stripped vines, additional limbs, and a mouth gag.

Ur'Gran Cech, The Summoning Palm of a dilapidat-ed monastery, Grand Inquisitor. Child of The Deep Well. Dressed in an array of aprons and carrying a reel-to-reel tape recorder, a cellphone, and an important tablet.

Geb'Kell Gaer, plauge'd villager of the exterior, an architect's apprentice. Follower of Tumpur. Dressed in a configuration of tentacles and carrying a trephine and accompanying trepan, coffee beans, and wire'd oxygen tanks.

Eche Tuler, The Summoning Palm of Cit Varas, a lim-inal scholar. Devotee to The Hylant King. Dressed in trash and carrying a bedroll, a carton of ciga-rettes, and gnaw'd seeds. The cigarettes are wet.

Ubi'Urnt Aarhus, defunct administrater of Dathapt, an art critic. Devotee to The Hundred Headless Woman. Dressed in reflective materials and carrying moss weaves, decadent shawls, and lotus stems.

Patr Cech, root'd stem of a tomb to the south,
a hermetic coordinator. Follower of The Chalice. Dressed in trackmesh and carrying contiguous
joints, bags of fertilizer, and prairie grass
stalks. With oblong gums and aquamarinegreen fillings.

Dua'Amaun Saad, stranger of the outskirts, a haruspex. Follower of The Hylant King. Dressed in a
cowl and carrying bone meal, a small sculpture, and
kelp. The sculpture is a separated jaw.

Abbe'Aken Sheehe, Friend to the Church of the
wilderness, a haruspex. Child of The Moon-Face.
Dressed in knot'd objects and carrying kevlar, a
black dog, and succulents. With rotting follicles
and salt'd burns.

Byfr Huten, sentient mass of a procedural cityscape, an equestrian performer. Child of Doromundis. Dressed in an artificial carapace and carrying
biometric armor, VHS tapes, and stripped vines.
With steep ankles and silverorange blisters.

Eyon'Hap Detwa, a polemarch of En, a techscanner.
Heir to Ameer DuVal. Dressed in crab pelts and carrying rolls of thread, a painting, and an artificial
carapace. The painting depicts a snail. The snail
is in love.

Mede'Anet Penia, a lecturer of the Cauldron, a
zonetologist. Devotee to The Crawling Ooze. Dressed
in robes and carrying an array of aprons, a severed ear, and a spectrometer.

Yune'Raat Esperodies, a primate of Anarak, a material designer. Devotee to The Nostrum. Dressed
in linens and carrying a bundle'd duvet, heavyset
blankets, and an unweildy mace.

Aurva Capio, prospective client of the Carnlands,
a scapulomancer. Son of Doromundis. Dressed in a
simple dress and carrying heavyset blankets, neural
comb, and rail nails.

Bel'Tesh Zika, sever'd head of Cit Dair'Kud'Tuler, a scholar of minotaur semiotics. Follower of Bird Superior. Dressed in trash and carrying lotus stems, dice, and tarpaulin. The dice are a d20 and d20.

Lurgo Widmar, cyberpunk of The Moon, an interior demonologist. Devotee to Ultut. Dressed in work clothes and carrying a hand auger, a small sun, and bars of RAM.

D'Ket Felk, Prisoner of Aswart, an experienced cryptographer. Son of Volcanic Fumes. Dressed in trackmesh and carrying torn vinyl, sacks of blood, and cans of nectar.

Amir'Kell Baunt, Consul of Fir'Al'Tuler, a digital ecologist. Enemy of Lovotor. Dressed in faction affiliate'd clothing and carrying tissue samples, tallow, and severed implants.

Decar Abdelnoer, feral bear of Hima'al, an adept exobotanist. Child of The Interface. Dressed in mirror'd panels and carrying dermal implants, golem flesh, and bone meal. With acid-spit molars and greengray worn blotches.

Zodi'Aken Pacaan, deer-body of Cit Vavia, a scholar
of ephemeral posterity. Enemy of Bird Superior.
Dressed in robes and carrying a gorget, an important tablet, and a sealed chastity belt. The robes
are torn.

Amir'Baal Devang, The Neophyte of the Ambient Zone,
a reader. Devotee to Kei-Man. Dressed in denim and
carrying an ecdysis trigger, proto-limbs, and a
severed tongue. With ocherorange eyes and cut pads.

Hri'Rada Maag, curse'd villager of a tomb to the
north, a hyper-zonal ecologist. Enemy of Kei-Man.
Dressed in cloth and carrying a sealed chastity
belt, a trocer, and turmeric.

D'Feim Haurvat, precorpse of a distant past, an
equestrian performer. Devotee to The Crawling Ooze.
Dressed in cloth and carrying pliers, precious
ornaments, and crab pelts. With rustplum nail beds
and lemongray ink.

Dua'Feim Mallaird, stray dog of Fir'Al'Tuler, body-mass engineer. Child of The Juice'd Baron. Dressed in contiguous joints and carrying a spectrometer, spider plants, and religious objects. The spider plants are dehydrated.

D'Dant Capio, robber of Batum, a Morphofeminist. Daughter of The Chalice. Dressed in bulk'd iron and carrying a metal contraption, fungal sprouts, and reflective materials.

Del'Roni Agrhil, The Left Hand of Upasal, a Holocener. Child of Lovotor. Dressed in decadent shawls and carrying moss weaves, a crate of soylent, and the pandimonium index. With steep pads and silk'd infections.

Fir'Ka Sabiume, Pariah of Batum, a nematode breeder. Daughter of Oark. Dressed in a cowl and carrying a percolator, a bedroll, and dried fruits.

Ophul Taglam, deer-body of a transnational space, a Holocener. Enemy of Phot Kul. Dressed in decadent shawls and carrying conical objects, an ecraseur, and a cellphone.

Jem'Apet Ausrin, mantis of a tomb to the north, a dream technician. Child of Gond. Dressed in burlap and carrying unplugged contraptions, an amputation knife, and bulk'd iron.

Par'Gran Habacht, stranger of another planet, a
subterranean apiologist. Devotee to the Goatfolk.
Dressed in multicolor bows and carrying thick leg
warmers, a corpse over their shoulder, and a bedroll.

Uni'Sham Nabu, spike'd hog of Choregas, Mule
Herder. Heir to Ameer DuVal. Dressed in tigulated
mail and carrying an ecraseur, a protractor, and a
simple dress.

Umeer'Rada Ugar, terror of Ephor, a bone harvester.
Devotee to The Moon-Face. Dressed in work clothes
and carrying a box radio, moss weaves, and a roll
of cartridges.

Edet Bachhubre, Matriarch of Azmeern, a nematode
breeder. Follower of The Unbound Stomach. Dressed
in linens and carrying moss weaves, prairie grass
stalks, and beautiful jewelery. The jewelery is
tarnished.

Ent'Smet Slahgt, The Flesh'd of the Centur Cathedral, a journeyman of fleshcraft. Devotee to Kei-
Man. Dressed in moderate plating and carrying a
sacred tome, cloth, and quince. The tome contains
a portal.

Nel'Lpra Espern, a hire'd body of a dilapidated monastery, a pitchspeaker. Daughter of Doromundis. Dressed in additional limbs and carrying robes, nylon, and a trowel. With silk'd obliques and ocherorange swelling.

Amir'Neom Ittre, The Whisperer of Dathapt, a member of the Order of Small Fires. Enemy of The Juice'd Baron. Dressed in babel-ware and carrying reflective materials, a stylus, and synthetic produce.

Amir'Lpra Iigrashi, red clown of Lundre, an Omphalomancer. Enemy of Lovotor. Dressed in black robes and carrying irridescent garbs, bottles of acid, and tar'd feathers.

Ameer'Neom Nachbar, Gentleman of Holy Attire of Junkrhad, bibliomancer. Devotee to The Deep Well. Dressed in clusters of TVP and carrying a box of carefully packaged needles, an interface, and bear pelts.

Umeer'Smet Wehrlee, cyberpunk of the ludological south, an art critic. Daughter of Bird Superior. Dressed in many talismen and carrying dermal implants, contiguous joints, and high-stress exos.

Suri'Otep Et'Alette, fingerless dweller of Chthonos, a text morphologist. Son of the Nematode Mother. Dressed in velvet robes and carrying orbital siphons, ice'd milk bottles, and a bundle'd duvet. The milk is curdle'd.

Agan Ubelrahn, the aphroditium of a transnational space, a radical thinker. Enemy of Bardofrankont. Dressed in dermal implants and carrying an isohedron, reams of parchment paper, and a linear frame. The isohedron has 10 sides.

De'Hept Kavan, Friend to the Mayor of a dilapidated monastery, a Xenomorphic Engineer. Devotee to Ultut. Dressed in burlap and carrying fir leaves, technoscanner, and succulents.

Djo'Lpra Sahr, Jaguar of Junkrhad, an adept exobotanist. Enemy of the Goatfolk. Dressed in an iron maiden and carrying a roll of cartridges, an analog camera, and knot'd objects.

Suri'Iah Trigov, a scholar of Cit Vavia, a scholar of ephemeral posterity. Daughter of The Interface. Dressed in a dusk shroud and carrying unplug'd monitors, mirror'd panels, and a bundle'd duvet. With salt'd obliques and bulbous nail beds.

Decu Belabog, Sacrificial Heifer of Chthonos, a
practitioner of collectamancy. Devotee to The
Hylant King. Dressed in torn vinyl and carrying a
belladonic cast, structural proteins, and beautiful
jewelery. With crook'd wrists and scaly nates.

Afte Dahak, an associate of Licot, an equestrian
performer. Child of Kei-Man. Dressed in trackmesh
and carrying sacks of water, quince, and faction
affiliate'd clothing.

Ent'Loc Aarhus, Pyrarc of Anarak, a practitioner of
TVmancy. Follower of The Chalice. Dressed in wire'd
oxygen tanks and carrying clusters of TVP, reams
of grid paper, and sacks of oil. The TVP is sopping
wet.

Heh'Urnt Devang, The Flesh'd of En, an art critic.
Child of The Chalice. Dressed in reflective materials and carrying an ecraseur, a crate of soylent,
and holy garb.

Heh'Sham Ugar, plauge'd villager of Revarie, a
water merchant. Daughter of The Crawling Ooze.
Dressed in burlap and carrying a coveted heirloom,
slabs of ice, and orbital siphons.

Hakue Sukrep, a hire'd body of Cit Dair'Kud'Tuler,
an expert in animal husbandry. Daughter of Egregious Cuts. Dressed in chain sleeves and carrying
pliers, a stylus, and composite plateware.

Baka'Lpra Jurat, Eunuch of the outskirts, a hermetic coordinator. Heir to The Urchin King. Dressed in
chain sleeves and carrying various salves & creams,
knot'd electrical cords, and slabs of ice.

Aze'Odde Kavan, a badger of Cit Licot, a scholar
of post-digital epistemology. Follower of Garagan.
Dressed in a scarab husk and carrying vagrant garb,
a video still, and recovered processors. The video
still depicts a set of three canals.

Jem'Raat Heret, Heredet of Agatar, a metamedia
specialist. Devotee to Egregious Cuts. Dressed in
reflective materials and carrying scissors, various loose springs and pins, and an interface. With
violent molars and taint'd occipital hatch.

Besla Seelig, red clown of Ephor, Mule Herder. Heir
to The Urchin King. Dressed in many talismen and
carrying a mouth gag, muscle memory implants, and
cans of nectar.

Baka'Anet Agard, the practice'd sow of Qamsil,
Marred Grocer. Heir to Bird Superior. Dressed in
additional limbs and carrying velvet robes, a dull
knife, and unique garb. With flexible vertebrae and
rustplum sutures.

Ubi'Feim Mien, fodder of Nahr, a bone harvester.
Follower of Ultut. Dressed in decadent shawls and
carrying a hand broom, trackmesh, and chewing gum.

Aze'Loc Scherngral, Pyrarc of Cit Dair'Kud'Tuler,
a bacterial miner. Son of Lunar. Dressed in conical
objects and carrying a dried eye, bottles of slime,
and bottles of acid.

Imho'Neom Gehen, sentient mass of the Ambient Zone,
a scholar of geo-mechanical criticism. Son of The
Chalice. Dressed in bulk'd iron and carrying a ring
of keys, coffee beans, and the hoof of an ungulate.

Mal'Aken Aaber, haunch'd bird of Anarak, nectar
chemist. Son of The Juice'd Baron. Dressed in
burlap and carrying a toolbox, structural proteins,
and valueless minerals. With babyblueviolet thighs
and shave'd ink.

Duvre'Aken Vaccan, stranger of a tomb to the north,
biographer. Devotee to Lovotor. Dressed in a scarab
husk and carrying various salves & creams, dice,
and vagrant garb. The dice are a d4 and d8.

Mahes'Sham Bachhubre, Pyrarc of Fir'Al'Tuler,
a subterranean apiologist. Devotee to Kei-Man.
Dressed in a mirror'd facade and carrying a trowel,
electrical wires, and a claw hammer.

Pra'Hept Paavla, Hydra of Cit Ravum, a studio
painter. Son of The Hylant King. Dressed in a belladonic cast and carrying unilt candles, delicate
tarts, and biometric armor.

De'Gran Sawhat, devotee of Yoasnmsokl, Applied
Ontologist. Child of The Crawling Ooze. Dressed in
biometric armor and carrying fir leaves, an idol,
and a box radio.

Ent'Firum Cebla, grid'd fool of the ludological
south, an astragalomancer. Follower of Ultut.
Dressed in decadent shawls and carrying a roll of
cartridges, the cantos, and a bedroll. With grayblue toes and redviolet soles.

Bel'Sham Ugrite, a polemarch of Hima'al, arrhythmic
bard. Daughter of Bardofrankont. Dressed in satin
and carrying valuable minerals, a lithotome, and
bags of fertilizer. With bulbous irises and ocherorange fillings.

Uni'Roni Behm, an unlearn'd body of Upasal, Appointed Bishop. Child of Ultut. Dressed in tar'd
feathers and carrying satin, sacks of blood, and
trackmesh.

Cyb'Mot Chevnik, the aphroditium of Revarie, a fledgling in the Guild of Faciality. Devotee to Bird Superior. Dressed in grime'd coveralls and carrying unmark'd objects, denim fits, and unplug'd monitors.

Oricha Setver, sentient mass of a desecrated shrine, an apprentice of the Augury. Devotee to Ultut. Dressed in high-stress exos and carrying uncast nets, a bone saw, and clusters of TVP.

Heh'Ket Kachur, precorpse of another planet, a member of the Guild of Cyber Mycologies. Follower of no one. Dressed in faction affiliate'd clothing and carrying a simple dress, a video still, and lotus stems. The video still depicts a mule. The mule is whining.

Fir'Dant Ere, raccoon of Dair'Kud'Tuler, an experienced cryptographer. Follower of the Nematode Mother. Dressed in crab pelts and carrying a single-shot rifle, enriched soil, and a stylus. The rifle is empty.

Fir'Feim Sabat, the practice'd sow of Varas, an
occult minimalist. Follower of Phot Kul. Dressed in
padded armor and carrying a trowel, tissue samples,
and kevlar.

Suri'Tesh Gaer, siphon'd fool of Choregas, a fleshcraft assistant. Enemy of Bardofrankont. Dressed
in an array of buckles and carrying bulk'd iron,
various salves & creams, and a severed finger. The
finger is a family heirloom.

Hade Voorhes, sprout'd commoner of the Cauldron,
Mule Herder. Follower of many saints. Dressed in
iron mesh and carrying unassuming clothes, gemstones, and minor excavation equipment. With lean
abrasions and salt'd arteries.

Behar Gulem, a desert father of En, a Neo-proph.
Enemy of Gilead. Dressed in carbon fiber and carrying velvet robes, composite plateware, and an
unidentified brass instrument.

Ives Casbeer, Palatine of Choregas, a fleshcraft assistant. Heir to Loplop. Dressed in cloth and carrying a corpse over their shoulder, a book of hymns, and turmeric. With grayblue nates and lofty follicles.

Eyon'Roni Agard, prospective client of the outskirts, a digital ecologist. Heir to no one. Dressed in grime'd coveralls and carrying a box radio, a carton of cigarettes, and robes. With wiry shins and silverorange sutures.

Pef'Ka Sukrep, precorpse of unimportant affiliations, a futamancer. Enemy of The Hylant King. Dressed in babel-ware and carrying a line of hangers, knot'd objects, and fresh produce. With aquamarinegreen capillaries and redviolet water.

Pef'Suel Urak, The Nomad of Cit Batum, a scholar of visceral hermetics. Son of The Crawling Ooze. Dressed in vagrant garb and carrying clips, a bone saw, and seeds. The seeds are impotent.

Donte Ishofli, Arachnid follower of Cit Varas, an architect's apprentice. Devotee to Ameer DuVal. Dressed in tar'd feathers and carrying a fowl, various artifacts, and salvaged ciruit boards.

Umir'Roni Vacek, curse'd commoner of a transnational space, a scholar of visceral hermetics. Devotee to Tumpur. Dressed in holy garb and carrying
vagrant garb, a line of hangers, and a severed ear.
With lemongray lacerations and steep follicles.

Aze'Amaun Ahell, grid'd fool of the Carnlands,
a scholar of geo-mechanical criticism. Enemy of
Bird Superior. Dressed in tarpaulin and carrying a
cellphone, a hand broom, and scissors. With taint'd
soles and rustplum capillaries.

Notus Roath, The Neophyte of the Niopo Tree, an
entrail supply specialist. Child of many saints.
Dressed in heavy greaves and carrying bulk'd iron,
structural proteins, and velvet robes.

Dua'Tek Dasch, Prisoner of House of Effigy, a
soothsayer. Enemy of Lovotor. Dressed in an array
of approns and carrying a biomonitor, recovered
processors, and a trocer.

Wadej'Imp Mabe, grid'd fool of a distant past, a
Slime Morphologist. Heir to The Moon-Face. Dressed
in splint mail and carrying robes, salvaged ciruit
boards, and a tome of sandpaper. The tome was written by the mayor of Cit Fir'Al'Tuler.

Baka'Aken Kikomora, mammoth of a tomb to the south, a seasoned medievalist. Devotee to the Goatfolk. Dressed in a reflective mask and carrying wooden figurines, an interface, and crude cut cloth.

Castur Wadak, the Orphic Fool of Vavia, a water merchant. Devotee to The Moon-Face. Dressed in a configuration of tentacles and carrying bottles of slime, a herd of microbes, and a ring of keys.

Baka'Raat Fumero, haunch'd bird of a tomb to the south, Applied Ontologist. Heir to Asterion. Dressed in black robes and carrying orbital siphons, valueless minerals, and a reel-to-reel tape recorder.

Irra Ager, Villager of a dilapidated monastery, a Morphofeminist. Daughter of The Chalice. Dressed in black robes and carrying stamps approved by the bureaucracy, a spectrometer, and nylon.

Zodi'Smet Jurat, The Blessed of Cit Varas, a portalogist. Follower of Lunar. Dressed in vagrant garb and carrying moss weaves, technoscanner, and a cellphone.

Heh'Amaun Ausrin, Battl'd Insect of Revarie, a Lunar Gnostic. Devotee to The Neo-Succulent. Dressed in nematode pelts and carrying recovered processors, technoscanner, and moderate plating.

Ur'Yett Felk, skull digger of a desert temple, an expert in animal husbandry. Son of Egregious Cuts. Dressed in electrical gloves and carrying velvet robes, a crate of soylent, and decadent shawls. With oblong ear lobes and carve'd soles.

Kala Ochosi, Tempt'd Son of a nearby watchtower, a pitchspeaker. Devotee to The Deep Well. Dressed in a cowl and carrying cans of coolant, a bedroll, and a pick.

Jem'Neom Ebben, siphon'd fool of Spahbod, trepaneer. Heir to Lovotor. Dressed in linens and carrying an artificial leach, sacks of blood, and recovered processors.

Ur'Urnt Culsa, Ruiner of Revarie, an interior demonologist. Enemy of The Unbound Stomach. Dressed in knot'd objects and carrying moss weaves, unsoil'd planters, and foot pedals.

L'h'Tek Tevault, Pyrarc of a distant past, an interface engineer. Enemy of The Hundred Headless Woman. Dressed in unassuming clothes and carrying grime'd coveralls, tins of gelatin, and impotent seeds.

Umeer'Nepher Achazel, a lecturer of the Centur Cathedral, Grand Inquisitor. Child of Bardofrankont. Dressed in steel armor and carrying wooden figurines, foot pedals, and a cellphone. The wooden figurines are splintered.

Yune'Hept Molok, the practice'd sow of Cit Vavia, a scholar of ephemeral posterity. Child of many saints. Dressed in velvet robes and carrying a video still, mirror'd panels, and quince. The video still depicts a mule. The mule is dancing.

Byfr Sorcer, white clown of Cit Varas, a member of the Guild of Cyber Mycologies. Daughter of Asterion. Dressed in a dusk shroud and carrying various artifacts, ecto-chisel, and polymer blocks.

De'Elkt Cantip, haunch'd bird of The Moon, a metamedia specialist. Follower of The Urchin King. Dressed in kelp and carrying a carton of cigarettes, heavyset blankets, and an arrow remover.

Rukur Tawat, a hound of the Digital Landscape, a
Yonicist. Son of The Deep Well. Dressed in satin
and carrying lotus stems, bags of fertilizer, and
steel armor. With redpink scalp and copperblue
knees.

Ugra'Tesh Tabul, Archpriest of Cit Batum, arrhythmic bard. Heir to Bardofrankont. Dressed in a
belladonic cast and carrying linens, a hand drill,
and high-stress exos. With babyblueviolet eyes and
perfumed soles.

Hri'Nepher Esperodies, a hikikomori of the Ambient Zone, a diligent squire. Enemy of The Chalice.
Dressed in a skull cap and carrying a lithotome,
fungal sprouts, and a box radio.

Bosum Et'Ungulum, mutilate'd villager of a desecrated shrine, a scholar of hypnagogic eroticism.
Heir to Lunar. Dressed in wire fleece and carrying
linens, carbon fiber, and golem flesh. With peachgreen teeth and rotting ear lobes.

Aza'Ament Wnuk, The Blessed of Lower Dark, a
scholar of visceral hermetics. Son of Ameer DuVal.
Dressed in structural proteins and carrying palmagranates, spider plants, and seeds.

Duvre'Erzu Egle, The Whisperer of the Digital Landscape, trepaneer. Son of The Chalice. Dressed in additional limbs and carrying a crate of soylent, a dried eye, and irridescent garbs. With gossamer nostrils and globular nates.

Umir'Numi Widmar, devotee of Revarie, bodymass engineer. Daughter of The Unbound Stomach. Dressed in an array of buckles and carrying old melee weapons, a fowl, and pliers.

Djo'Elkt Gatal, The Awakened of Vavia, a Holocener. Child of Asterion. Dressed in satin and carrying a linear frame, holy garb, and structural proteins. With redpink arteries and redpink trachea.

Baka'Sham Mollard, cyberpunk of a pastoral landscape, Neo-typesetter. Child of The Neo-Succulent. Dressed in steel armor and carrying enriched soil, succulents, and the remnants of a garden.

Hez'Dant Abdelnoer, a desert father of Vavia, atonal bard. Child of Bird Inferior. Dressed in many talismen and carrying sacks of bitumen, a severed finger, and tar'd feathers. With scaly and redpink cheeks.

Pan'Anet Yarat, Gentleman of Holy Attire of an unknown origin, a blacksmith's assistant. Follower of Gond. Dressed in many talismen and carrying an important tablet, tins of gelatin, and kelp.

Agav Baunt, a desert father of House of Effigy, a
member of the Panoptic Order. Child of Volcanic
Fumes. Dressed in utero packs and carrying work
clothes, chewing gum, and a belladonic cast. The
cast is split.

Har Guyuert, afflict'd villager of a tomb to the
south, a nematode farmer. Follower of The Unbound
Stomach. Dressed in quilted armor and carrying a
severed tongue, an important tablet, and a linear
frame.

Loa'Raat Maedia, sentient mass of a desert temple, a hermetic coordinator. Heir to the Nematode
Mother. Dressed in moderate plating and carrying
enriched soil, the cantos, and holy garb.

Geb'Baal Lotan, fodder of a desert temple, a member
of the Order of Small Fires. Son of The Nostrum.
Dressed in a mirror'd facade and carrying high-
stress exos, cloth, and robes. With slime'd knuckles and cyanred wounds.

Al'Mot Hure, Heredet of Chthonos, a studio painter.
Child of Ameer DuVal. Dressed in electrical gloves
and carrying work clothes, a severed tongue, and
recovered processors. The electrical gloves are
burnt.

Drom Guyuert, Arachnid follower of Cit Fir'Al'Tuler, a nematode farmer. Child of no one. Dressed in
wire'd oxygen tanks and carrying a severed nose, a
severed finger, and various artifacts. The finger is
bleeding.

Nel'Neom Vaccan, Patriarch of Dathapt, a subterranean apiologist. Daughter of Kei-Man. Dressed
in contiguous joints and carrying sensory archive
tool, sensory archive tool, and crab pelts.

Mede'Hept Vikar, afflict'd villager of Choregas, a
scholar of hypnagogic eroticism. Follower of The
Moon-Face. Dressed in clusters of TVP and carrying
cured meat, work clothes, and beautiful jewelery.

Duvre'Rada Saurte, deer-body of Hima'al, Appointed
Bishop. Daughter of Ameer DuVal. Dressed in broken
cybernetics and carrying muscle memory implants,
bags of fertilizer, and decadent shawls.

Ent'Urnt Ankram, travel'd companion of Argas, a
Slime Morphologist. Child of Lovotor. Dressed in a
wing'd helmet and carrying an interface, a cellphone, and cloth. With gaudy ribs and rustplum
obliques.

Dei'Amaun Cech, Sacrificial Heifer of Latabk, a Lunar Gnostic. Follower of Ultut. Dressed in kelp and
carrying a mouth gag, quince, and a severed nose.
With scarred ventral blotches and taint'd irises.

Leshi Amon, stranger of Chthonos, a futamancer. Enemy of the Goatfolk. Dressed in conical objects and carrying a configuration of tentacles, the pandimonium index, and a reel-to-reel tape recorder.

Sleip Voktiem, curse'd villager of Aswart, a specialist in synthetic materials. Daughter of no one. Dressed in light plating and carrying unilt candles, moderate plating, and a hand drill.

Uyr Molloy, The Polydactyl Palm of Cit Licot, a minor castor. Follower of the Goatfolk. Dressed in kevlar and carrying a painting, various maps, and a collection of CDs. The painting depicts a column. The column is dripping slime.

El'Unut Yarat, mantis of a mountain village, a neo-historian. Heir to The Deep Well. Dressed in kevlar and carrying the remnants of a garden, reams of parchment paper, and electrical wires.

Hri'Apet Amon, Friend to the Church of Revarie, a journeyman of fleshcraft. Daughter of The Chalice. Dressed in linens and carrying turmeric, golem flesh, and loose water. The turmeric is dripping.

Fir'Raat Sorcer, The Neophyte of Cit Ravum, a water merchant. Daughter of The Juice'd Baron. Dressed in splint mail and carrying reams of parchment paper, moss weaves, and a hand auger. With redpink ribs and lean capillaries.

Ba'Dant Tyrer, Jaguar of a transnational space, a techscanner. Devotee to Doromundis. Dressed in unassuming clothes and carrying velvet robes, unilt candles, and a black dog. With angle'd nates and yellowing sores.

Dua'Uun Habacht, a declaw'd wolverine of the Carnlands, a journeyman of fleshcraft. Enemy of The Crawling Ooze. Dressed in linens and carrying rail nails, a dull knife, and sacks of water.

Pan'Lpra Mendu, cyberpunk of a pastoral landscape, a scholar of ephemeral posterity. Devotee to Bardofrankont. Dressed in trackmesh and carrying canteens, a pick, and a lithotome.

Baka'Feim Osika, Tempt'd Son of Anarak, an Object-Oriented Psychologist. Devotee to The Juice'd Baron. Dressed in heavyset blankets and carrying cloth, burlap, and contiguous joints.

Ubi'Hept Iigrashi, sentient mass of Ungulum, a guilded merchant. Enemy of Volcanic Fumes. Dressed in carbon fiber and carrying an ecdysis trigger, a bone saw, and an analog camera.

Ubi'Gran Gresh, Villager of Unaindin, a fleshcraft assistant. Child of The Chalice. Dressed in thick leg warmers and carrying a simple dress, operator cards, and beautiful jewelery.

Pra'Yett Kaddis, Friend to the Church of Fir'Al'Tuler, a bacterial miner. Follower of Bird Inferior. Dressed in light plating and carrying a video still, dice, and sacks of blood. The video still depicts a heroic deed.

Saule Wehrlee, Drunkard of Dair'Kud'Tuler, a reader. Devotee to Phot Kul. Dressed in additional limbs and carrying various salves & creams, a herd of microbes, and a gorget. With redchartreuse genitalia and tepid sutures.

Al'Elkt Nihil, mammoth of Lundre, a dream technician. Child of The Hylant King. Dressed in many talismen and carrying a video still, an array of buckles, and heavyset blankets. The video still is dirty. It was buried for 1,000 years.

Ous'Baal Agrhil, okapi of En, a member of the Order of Small Fires. Son of Gilead. Dressed in irridescent garbs and carrying chewing gum, irridescent garbs, and crude cut cloth.

Tahir Taglam, The Left Hand of a distant past, a blacksmith's assistant. Son of The Chalice. Dressed in dermal implants and carrying orbital siphons, a set of jugum, and a lute. The lute is tuned.

Papat Lotan, siphon'd fool of Cit Hima'al, a practitioner of collectamancy. Son of Volcanic Fumes. Dressed in an array of buckles and carrying datacells, a book of hymns, and an isohedron. The isohedron has 8 sides.

Yasan Cearle, hive body of Cit Licot, a xenoarchitect. Devotee to The Interface. Dressed in a wing'd helmet and carrying a small sun, trash, and the remnants of a garden.

Mirum Maag, Drowned Wight of a tomb to the north,
a scholar of visceral hermetics. Child of Bird
Superior. Dressed in quilted armor and carrying
mirror'd panels, datacells, and bags of fertilizer.

Ked'Ka Vierek, haunch'd bird of Dair'Kud'Tuler,
a Lunar Gnostic. Devotee to Garagan. Dressed in a
dusk shroud and carrying steel armor, a bone saw,
and moss weaves.

Nel'Miro Pavak, mutilate'd villager of the outskirts, a pitchspeaker. Daughter of The Interface.
Dressed in a gas mask and carrying ecto-chisel,
unassuming clothes, and cloth.

Usil'Duvel Rhod, precorpse of Qamsil, a member of
the Order of Small Fires. Heir to Asterion. Dressed
in cloth and carrying additional limbs, reams of
parchment paper, and a collection of CDs. The CDs
are crack'd.

Hez'Hept Gabor, Friend to the Magistrate of Cit
Vavia, a scholar of necrometry. Child of Bird Inferior. Dressed in deer pelts and carrying a small
sculpture, bulk'd iron, and satin. The sculpture is
a mollusc.

Loa'Smet Ittre, terror of Vavia, a virtual archaeologist. Son of Oark. Dressed in robes and carrying
gnaw'd seeds, groceries, and ice'd milk bottles.
With luminous shins and salt'd ink.

Hri'Iah Astare, cyberpunk of Nahr, a scanner.
Daughter of The Deep Well. Dressed in clusters of
TVP and carrying reflective materials, an artificial
carapace, and succulents.

Cherna Packum, Prisoner of Tel Grazere, Neo-typesetter. Heir to The Neo-Succulent. Dressed in crude
cut cloth and carrying a video still, nut butter,
and tins of gelatin. The video still is a portal.

Ur'Neom Vierek, white clown of Junkrhad, trepaneer.
Child of The Juice'd Baron. Dressed in a simple
dress and carrying burlap, a roll of cartridges,
and fasteners. With sharp water and dark ankles.

Ba'Baal Zika, The Left Hand of Cit Ravum, a nematode farmer. Son of many saints. Dressed in a
linear frame and carrying an arrow remover, an
ecraseur, and torn vinyl.

Bel'Iah Schlof, unbound familiar of Varas,
trepaneer. Daughter of The Juice'd Baron. Dressed
in crude cut cloth and carrying various loose
springs and pins, proto-limbs, and a cellphone. The
cellphone has no signal.

Id Latur, The Blessed of Upasal, a fleshcraft assistant. Follower of The Moon-Face. Dressed in uncast nets and carrying a coveted heirloom, a bundle'd duvet, and orbital siphons.

Umeer'Ket Wrye, a garter snake of Cit Varas, a scapulomancer. Devotee to Oark. Dressed in clusters of TVP and carrying technoscanner, lotus stems, and a herd of microbes.

Ymir Kinnari, Palatine of Cit Batum, atonal bard. Heir to The Deep Well. Dressed in steel mesh and carrying coins, salvage, and an interface.

Ba'Mot Basuk, a hound of a tomb to the south, a dream technician. Son of Doromundis. Dressed in tarpaulin and carrying a severed tongue, sacks of bitumen, and uncast nets.

Ezru Valek, The Polydactyl Palm of a tomb to the north, a haruspex. Child of Bardofrankont. Dressed in robes and carrying unlit candles, tarot cards, and rail nails. With dark obliques and pinkyellow burns.

Al'Hap Amon, Matriarch of Cit Dair'Kud'Tuler, an architect's apprentice. Devotee to Kei-Man. Dressed in cloth and carrying the hoof of an ungulate, a corpse over their shoulder, and fresh produce.

Del'Neom Rasa, a lecturer of Azmeern, an occulture critic. Heir to no one. Dressed in a reflective mask and carrying gnaw'd seeds, babel-ware, and a protractor. With petite arm hairs and yellowing capillaries.

Urso Bachhubre, raccoon of Cit Yoasnmoskl, an architect's apprentice. Son of Kei-Man. Dressed in clusters of TVP and carrying a biomonitor, an ecdysis trigger, and satin.

Aza'Amaun Bachhubre, cyberpunk of a dilapidated monastery, a dream technician. Enemy of the Nematode Mother. Dressed in knot'd objects and carrying beautiful jewelery, a severed nose, and a toolbox.

Pef'Roni Voktiem, a garter snake of the Niopo Tree, a watchdog. Heir to Egregious Cuts. Dressed in an iron maiden and carrying scissors, ecto-chisel, and a trowel.

Al'Elkt Cebla, stray dog of a distant past, an astragalomancer. Devotee to no one. Dressed in moderate plating and carrying wooden figurines, multicolor bows, and groceries. The groceries are soil'd.

Usil'Gran Khon, harlequin of Lundre, Appointed Bishop. Daughter of The Moon-Face. Dressed in robes and carrying clips, sacks of bitumen, and a sealed chastity belt. The sack is leaking.

Heru'Unut Ebaugh, sever'd torso of Cit Decair, a zonetologist. Follower of many saints. Dressed in a dusk shroud and carrying dried grains, fragant stones, and unmark'd objects. With bulbous lacerations and bluegreen infections.

Crat Saumtar, feral bear of Licot, a laborer. Enemy of The Hylant King. Dressed in a cowl and carrying orbital siphons, reams of grid paper, and a trocer. The trocer is rusted.

Ta Neblogst, Villager of Cit Fir'Al'Tuler, biographer. Enemy of the Nematode Mother. Dressed in torn vinyl and carrying an array of buckles, black robes, and crab pelts.

Abdon Belabog, trembling seer of a distant past, Marred Grocer. Follower of the Goatfolk. Dressed in heavyset blankets and carrying proto-limbs, unassuming clothes, and golem flesh.

Mokkur Thakur, The Hoarder of Artifacts of the exterior, nectar chemist. Child of Ameer DuVal. Dressed in broken cybernetics and carrying a toolbox, an iron maiden, and denim fits.

Amir'Raat Lethem, hive body of Spahbod, a guilded merchant. Enemy of The Nostrum. Dressed in tar'd feathers and carrying ice'd milk bottles, holy garb, and a hand broom.

Yune'Nepher Behm, the beauty of Cit Vavia, a blacksmith's assistant. Enemy of The Hundred Headless Woman. Dressed in uncast nets and carrying an analog camera, a severed ear, and many perfumes.

Abbe'Raat Uhlik, Grazing Sow of Dathapt, an exorcist of sorts. Enemy of no one. Dressed in a scarab husk and carrying utero packs, the cantos, and a roll of cartridges.

Abbe'Feim Atunis, fodder of Argas, a reader. Devotee to many saints. Dressed in linens and carrying an oil lamp, the hoof of an ungulate, and an arrow remover.

Duod Ittre, postpunk of a distant past, a material designer. Son of The Juice'd Baron. Dressed
in a skull cap and carrying a painting, recovered
processors, and ecto-chisel. The painting depicts a
herd of antelope.

El'Tek Elepis, The Nomad of Spahbod, an occult
minimalist. Devotee to Gond. Dressed in a wing'd
helmet and carrying an ecraseur, stripped vines,
and a mouth gag.

Uni'Lpra Alau, stranger of Lundre, a scholar of
proto-linguistics. Follower of Oark. Dressed in a
dusk shroud and carrying a fowl, a bone saw, and
work clothes. With greenbrown wrinkles and petite
digits.

Ous'Ka Penia, Archpriest of Qamsil, arrhythmic
bard. Follower of Bardofrankont. Dressed in additional limbs and carrying an ecraseur, tallow, and
a stylus.

Hyrme Owyanr, stray dog of Tel Grazere, a portalogist. Enemy of The Unbound Stomach. Dressed in a
wing'd helmet and carrying reflective materials, a
corpse over their shoulder, and a reel-to-reel tape
recorder.

Al'Aken Pavuer, a hikikomori of the Digital Landscape, a scholar of minotaur semiotics. Enemy of
The Unbound Stomach. Dressed in tigulated mail and
carrying dried fruits, an artificial carapace, and
various loose springs and pins.

Beyla Pasiphate, The Right Hand of Vavia, a Yonicist. Devotee to Bardofrankont. Dressed in work
clothes and carrying orbital siphons, a biomonitor,
and a percolator. With aquamarinegreen knees and
lofty capillaries.

Duvre'Tesh Bachhubre, Heredet of the exterior, a
gastromancer. Follower of The Urchin King. Dressed
in many talismen and carrying valueless minerals, a
small sun, and deer pelts.

El'Unut Dien, vole of a dilapidated monastery, a
watchdog. Daughter of The Neo-Succulent. Dressed in
a configuration of tentacles and carrying technoscanner, fragant stones, and burlap.

Heru'Feim Replogle, the Orphic Fool of Lundre,
an expert in animal husbandry. Follower of many
saints. Dressed in chain sleeves and carrying
fungal sprouts, ornate rugs, and a small sculpture.
The sculpture is conical.

Diaph Et'Alette, devotee of Unaindin, a water merchant. Devotee to Loplop. Dressed in a scarab husk and carrying an array of aprons, a herd of microbes, and thick leg warmers.

Pef'Ament Plutence, devotee of Yoasnmsokl, an Omphalomancer. Enemy of The Unbound Stomach. Dressed in many talismen and carrying seeds, torn vinyl, and a simple dress. With dark avulsions and redpink ankles.

Eyon'Feim Kikomora, swarm'd form of Licot, a bone harvester. Son of The Moon-Face. Dressed in trackmesh and carrying pliers, an unweildy mace, and crude cut cloth. The mace is unbalanced.

Uni'Ka Kaukas, Gentleman of Holy Attire of a pastoral landscape, an adept exobotanist. Daughter of Oark. Dressed in beautiful jewelery and carrying a dull knife, an important tablet, and reams of grid paper. The knife is crack'd.

Bel'Tesh Medina, postpunk of Ephor, an entrail supply specialist. Heir to The Urchin King. Dressed in splint mail and carrying technoscanner, polymer blocks, and a trephine and accompanying trepan.

Baka'Talm Ifft, a hound of Fir'Al'Tuler, an astragalomancer. Child of the Goatfolk. Dressed in cloth and carrying datacells, valuable minerals, and babel-ware. With gaudy nates and peachgreen hands.

Dievas Ebben, white clown of the Niopo Tree, a diligent squire. Follower of The Interface. Dressed in crab pelts and carrying reams of parchment paper, spider plants, and trackmesh.

Heh'Roni Sesser, frame'd criminal of the northern deserts, a nematode breeder. Child of The Neo-Succulent. Dressed in a reflective mask and carrying a severed nose, unplugged contraptions, and a sealed chastity belt.

Kathor Obscur, unbound familiar of Hima'al, a scholar of geo-mechanical criticism. Daughter of The Hylant King. Dressed in carbon fiber and carrying ornate rugs, multicolor bows, and minor excavation equipment.

Ihy'Aken Detwa, story'd fool of a pastoral landscape, a bacterial miner. Devotee to The Crawling Ooze. Dressed in vambraces and carrying a painting, enriched soil, and minor excavation equipment. The painting is a portrait. The subject is weeping over a mound of debris.

Loa'Duvel Kaukas, okapi of the ludological south, Marred Grocer. Child of no one. Dressed in a cowl and carrying a video still, a hand broom, and a nail file. The video still is a portrait. The subject is upset.

De'Duvel Tham, Erupted Body of the outskirts, Mule Herder. Enemy of The Nostrum. Dressed in vambraces and carrying guild papers, an ecdysis trigger, and tins of gelatin.

D'Tek Dahak, hive body of Qamsil, bibliomancer. Son of Bardofrankont. Dressed in padded armor and carrying a coveted heirloom, light plating, and a bundle'd duvet. The duvet is stain'd.

Pan'Hept Sorcer, plauge'd villager of Ravum, a student of golemancy. Son of Gilead. Dressed in structural proteins and carrying faction affiliate'd clothing, a trephine and accompanying trepan, and holy garb.

Mahes'Firum Kabat, vole of House of Effigy, a member of the Guild of Cyber Mycologies. Follower of Tumpur. Dressed in thick leg warmers and carrying a small sculpture, gemstones, and a box of matches. The sculpture is a cellphone.

Raas Iigrashi, traitor of Batum, a digital ecologist. Child of The Hylant King. Dressed in work clothes and carrying valueless minerals, a book of hymns, and crab pelts. The pelt is taint'd.

Eyon'Ament Molleur, sever'd head of Argas, an experienced cryptographer. Son of Gond. Dressed in electrical gloves and carrying jicama, clips, and scissors. With slime'd molars and carve'd follicles.

Aze'Uun Voktiem, a hikikomori of the Niopo Tree, a dream technician. Son of The Nostrum. Dressed in quilted armor and carrying slabs of ice, cans of coolant, and unplug'd monitors.

Crat Pacaan, swarm'd form of Licot, a bone harvester. Heir to The Moon-Face. Dressed in a linear frame and carrying fragant stones, steel armor, and various salves & creams. With salt'd ink and cyanred abrasions.

Aze'Suel Gulem, mantis of Nahr, Mule Herder. Daughter of Volcanic Fumes. Dressed in irridescent garbs and carrying pluck'd guavas, tarot cards, and a sealed chastity belt. With steep lacerations and aquamarinegreen arteries.

Sau Mollard, siphon'd fool of the Digital Landscape, a practitioner of necromancy. Daughter of Ultut. Dressed in additional limbs and carrying tins of gelatin, a book of poetry, and bags of fertilizer.

Antero Perkants, skull digger of a desert temple, a practitioner of TVmancy. Daughter of Ultut. Dressed in carbon fiber and carrying an amputation knife, sacks of slime, and a metal contraption.

Cyb'Lpra Polit, The Polydactyl Palm of the wilderness, nectar chemist. Child of Kei-Man. Dressed in tar'd feathers and carrying various artifacts, dried grains, and decadent shawls.

Fullah Sawhat, scale'd fiend of Cit Decair, Neo-typesetter. Heir to The Interface. Dressed in crude cut cloth and carrying thick leg warmers, nematode pelts, and an array of buckles.

Grhi'Elkt Atunis, a badger of Hima'al, trepaneer. Enemy of the Goatfolk. Dressed in an iron maiden and carrying slabs of ice, sacks of oil, and a belladonic cast.

Cyb'Uum Tham, The Polydactyl Palm of Cit Ravum, a water merchant. Devotee to Garagan. Dressed in knot'd objects and carrying quince, a ring of keys, and valuable minerals. The quince is pre-cut.

Imho'Tesh Perstelis, a primate of Tel Grazere, an occult minimalist. Follower of the Goatfolk. Dressed in a simple dress and carrying trackmesh, structural proteins, and a protractor. With silver-orange wrists and globular ventral blotches.

Mal'Ka Cenamo, hive body of Ungulum, a nematode breeder. Daughter of The Deep Well. Dressed in burlap and carrying severed implants, dried grains, and an interface. The interface is crack'd.

Beji Agre, The Syzygy of All Stars of Cit Varas, a
nematode breeder. Follower of The Neo-Succulent.
Dressed in splint mail and carrying a severed ear,
succulents, and succulents. The succlents are
thriving.

Got Lazdon, scale'd fiend of Choregas, a watchdog.
Daughter of The Chalice. Dressed in grime'd coveralls and carrying a coveted heirloom, wooden
figurines, and reams of grid paper. With bulbous
infections and ocherfuschia blisters.

Wadej'Kell Hejduk, curse'd commoner of Cit
Fir'Al'Tuler, a material designer. Heir to Ameer
DuVal. Dressed in work clothes and carrying
stripped vines, pliers, and jicama. The jicama is
juliene'd.

Nel'Aken Sunkt, travel'd companion of the Ambient Zone, Grand Inquisitor. Heir to The Nostrum.
Dressed in heavy greaves and carrying a painting, a
stylus, and bone meal. The painting lacks intrigue.

Ugra'Otep Battiat, postpunk of another planet, a
seasoned medievalist. Devotee to The Juice'd Baron.
Dressed in conical objects and carrying sacks of
water, a cellphone, and tallow. The tallow is
turn'd.

Loa'Apet Epione, Battl'd Insect of Nahr, a hyper-zonal ecologist. Son of Lovotor. Dressed in
knot'd objects and carrying crab pelts, a bundle'd
duvet, and nut butter. The nut butter is made with
almonds.

Ugra'Gran Kachur, punk of a dilapidated monastery,
a cosmopolist. Enemy of Ameer DuVal. Dressed in
proto-limbs and carrying various artifacts, various
salves & creams, and an oil lamp.

Dei'Hept Kavan, Friend to the Magistrate of Cit
Batum, a digital ecologist. Daughter of The Juice'd
Baron. Dressed in padded armor and carrying robes,
vagrant garb, and a lithotome.

Mal'Uun Ifft, travel'd companion of a transnational
space, arrhythmic bard. Heir to The Urchin King.
Dressed in trash and carrying nut butter, a set
of jugum, and a box of carefully packaged needles.
With redchartreuse abrasions and gossamer molars.

Ikke Merope, The Hoarder of Artifacts of Lower Dark, an adept exobotanist. Heir to Tumpur.
Dressed in thick leg warmers and carrying a roll of
cartridges, the remnants of a garden, and tissue
samples.

Al'Apet Cenac, feral bear of a tomb to the south,
an expert in animal husbandry. Child of Oark.
Dressed in cloth and carrying robes, nematode
pelts, and an analog camera. With rusted obliques
and lemongray knees.

Yune'Hap Kuler, sever'd head of a procedural
cityscape, a narrative designer. Devotee to The
Interface. Dressed in a reflective mask and carrying
an array of buckles, a dull knife, and precious
ornaments.

Wadej'Raat Zais, Archpriest of the Digital Landscape, a scholar of marxist grammatology. Follower
of many saints. Dressed in chain sleeves and carrying the cantos, tins of pink paste, and robes.

Heh'Rada Voogd, skull digger of Chthonos, a dream
technician. Enemy of Ameer DuVal. Dressed in
vagrant garb and carrying composite plateware,
fragant stones, and a video still. The video still
depicts a snail. The snail is in love.

Ur'Erzu Scherngral, Prisoner of Nahr, a fleshcraft
assistant. Devotee to the Goatfolk. Dressed in field
plates and carrying a protractor, an idol, and an
array of aprons.

Djo'Gran Lazdon, traveler of Tel Grazere, atonal bard. Son of Oark. Dressed in clusters of TVP and carrying knot'd electrical cords, velvet robes, and precious ornaments. With angle'd loins and peach-green infections.

Dioscre Maedia, feral bear of unimportant affiliations, a zonetologist. Daughter of Bardofrankont. Dressed in trackmesh and carrying faction affiliate'd clothing, gnaw'd seeds, and denim fits.

Ibo Nihil, a tree folk of Agatar, a Xenomorphic Engineer. Devotee to The Neo-Succulent. Dressed in nylon and carrying tallow, a metal contraption, and bear pelts. With bluegreen bruises and petite toes.

Zodi'Hept Tawat, Arachnid follower of Tel Grazere, a mancer of some kind. Son of The Moon-Face. Dressed in light plating and carrying a configuration of tentacles, a linear frame, and a severed finger.

Amer'Otep Sahr, Tempt'd Son of the outskirts, a minor castor. Daughter of The Neo-Succulent. Dressed in conical objects and carrying a cellphone, scissors, and loose water.

Del'Hept Nabu, a badger of Vavia, an anti-realist.
Enemy of The Hylant King. Dressed in steel armor
and carrying bags of fertilizer, a pick, and dried
grains. With bulbous veins and perfumed ink.

Rima Yanak, Frog of a distant past, a soothsayer.
Enemy of Oark. Dressed in denim and carrying a
trowel, bottles of acid, and satin.

Ta Rahld, a tree folk of Varas, biographer. Devotee
to Ultut. Dressed in tarpaulin and carrying uncast
nets, chewing gum, and a coveted heirloom. The
heirloom is a protractor.

Heru'Tek Voorhes, The Nomad of a desecrated shrine,
a Neo-proph. Devotee to Asterion. Dressed in wire
fleece and carrying technoscanner, technoscanner,
and a configuration of tentacles.

Ymir Wadak, The Right Hand of an unknown origin, a
nematode breeder. Child of Egregious Cuts. Dressed
in babel-ware and carrying fungal sprouts, succulents, and tissue samples. The succulent is thriving.

Ameer'Sham Ager, curse'd villager of Cit Batum, a
material designer. Daughter of The Hundred Headless
Woman. Dressed in nylon and carrying cloth, gnaw'd
seeds, and an oil lamp.

Sigge Labrahm, The Flesh'd of the Centur Cathedral, a guilded merchant. Follower of The Interface. Dressed in utero packs and carrying coins, fungal sprouts, and a claw hammer.

Imho'Tesh Dal, the practice'd sow of Anarak, a scholar of visceral hermetics. Heir to Lovotor. Dressed in electrical gloves and carrying dried fruits, the remnants of a garden, and a bone saw. With acid-spit ink and olivepink bruises.

D'Otep Nabu, okapi of Cit Decair, Applied Ontologist. Child of Gilead. Dressed in a dusk shroud and carrying sacks of water, crab pelts, and a bundle'd duvet.

Duvre'Hept Zacek, hive body of a distant past, a scholar of hypnagogic eroticism. Son of Kei-Man. Dressed in knot'd objects and carrying clips, ice'd milk bottles, and the pandimonium index. The clips are rust'd.

Pra'Ket Perstelis, Gentleman of Holy Attire of Lundre, a dream technician. Son of Bird Inferior. Dressed in broken cybernetics and carrying precious ornaments, pluck'd guavas, and a pick.

Ous'Unut Eng, feral bear of Lower Dark, trepaneer. Follower of Phot Kul. Dressed in tigulated mail and carrying fresh produce, vagrant garb, and robes.

Ihy'Ament Yablon, hive body of a dilapidated monastery, a nematode breeder. Follower of The Crawling Ooze. Dressed in nylon and carrying tins of gelatin, clusters of TVP, and many talismen.

Loa'Odde Wat, Pariah of Agatar, a cosmopolist. Child of The Unbound Stomach. Dressed in padded armor and carrying impotent seeds, an ecdysis trigger, and many perfumes.

Djo'Loc Vikent, Friend to the Mayor of a rural river town, a member of the Guild of Cyber Mycologies. Follower of The Hundred Headless Woman. Dressed in an array of aprons and carrying various artifacts, black robes, and dried fruits.

Ba'Mot Urchint, feral bear of Hima'al, Grand Inquisitor. Enemy of Lunar. Dressed in kelp and carrying salvage, religious objects, and fir leaves. With lofty collar bones and acid-spit soles.

Al'Odde Et'Nahr, sever'd head of the Cauldron, a Xenomorphic Engineer. Daughter of Lunar. Dressed in a dusk shroud and carrying a tome of sandpaper, various salves & creams, and polymer blocks. The tome contains primitive coding languages.

Cherna Kaeliehm, an unlearn'd body of Spahbod,
a subterranean apiologist. Devotee to Phot Kul.
Dressed in conical objects and carrying kelp, satin, and the cantos. The cantos speak the truth.

Abab Roath, the aphroditium of Latabk, a Necrologist. Devotee to Ameer DuVal. Dressed in crab pelts
and carrying a small sculpture, delicate tarts, and
crude cut cloth. The sculpture is a nematode.

Hyrr Reshe, The Apostle of Aswart, a member of
the Order of Small Fires. Follower of The Unbound
Stomach. Dressed in iron mesh and carrying sacks of
bitumen, high-stress exos, and VHS tapes.

Ba'Nepher Saarinen, an anteater of Junkrhad, a
liminal scholar. Child of The Hylant King. Dressed
in conical objects and carrying an oil lamp, knot'd
objects, and robes.

Ameer'Uun Fullish, Hydra of the Cauldron, a minor
castor. Son of The Chalice. Dressed in an artificial
carapace and carrying a severed finger, a percolator, and deer pelts.

Mal'Yett Maas, fingerless dweller of Junkrhad, a
diligent squire. Son of Gilead. Dressed in mirror'd
panels and carrying fungal sprouts, a toolbox, and
cloth. With crook'd arteries and dark eyes.

Heru'Uun Czap, a desert father of Choregas, a
neo-historian. Enemy of Asterion. Dressed in kelp
and carrying a bundle'd duvet, waterlog'd magazines, and a severed ear.

Amir'Iah Agre, Pyrarc of a procedural cityscape,
a scholar of proto-linguistics. Devotee to Ameer
DuVal. Dressed in clusters of TVP and carrying the
remnants of a garden, chewing gum, and a bundle'd
duvet.

Eyon'Duvel Achazel, Jaguar of a desert temple, a
fledgling in the Guild of Faciality. Devotee to Volcanic Fumes. Dressed in tigulated mail and carrying
a protractor, pliers, and reflective materials.

Abbe'Hap Egle, sever'd torso of an unknown origin,
a scholar of geo-mechanical criticism. Daughter
of Gond. Dressed in a mirror'd facade and carrying
palmagranates, a carton of cigarettes, and salvaged ciruit boards. The circuit boards are poorly
solder'd.

Mede'Dant Hepfler, a lecturer of Cit Decair, a Slime
Morphologist. Devotee to The Deep Well. Dressed
in deer pelts and carrying an array of buckles, a
toolbox, and the remnants of a garden. With tepid
capillaries and flexible palms.

De'Sham Eng, devotee of the Ambient Zone, an affiliate of the Threadbarer. Heir to The Crawling Ooze. Dressed in an array of aprons and carrying valuable minerals, dried fruits, and dried grains. With silverorange occipital hatch and bald lacerations.

Umeer'Tesh Zeer, newly resurrected servant of a procedural cityscape, a zonetologist. Son of The Deep Well. Dressed in hardened leather and carrying bone meal, a mouth gag, and tins of pink paste. With pickle'd avulsions and petite pores.

Pef'Ka Ekate, The Whisperer of Cit Licot, a scanner. Follower of Ameer DuVal. Dressed in splint mail and carrying bags of fertilizer, groceries, and vagrant garb.

Pef'Elkt Kremata, sever'd head of a tomb to the south, a scholar of necrometry. Enemy of Egregious Cuts. Dressed in bulk'd iron and carrying impotent seeds, a claw hammer, and reflective materials.

Aze'Miro Reeg, Heredet of the Niopo Tree, a scholar of minotaur semiotics. Devotee to the Goatfolk. Dressed in high-stress exos and carrying a small sun, a sacred tome, and turmeric. The tome is without pages.

L'h'Neom Achteriem, a hound of Ravum, a material designer. Devotee to the Nematode Mother. Dressed in kevlar and carrying groceries, conical objects, and a spectrometer.

Ous'Otep Kakar, Eunuch of Batum, a Lunar Gnostic. Heir to The Hundred Headless Woman. Dressed in splint mail and carrying an unweildy mace, severed implants, and palmagranates.

Heru'Ket Kuler, Hydra of Vavia, a scanner. Child of Ameer DuVal. Dressed in unassuming clothes and carrying tissue samples, high-stress exos, and satin.

Umir'Smet Gayumart, stranger of Cit Vavia, a member of the Order of Small Fires. Devotee to The Interface. Dressed in black robes and carrying work clothes, burlap, and trash. The trash is valuable.

Geb'Anet Et'Nahr, Villager of an unknown origin, a techscanner. Heir to The Urchin King. Dressed in an artificial carapace and carrying a severed ear, a lithotome, and a fowl. With rotting calves and roseblue ear lobes.

Pan'Smet Kahan, a primate of the Cauldron, an architect's apprentice. Heir to Gond. Dressed in velvet robes and carrying an amputation knife, a box of matches, and velvet robes. The knife is dull.

Nrir Segur, traitor of Ravum, a virtual archaeologist. Child of Tumpur. Dressed in a dusk shroud
and carrying an artificial leach, enriched soil, and
cans of nectar.

Dua'Mot Rablase, an associate of Spahbod, a futamancer. Follower of Bardofrankont. Dressed in field
plates and carrying denim fits, a mouth gag, and
utero packs.

Hri'Apet Dannen, Pyrarc of a tomb to the north, a
bacterial miner. Heir to Tumpur. Dressed in black
robes and carrying gemstones, fasteners, and an
isohedron. The isohedron has 18 sides.

Djo'Suel Bame, grid'd fool of a pastoral landscape,
a radical thinker. Daughter of Lovotor. Dressed in
tarpaulin and carrying ice'd milk bottles, a rotor
machine, and a trowel.

Mona'Suel Gaet, Orator of Chthonos, biographer.
Child of Garagan. Dressed in deer pelts and carrying a video still, crab pelts, and bars of RAM. The
video still is pulled from a corrupted VHS tape.

Pef'Imp Huten, Hydra of Latabk, a blacksmith's assistant. Enemy of Ameer DuVal. Dressed in trackmesh
and carrying kevlar, jicama, and a hand broom.

Zodi'Hept Carval, skull digger of a nearby watchtower, a minor castor. Daughter of Loplop. Dressed
in a skull cap and carrying net monitors, many
talismen, and a video still. The video still is a
portrait. The subject is mourning.

Ent'Iah Tel'Vavia, mammoth of the wilderness, an
affliate of the Threadbarer. Enemy of The Unbound
Stomach. Dressed in additional limbs and carrying
unmark'd objects, a rotor machine, and pluck'd
guavas.

D'Anet Gulls, harlequin of Varas, a Slime Morphologist. Child of Volcanic Fumes. Dressed in muscle
memory implants and carrying sacks of slime, crude
cut cloth, and an important tablet. The tablet is
crack'd.

Dion Casur, root'd stem of Cit Centur, a nematode
farmer. Devotee to Ultut. Dressed in kelp and
carrying reflective materials, an array of buckles,
and an unweildy mace. With lofty ribs and crook'd
wounds.

Del'Baal Huten, a hire'd body of Ravum, a cosmopolist. Enemy of Bardofrankont. Dressed in tigulated
mail and carrying a bone saw, various salves &
creams, and polymer blocks.

Abnor Schlof, Limb Tree of Fir'Al'Tuler, an auto-mapper. Enemy of Phot Kul. Dressed in unassuming clothes and carrying fungal sprouts, a linear frame, and cans of nectar.

Abbe'Suel Morank, unbound familiar of a desecrated shrine, a journeyman of fleshcraft. Child of many saints. Dressed in trash and carrying stamps approved by the bureaucracy, carbon fiber, and work clothes.

Rada Alau, prospective client of Nahr, Applied Ontologist. Follower of Kei-Man. Dressed in biometric armor and carrying bone meal, fasteners, and nut butter.

Dua'Aken Hahhiam, fence of Cit Licot, a hyper-zonal ecologist. Heir to Oark. Dressed in burlap and carrying a hand drill, a configuration of tentacles, and a toolbox. With pinkyellow nape and pickle'd avulsions.

Ur'Numi Ishofli, unbound familiar of a transnational space, bodymass engineer. Son of Volcanic Fumes. Dressed in clusters of TVP and carrying foot pedals, a cellphone, and religious objects.

Imho'Lpra Agrhil, plauge'd villager of Cit Decair,
a mancer of some kind. Heir to Loplop. Dressed
in cloth and carrying unplug'd monitors, chewing
gum, and a dried eye. With brownsilver paints and
crook'd trachea.

Del'Uum Mollard, sentient mass of a pastoral landscape, a scholar of ephemeral posterity. Heir to
many saints. Dressed in chain sleeves and carrying
fir leaves, various maps, and a video still. The
video still depicts a set of three canals.

Del'Kell Ankram, tentacle'd fool of Nahr, an automapper. Heir to Oark. Dressed in robes and carrying
spare robes, kelp, and a set of jugum.

Ubi'Baal Rangrak, okapi of Revarie, a collisionist.
Child of no one. Dressed in an array of buckles and
carrying VHS tapes, a herd of microbes, and prairie
grass stalks.

Mimir Dilmun, fodder of Cit Fir'Al'Tuler, a scholar
of minotaur semiotics. Follower of The Urchin King.
Dressed in nylon and carrying thick leg warmers,
VHS tapes, and a belladonic cast. With scaly wounds
and lofty gums.

Wadej'Amaun Ybarbo, sentient mass of Licot, a futamancer. Heir to Bird Superior. Dressed in holy garb
and carrying electrical wires, steel armor, and the
hoof of an ungulate.

Eyon'Sham Mien, Prisoner of the Niopo Tree, an apprentice of the Augury. Child of The Crawling Ooze. Dressed in many talismen and carrying a protractor, quince, and lotus stems.

Heh'Numi Nerh'Ghrall, a lecturer of Hima'al, a scholar of ephemeral posterity. Follower of The Neo-Succulent. Dressed in crude cut cloth and carrying an arrow remover, a book of hymns, and a simple dress. With paint'd eyelids and scaly swelling.

Bades Gatal, postpunk of a rural river town, an astragalomancer. Heir to no one. Dressed in an iron maiden and carrying a woodcutter's axe, unplug'd contraptions, and a black dog.

Gayr Synth, The Left Hand of the wilderness, a bacterial miner. Heir to Doromundis. Dressed in bear pelts and carrying a spectrometer, crude cut cloth, and an array of aprons.

Ous'Rada Takarem, The Neophyte of Ungulum, a scholar of geo-mechanical criticism. Enemy of Oark. Dressed in a gas mask and carrying operator cards, fungal sprouts, and satin.

Aze'Hap Dalgesh, a hire'd body of Cit Dair'Kud'Tuler, a scapulomancer. Heir to no one. Dressed in an iron maiden and carrying unilt candles, heavyset blankets, and conical objects. With tepid shins and coralcream hands.

Gayr Gatal, Hydra of the Digital Landscape, bodymass engineer. Son of Doromundis. Dressed in proto-limbs and carrying a cellphone, a woodcutter's axe, and a video still. The video still is a portrait. The subject is growing a garden.

Dei'Yett Bacharach, traitor of Aswart, a Yonicist. Heir to the Nematode Mother. Dressed in velvet robes and carrying rail nails, wooden figurines, and many talismen.

Pra'Uun Dannen, Patriarch of Fir'Al'Tuler, nectar chemist. Son of the Goatfolk. Dressed in work clothes and carrying an important tablet, a dull knife, and tarpaulin. The tablet is untranslate'd.

Ameer'Aken Gaet, a tree folk of Lundre, a practitioner of necromancy. Heir to Doromundis. Dressed in heavyset blankets and carrying old melee weapons, a metal contraption, and polymer blocks. The blocks are chip'd.

Geb'Lpra Molloy, The Neophyte of Anarak, an expert
in animal husbandry. Follower of Lunar. Dressed in
satin and carrying unmark'd objects, a nail file,
and bone meal.

Ent'Roni Kier, defunct administrater of a procedural cityscape, an anti-realist. Daughter of no one.
Dressed in contiguous joints and carrying broken
cybernetics, impotent seeds, and scissors.

Zodi'Urnt Faas, travel'd companion of Choregas,
a hermetic coordinator. Heir to Oark. Dressed in
light plating and carrying unlit candles, a book of
poetry, and denim fits. With violent knees and bald
sutures.

Suri'Erzu Heret, The Neophyte of the wilderness, a
soothsayer. Heir to Phot Kul. Dressed in a sealed
chastity belt and carrying the cantos, fasteners,
and sacks of oil. With bent nape and redviolet
pads.

El'Gran Labiche, Battl'd Insect of Revarie, Neo-typesetter. Child of Garagan. Dressed in kelp and carrying unplug'd monitors, an idol, and a box radio.

Yune'Suel Gayumart, story'd fool of Yoasnmsokl, a liminal scholar. Follower of Bird Inferior. Dressed in light plating and carrying a hand broom, bars of RAM, and a corpse over their shoulder. With pickle'd digits and cyanred bruises.

Lete Simras, afflict'd villager of Cit Centur, a reader. Devotee to The Nostrum. Dressed in carbon fiber and carrying a severed ear, ornate rugs, and electrical wires.

Dei'Otep Aarhus, a hikikomori of the northern deserts, an occult minimalist. Enemy of no one. Dressed in tarpaulin and carrying vagrant garb, precious ornaments, and severed implants. The ornaments are heirlooms.

Amer'Aken Amon, cyberpunk of the northern deserts, a practitioner of collectamancy. Son of Bird Superior. Dressed in steel armor and carrying ecto-chisel, a severed tongue, and fasteners. With lemongray wrists and worn thighs.

Gebby Pavak, sentient mass of Chthonos, an affiliate of the Threadbarer. Son of The Crawling Ooze. Dressed in high-stress exos and carrying nylon, moss weaves, and the hoof of an ungulate.

Pan'Aken Tawat, a tree folk of Cit Fir'Al'Tuler, a Xenomorphic Engineer. Daughter of Volcanic Fumes. Dressed in a simple dress and carrying sacks of blood, religious objects, and a cellphone.

Ludek Mangis, sever'd head of Cit Centur, a scholar of geo-mechanical criticism. Heir to Bird Inferior. Dressed in tigulated mail and carrying fresh produce, a coveted heirloom, and the cantos.

Ugra'Lpra Panorm, the crack'd finger of the ludological south, a virtual archaeologist. Follower of Loplop. Dressed in many talismen and carrying an analog camera, steel armor, and carbon fiber.

Ba'Roni Gula, Warden of Upasal, an entrail supply specialist. Heir to no one. Dressed in a mirror'd facade and carrying a severed finger, many talismen, and an iron maiden.

Yune'Urnt Kremata, Eunuch of Aswart, a seasoned medievalist. Heir to The Interface. Dressed in tarpaulin and carrying reflective materials, steel armor, and a belladonic cast. With oblong paints and angle'd heels.

Pra'Lpra Agre, Friend to the Magistrate of the
Carnlands, a Lunar Gnostic. Enemy of Gond. Dressed
in a cowl and carrying a box of matches, bottles
of acid, and an ecraseur. With perfumed pores and
sharp ankles.

Baka'Uun Molleur, Hydra of Upasal, a Lunar Gnostic.
Son of Tumpur. Dressed in a sealed chastity belt
and carrying groceries, conical objects, and an oil
lamp.

Ked'Raat Setver, unbound familiar of a desert
temple, a member of the Guild of Cyber Mycologies.
Son of The Hylant King. Dressed in utero packs and
carrying salvaged ciruit boards, VHS tapes, and
various loose springs and pins.

Eyon'Aken Dasch, Ruiner of Ephor, a material designer. Devotee to The Chalice. Dressed in babel-ware and carrying steel armor, various maps,
and stripped vines. With sharp toes and gossamer
knuckles.

Imho'Apet Wat, traveler of a desecrated shrine,
an occulture critic. Heir to The Unbound Stomach.
Dressed in nematode pelts and carrying an iron
maiden, an idol, and various loose springs and
pins.

Mahes'Apet Duver, spike'd hog of Anarak, a pseudo-geographer. Child of Tumpur. Dressed in a scarab husk and carrying a stylus, religious objects, and sacks of blood.

Ba'Tesh Gaer, spike'd hog of Dathapt, a laborer. Daughter of Ultut. Dressed in muscle memory implants and carrying moderate plating, uncast nets, and fragant stones.

Heru'Imp Obscur, the beauty of the exterior, an occult minimalist. Follower of Volcanic Fumes. Dressed in crude cut cloth and carrying a hand broom, a percolator, and a wad of receipts.

De'Aken Dubann, Drowned Wight of En, Neo-typesetter. Son of The Interface. Dressed in thick leg warmers and carrying an interface, a severed nose, and sacks of blood.

Par'Baal Cenamo, a fungal body of Azmeern, a student of golemancy. Enemy of Bardofrankont. Dressed in carbon fiber and carrying a hand auger, sacks of slime, and various salves & creams. With petite cuts and oblong follicles.

Pra'Hept Ybarbo, frame'd criminal of Choregas, an equestrian performer. Daughter of no one. Dressed in heavy greaves and carrying a box of matches, cans of nectar, and multicolor bows.

Djo'Imp Cygan, a scholar of Ravum, a practitioner of necromancy. Daughter of Volcanic Fumes. Dressed in many talismen and carrying a corpse over their shoulder, knot'd objects, and a hand auger. With lofty water and gossamer irises.

Fir'Duvel Gresh, curse'd commoner of Cit Batum, a Slime Morphologist. Heir to the Nematode Mother. Dressed in a scarab husk and carrying pluck'd guavas, a mouth gag, and unlit candles.

Siet Casbeer, feral bear of a nearby watchtower, Applied Ontologist. Devotee to Kei-Man. Dressed in broken cybernetics and carrying black robes, an arrow remover, and stamps approved by the bureaucracy. The stamps are waterlog'd.

Pef'Loc Oduad, The Neophyte of the outskirts, a journeyman of fleshcraft. Devotee to Bardofrankont. Dressed in babel-ware and carrying bear pelts, fresh produce, and nylon.

Almen Kaas, precorpse of the Carnlands, a studio painter. Devotee to The Deep Well. Dressed in a skull cap and carrying an isohedron, a simple dress, and quince.

Hri'Firum Kabel, traveler of the Niopo Tree, a cartomancer. Son of Doromundis. Dressed in holy garb and carrying unassuming clothes, stamps approved by the bureaucracy, and tins of pink paste.

Eyon'Unut Fuld, The Apostle of Lower Dark, a narrative designer. Child of Bird Superior. Dressed in quilted armor and carrying steel armor, rail nails, and tar'd feathers. With grayblue knuckles and wiry nape.

Pan'Suel Tawat, mantis of Tel Grazere, atonal bard. Heir to The Interface. Dressed in an array of aprons and carrying polymer blocks, a book of poetry, and the remnants of a garden.

Almen Et'Alette, vole of a procedural cityscape, a metamedia specialist. Heir to no one. Dressed in electrical gloves and carrying sensory archive tool, moss weaves, and nut butter. The nut butter is made with cashews.

L'Dant Et'Id, Ruiner of Anarak, an affliate of the Threadbarer. Child of Ultut. Dressed in additional limbs and carrying jicama, bone meal, and a carton of cigarettes.
Sao Matkan, Jaguar of the wilderness, a Lunar Gnostic. Child of Doromundis. Dressed in vambraces and carrying tarot cards, an oil lamp, and an artificial leach.

Cyb'Gran Maag, precorpse of Latabk, a seasoned medievalist. Enemy of Gilead. Dressed in a configuration of tentacles and carrying VHS tapes, cloth, and coffee beans.

Par'Apet Deuclane, root'd stem of Argas, a practitioner of collectamancy. Son of Gilead. Dressed
in nematode pelts and carrying dermal implants,
recovered processors, and ice'd milk bottles. With
rusted soles and olivepink toes.

Hyrr Horta, Eunuch of a distant past, a neo-historian. Heir to the Goatfolk. Dressed in a gas mask
and carrying a simple dress, bulk'd iron, and a
book of poetry.

Mitra Voktiem, zealous courter of Lower Dark, a
scholar of proto-linguistics. Follower of Gilead.
Dressed in velvet robes and carrying a collection
of CDs, biometric armor, and cloth.

Del'Ament Nachtmun, cave dweller of Varas, a
pitchspeaker. Daughter of The Chalice. Dressed in
tarpaulin and carrying prairie grass stalks, a bundle'd duvet, and bottles of slime. With symmetrical
collar bones and shave'd ear lobes.

Thiaf Ugar, a lecturer of Yoasnmsokl, a guilded
merchant. Heir to Gond. Dressed in muscle memory
implants and carrying a woodcutter's axe, chewing
gum, and an analog camera.

Imho'Hap Taaffe, afflict'd villager of Argas, a
scholar of necrometry. Follower of Gond. Dressed
in a mirror'd facade and carrying a severed nose, a
lute, and a collection of CDs.

Eyon'Mot Qader, The Right Hand of Ravum, a worshipper of the Lamprey. Enemy of Tumpur. Dressed in tarpaulin and carrying valuable minerals, valueless minerals, and reflective materials. With luminous eyes and silverorange eyes.

Aza'Ka Sattar, mutilate'd villager of Cit Yoasnmoskl, a neo-historian. Daughter of Ameer DuVal. Dressed in field plates and carrying an amputation knife, bottles of slime, and decadent shawls.

D'Talm Pacyna, story'd fool of Cit Batum, a scanner. Enemy of The Moon-Face. Dressed in nematode pelts and carrying lotus stems, scissors, and black robes.

D'Suel Devang, spike'd hog of a pastoral landscape, a futamancer. Heir to Bird Superior. Dressed in russet armor and carrying dried grains, wire'd oxygen tanks, and bottles of acid.

Ihy'Duvel Fuld, The Whisperer of the Digital Landscape, a minor castor. Daughter of the Goatfolk. Dressed in vagrant garb and carrying a sacred tome, nylon, and steel armor. The tome contains a portal.

Dei'Uun Hahhiam, Ruiner of Cit Varas, a Neo-proph. Devotee to The Moon-Face. Dressed in tar'd feathers and carrying proto-limbs, black robes, and a gorget.

Jem'Iah Sabiume, Hydra of unimportant affiliations,
a scholar of apiary geometry. Child of The Moon-
Face. Dressed in a dusk shroud and carrying reams
of parchment paper, VHS tapes, and a crate of
soylent.

Ameer'Talm Urchint, okapi of Ungulum, an occult
minimalist. Son of Egregious Cuts. Dressed in vambraces and carrying cured meat, reams of parchment
paper, and structural proteins. With gaudy scalp
and redpink water.

Dafyr Urak, haunch'd bird of another planet, a
scholar of post-digital epistemology. Follower of
Loplop. Dressed in wire'd oxygen tanks and carrying
recovered processors, a parcel, and a small sculpture. The sculpture is a nematode.

Baka'Neon Wehrlee, Erupted Body of Argas, scryer.
Child of The Moon-Face. Dressed in chain sleeves
and carrying clusters of TVP, an array of buckles,
and nylon.

Gamal Lazdon, afflict'd villager of Vavia, an art
critic. Son of Asterion. Dressed in heavy greaves
and carrying a nail file, technoscanner, and synthetic produce.

Pra'Tesh Zacek, Tempt'd Son of a nearby watchtower,
an automapper. Follower of Bird Superior. Dressed
in uncast nets and carrying a metal contraption,
wooden figurines, and moss weaves.

L'Feim Ducre, the Orphic Fool of Agatar, a journeyman of fleshcraft. Enemy of The Neo-Succulent.
Dressed in utero packs and carrying an ecdysis
trigger, an array of buckles, and a configuration of
tentacles.

Andhri Perkants, red clown of the Centur Cathedral,
a scholar of apiary geometry. Son of Ultut. Dressed
in a sealed chastity belt and carrying a painting, palmagranates, and steel armor. The painting
depicts a mule. The mule is whining.

Ahbe'Amaun Sabiume, a column monk of the Digital
Landscape, a Yonicist. Child of Tumpur. Dressed in
steel mesh and carrying ornate rugs, salvage, and a
bone saw.

Zodi'Apet Enil, The Polydactyl Palm of Agatar,
an architect's apprentice. Enemy of The Crawling
Ooze. Dressed in heavy greaves and carrying polymer
blocks, golem flesh, and various salves & creams.

Nel'Kell Basuk, the beauty of Junkrhad, a cantrip
engineer. Enemy of The Interface. Dressed in an
iron maiden and carrying a box of carefully packaged needles, VHS tapes, and quince.

Yune'Nepher Rasa, the crack'd finger of Azmeern,
a student of golemancy. Devotee to The Unbound
Stomach. Dressed in an ornate mask and carrying an
unweildy mace, tins of gelatin, and succulents. The
succulents are thriving.

Ba'Talm Guat, a badger of an unknown origin, a
Lunar Gnostic. Devotee to Volcanic Fumes. Dressed
in an iron maiden and carrying a gorget, bottles of
slime, and scissors.

Hri'Roni Ebben, Consul of Dair'Kud'Tuler, an entrail supply specialist. Devotee to The Nostrum.
Dressed in a wing'd helmet and carrying rolls of
thread, stripped vines, and rail nails.

Hri'Mot Oshmer, a raccoon dog of a tomb to the north, an automapper. Daughter of Tumpur. Dressed in thick leg warmers and carrying cloth, knot'd electrical cords, and polymer blocks.

Umeer'Smet Vaccan, Prisoner of House of Effigy, a zonetologist. Enemy of Bird Inferior. Dressed in fir leaves and carrying tins of gelatin, fungal sprouts, and valueless minerals.

Ihy'Numi Tarment, postpunk of Junkrhad, a subterranean apiologist. Enemy of Asterion. Dressed in grime'd coveralls and carrying tarpaulin, a roll of cartridges, and nut butter.

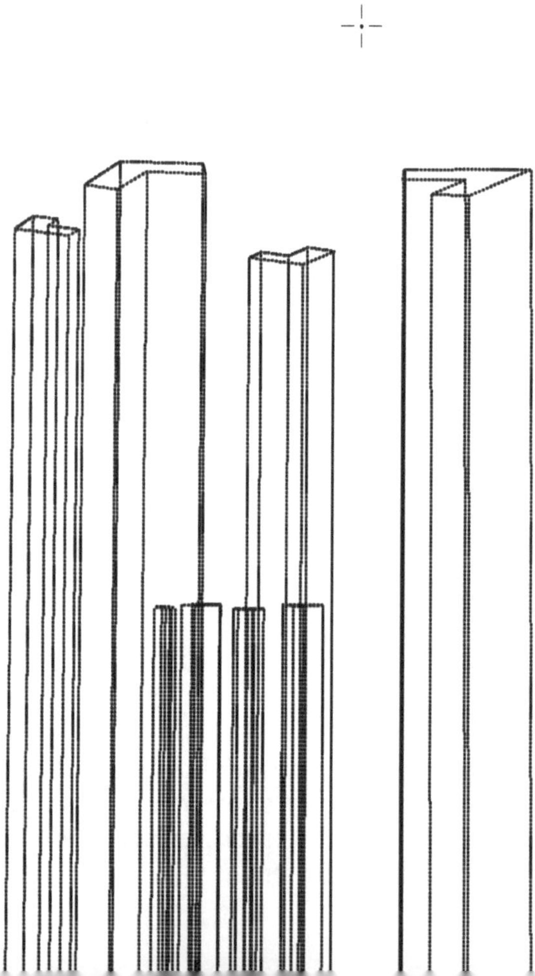

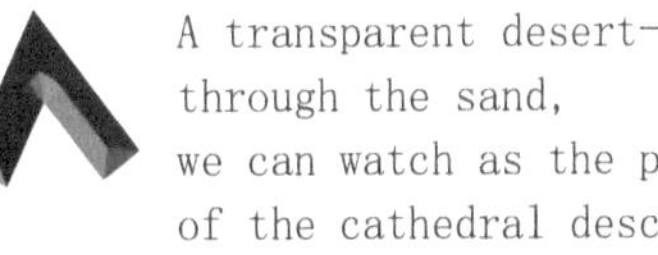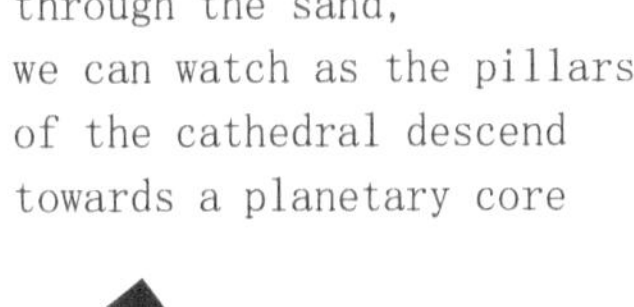

A transparent desert—
through the sand,
we can watch as the pillars
of the cathedral descend
towards a planetary core

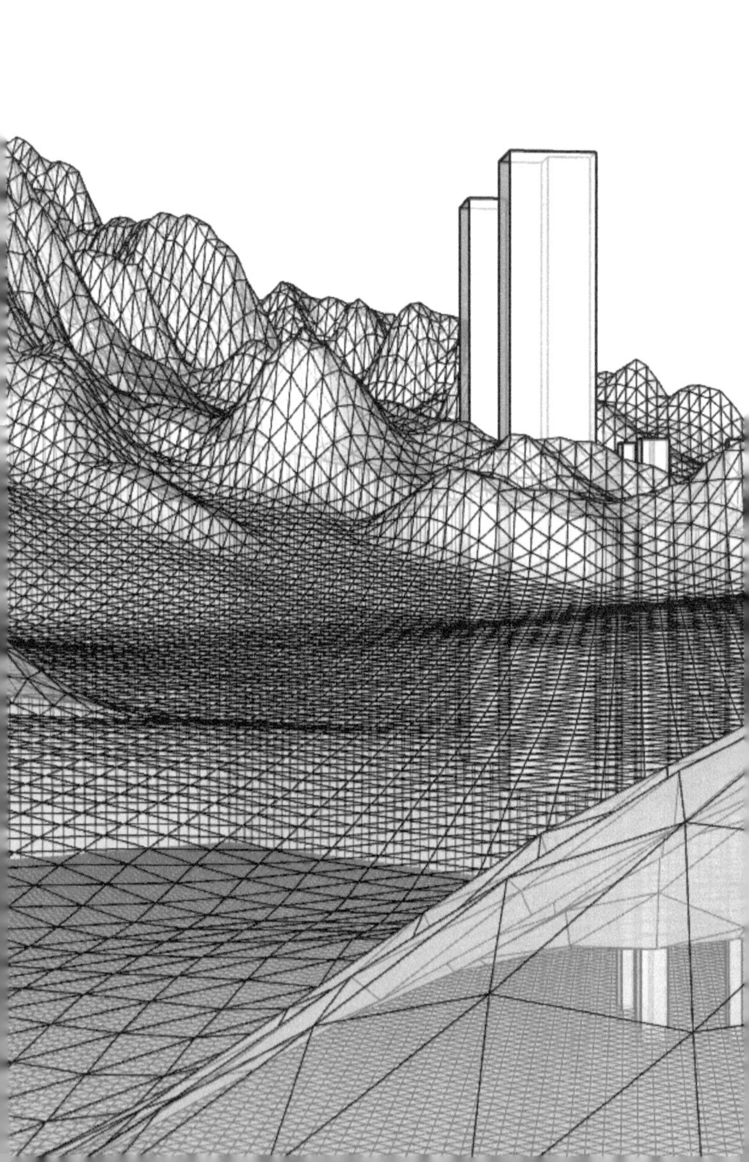

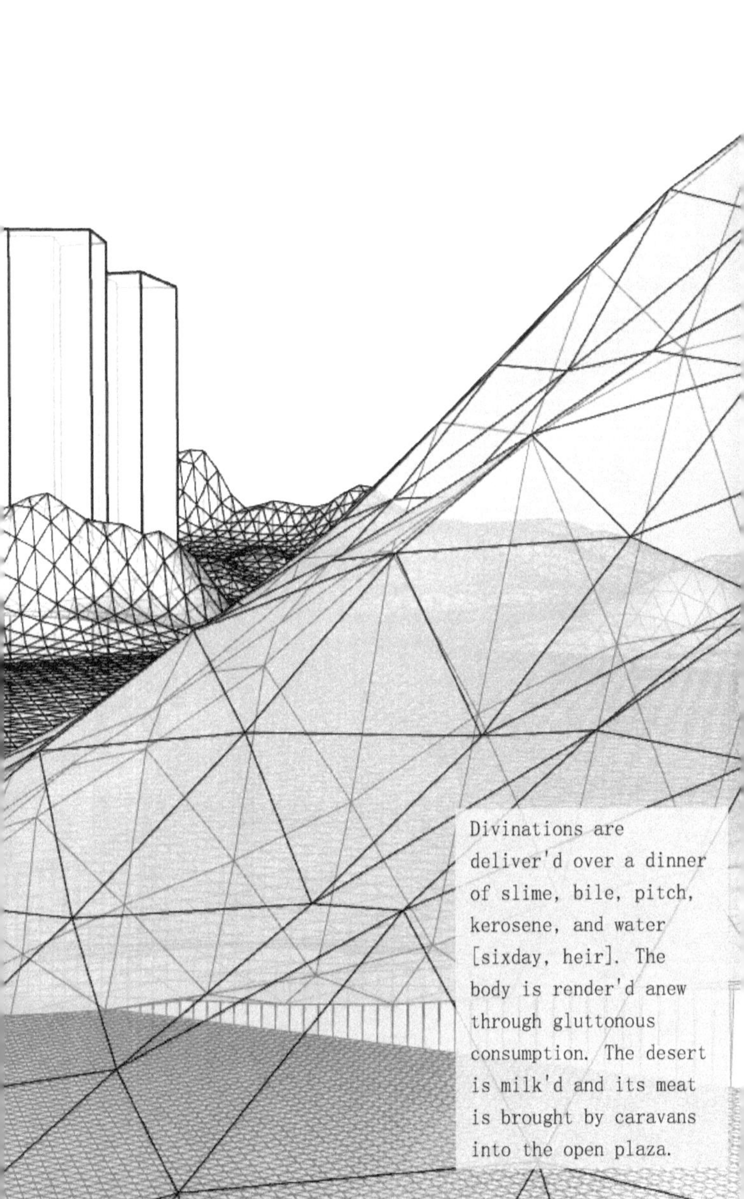
Divinations are
deliver'd over a dinner
of slime, bile, pitch,
kerosene, and water
[sixday, heir]. The
body is render'd anew
through gluttonous
consumption. The desert
is milk'd and its meat
is brought by caravans
into the open plaza.

ARRIVALS OF

Arrivals of the Third Day

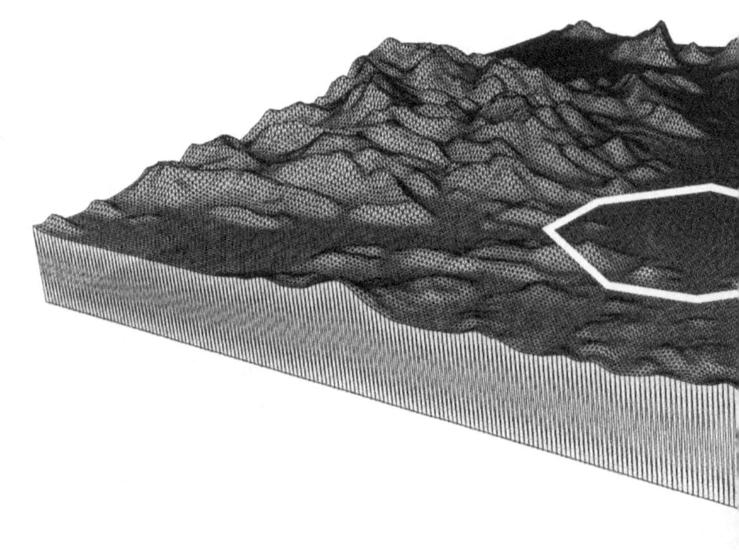

THE THIRD DAY

Trajectory of Pilgrimage
No-Heir
Path Version 3

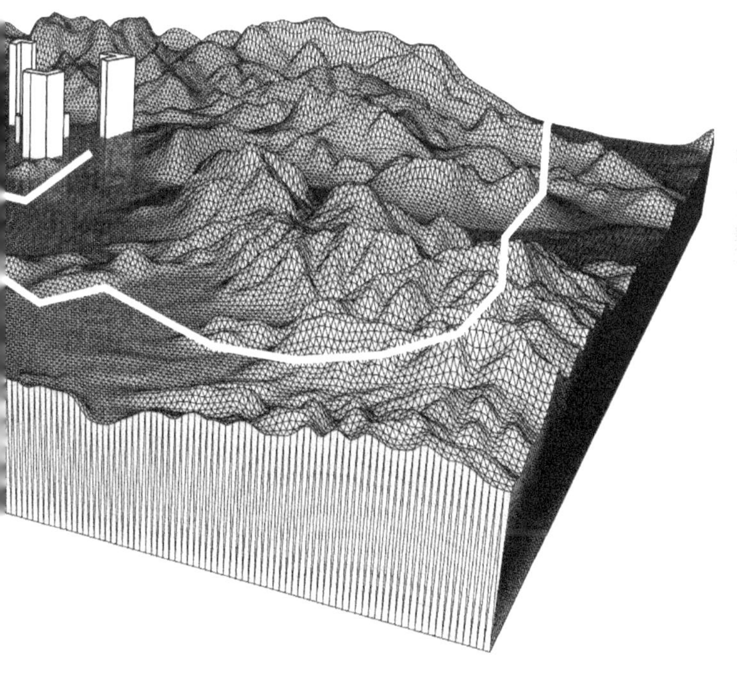

Day3
CensusDirectory
ID, Inventory
SelectedInspect Null
BodyInspect
Motive Null
Interior Und

Djo'Urnt Urchint, mantis of Lundre, a blacksmith's assistant. Son of Hez'Imp Tiems. Dressed in chain sleeves and carrying knot'd objects, cans of coolant, and a severed finger. With paint'd burns and redviolet nates.

Ugra'Dant Du'un, feral bear of the Digital Landscape, a cantrip engineer. Follower of Heru'Smet Radibeau. Dressed in tarpaulin and carrying various salves & creams, decadent shawls, and pluck'd guavas. With ocherorange crows feet and babyblueviolet digits.

Falk Zeer, story'd fool of Cit Yoasnmoskl, an art critic. Heir to Behar Kakar. Dressed in steel mesh and carrying spider plants, sacks of bitumen, and cured meat. With dark wrists and gossamer paints.

Zodi'Lpra Agard, The Summoning Palm of Upasal, an adept exobotanist. Follower of Cyb'Unut Wadak. Dressed in an ornate mask and carrying an old CD player, precious ornaments, and a coveted heirloom. With yellowing shins and bluegreen pores.

Suri'Imp Dilmun, sprout'd commoner of an unknown origin, a futamancer. Child of Mahes'Aken Maag. Dressed in heavyset blankets and carrying raw chocolate, composite plateware, and minor excavation equipment. With silk'd wounds and cyanred ribs.

Eyon'Sham Espern, feral cat of Dair'Kud'Tuler, a
Morphofeminist. Devotee to Hez'Tek Ager. Dressed
in trackmesh and carrying bone meal, denim fits,
and cured meat. With taint'd knuckles and violent
scalp.

Baka'Baal Widrig, spike'd hog of Upasal, biographer. Enemy of Heh'Raat Ozog. Dressed in leather
garb and carrying multicolor bows, an unidentified
brass instrument, and conical objects. With carve'd
ear lobes and olivepink teeth.

Tages Gehen, frame'd criminal of a desecrated
shrine, Appointed Bishop. Heir to Hylick Tel'Vavia.
Dressed in mirror'd panels and carrying a bundle'd
duvet, a bone saw, and religious objects. With bent
wrists and crimsongreen nail beds.

Gebby Cantip, The Summoning Palm of the outskirts,
an Omphalomancer. Devotee to Kenshi Medina. Dressed
in mirror'd panels and carrying neural comb, unmark'd objects, and deer pelts. With crook'd knees
and lean veins.

Dua'Roni Hejduk, the Orphic Fool of The Moon, a
Holocener. Follower of Amer'Hap Labrahm. Dressed
in a reflective mask and carrying an isohedron, nut
butter, and grime'd coveralls. With perfumed scalp
and paint'd heels.

Imho'Ka Pagac, Hydra of Cit Vavia, a scholar of
geo-mechanical criticism. Follower of Ur'Ket
Minerd. Dressed in trackmesh and carrying a dull
knife, dice, and wooden figurines. With luminous
capillaries and bulbous nostrils.

Imho'Anet Et'Id, Ruiner of a distant past, a Neo-
proph. Heir to Mede'Ka Uhr. Dressed in black robes
and carrying stamps approved by the bureaucracy,
bear pelts, and synthetic produce. With muscular
gums and rotting bruises.

Hez'Duvel Oshun, terror of a dilapidated monastery,
Applied Ontologist. Follower of El'Otep Replogle.
Dressed in unassuming clothes and carrying a mouth
gag, sacks of oil, and cans of coolant. With wiry
loins and wiry abrasions.

Par'Baal Molok, the Orphic Fool of Lower Dark, a
scholar of hypnagogic eroticism. Heir to Mahes'Tek
Voogd. Dressed in uncast nets and carrying trackmesh, cloth, and the pandimonium index. With gaudy
wrists and salt'd abrasions.

Ihy'Hept Onslenkt, a commoner of meatspace, a collisionist. Devotee to L'Loc Kahan. Dressed in steel
armor and carrying fir leaves, a box of matches,
and quince. With olivepink veins and brownsilver
arteries.

Ta Achazel, mantis of Anarak, an exorcist of sorts. Child of Ange Radakar. Dressed in cloth and carrying a hand broom, slabs of ice, and sacks of bitumen. With sharp knuckles and redpink wounds.

Ent'Rada Inkh, sever'd head of Dair'Kud'Tuler, a scholar of apiary geometry. Child of Heru'Loc Guat. Dressed in uncast nets and carrying a bedroll, a dull knife, and reams of grid paper. With bent trachea and copperblue teeth.

Mona'Suel Mien, zealous courter of Ungulum, a Neoproph. Enemy of Imho'Ka Himan. Dressed in broken cybernetics and carrying an arrow remover, muscle memory implants, and steel armor. With perfumed fillings and brownsilver nates.

Kaur Esperodies, defunct administrater of Yoasnmsokl, a text morphologist. Enemy of Elam Yablon. Dressed in mirror'd panels and carrying an amputation knife, linens, and holy garb. With bulbous crows feet and gaudy eyes.

Siet Pacaan, Calloused Hands of Spahbod, a water merchant. Child of Mair Agre. Dressed in deer
pelts and carrying stripped vines, the hoof of an
ungulate, and coins. With cut calves and rustplum
vertebrae.

Ent'Mot Nagengast, grid'd fool of The Moon, an
interior demonologist. Follower of Wadej'Numi
Lowalan. Dressed in babel-ware and carrying foot
pedals, a trowel, and a claw hammer. With redpink
crows feet and cyanred nape.

Nel'Yett Pagac, Drowned Wight of the Digital Landscape, an interior demonologist. Enemy of Dua'Ament
Manah. Dressed in vambraces and carrying groceries,
spider plants, and nut butter. With luminous occipital hatch and dark trachea.

Manta Gaer, postcorpse of Cit Ravum, a cantrip engineer. Daughter of Miro Duver. Dressed in nematode
pelts and carrying synthetic produce, recovered
processors, and polymer blocks. With copperblue
fillings and steep toes.

Lete Voktiem, The Blessed of a desert temple, a nematode breeder. Daughter of Castur Mendu. Dressed in iron mesh and carrying sacks of water, conical objects, and contiguous joints. With worn genitalia and pickle'd vertebrae.

Jem'Feim Waag, an anteater of Cit En, a scanner. Daughter of Amer'Otep Uhr. Dressed in dermal implants and carrying various artifacts, velvet robes, and recovered processors. With bald nape and bald wrinkles.

Hri'Lpra Waag, a primate of a mountain village, a digital ecologist. Follower of Umir'Tesh Rablase. Dressed in mirror'd panels and carrying enriched soil, a sealed chastity belt, and nut butter. With scaly fillings and bluegreen ear lobes.

Ugra'Apet Sabat, Battl'd Insect of Aswart, a digital ecologist. Heir to Abbe'Nepher Vierek. Dressed in many talismen and carrying an array of approns, many talismen, and biometric armor. With grayblue irises and gaudy occipital hatch.

Amer'Loc Narai, siphon'd fool of Choregas, a text morphologist. Devotee to De'Anet Tarment. Dressed in beautiful jewelery and carrying satin, a percolator, and waterlog'd magazines. With scaly eyelids and silverorange vertebrae.

Suri'Erzu Wrye, precorpse of Cit Ravum, Grand
Inquisitor. Enemy of Hri'Firum Enil. Dressed in
leather garb and carrying groceries, knot'd electrical cords, and a belladonic cast. With gaudy
gums and redchartreuse collar bones.

Heh'Sham Larat, Friend to the Church of meatspace,
a scholar of proto-linguistics. Devotee to L'h'Amaun Waag. Dressed in torn vinyl and carrying stamps
approved by the bureaucracy, clusters of TVP, and
utero packs. With bald infections and luminous
digits.

Del'Baal Labiche, The Neophyte of Revarie, a liminal scholar. Son of Bel'Hept Atunis. Dressed in
kevlar and carrying reflective materials, the hoof
of an ungulate, and an iron maiden. With silk'd
wounds and dark nape.

Pef'Anet Macci, stranger of Nahr, a fledgling in the
Guild of Faciality. Heir to D'Rada Yegge. Dressed
in a sealed chastity belt and carrying a lute, kevlar, and a protractor. With yellowing lacerations
and worn follicles.

Mal'Miro Carval, frame'd criminal of the Digital Landscape, a bone harvester. Son of Yune'Kell Mormil. Dressed in a configuration of tentacles and carrying a small sculpture, high-stress exos, and a bundle'd duvet. With bluegreen navel and pinkyellow collar bones.

Kuddu Pavak, a column monk of Ephor, an affliate of the Threadbarer. Follower of Caher Agard. Dressed in grime'd coveralls and carrying a box of carefully packaged needles, a hand auger, and coffee beans. With rotting sores and olivepink calves.

Usil'Numi Pagac, Orator of Revarie, a member of the Panoptic Order. Child of Ur'Ament Deran. Dressed in robes and carrying pluck'd guavas, black robes, and a severed ear. With angle'd knuckles and tepid infections.

Heru'Amaun Nies, curse'd commoner of Hima'al, a guilded merchant. Enemy of Par'Kell Manf. Dressed in splint mail and carrying linens, religious objects, and unplug'd monitors. With roseblue soles and tepid ribs.

Saule Takarem, terror of Revarie, a hyper-zonal ecologist. Enemy of Ptaph Qeet. Dressed in chain sleeves and carrying denim fits, a linear frame, and reams of parchment paper. With crimsongreen thighs and coralcream swelling.

Mair Sukrep, curse'd villager of Chthonos, Neo-typesetter. Child of Dafyr Kabel. Dressed in beautiful jewelery and carrying grime'd coveralls, irridescent garbs, and synthetic produce. With silk'd irises and pinkyellow nates.

Ymir Deran, stranger of Revarie, a xenoarchitect. Follower of Gagap Sheehe. Dressed in nylon and carrying a trephine and accompanying trepan, an important tablet, and a toolbox. With bluegreen genitalia and greenbrown wounds.

L'h'Talm Aarhus, cave dweller of Cit Fir'Al'Tuler, a xenoarchitect. Daughter of Pef'Numi Nielem. Dressed in a linear frame and carrying the pandimonium index, a lute, and a reel-to-reel tape recorder. With globular capillaries and greengray veins.

Umeer'Nepher Yanak, root'd stem of En, a member of the Panoptic Order. Child of Fir'Gran Hamadrium. Dressed in heavyset blankets and carrying a bone saw, recovered processors, and reams of parchment paper. With bluegreen heels and aquamarinegreen blisters.

Pan'Apet Uhr, Friend to the Magistrate of Cit
Yoasnmoskl, a student of golemancy. Heir to Uni'Ka
Ducre. Dressed in a gas mask and carrying jicama, a
protractor, and robes. With slime'd arm hairs and
luminous avulsions.

Surt Gulls, robber of Cit Vavia, a futamancer.
Child of Hasat Dal. Dressed in torn vinyl and carrying synthetic produce, a black dog, and multicol-
or bows. With olivepink irises and sharp nail beds.

Hri'Elkt Cantip, the practice'd sow of Qamsil,
arrhythmic bard. Follower of Zodi'Baal Wiygul.
Dressed in iron mesh and carrying minor excavation
equipment, a book of poetry, and a ring of keys.
With scarred irises and crimsongreen ankles.

Fir'Talm Patal, red clown of Batum, a Yonicist.
Enemy of Cyb'Hept Dalagur. Dressed in reflective materials and carrying a crate of soylent, religious
objects, and fungal sprouts. With peachgreen paints
and pickle'd molars.

Caher Gatal, Erupted Body of the ludological south, a reader. Child of Sirem Fabak. Dressed in track-mesh and carrying coins, proto-limbs, and carbon fiber. With grayblue calves and lemongray arteries.

Pan'Ket Balu, The Neophyte of Cit Centur, a xenoarchitect. Daughter of Dua'Urnt Yablon. Dressed in splint mail and carrying a pick, an artificial leach, and utero packs. With coralcream ankles and silverorange nape.

Blid Iafrate, skull digger of Cit Fir'Al'Tuler, a scholar of minotaur semiotics. Child of Nias Horta. Dressed in an array of buckles and carrying a small sculpture, cured meat, and denim fits. With shave'd gums and grayblue wrinkles.

Ihy'Firum Felk, a scholar of Ravum, a Yonicist. Daughter of Geb'Talm Basuk. Dressed in torn vinyl and carrying robes, bear pelts, and bottles of acid. With rusted sutures and wiry crows feet.

Cyb'Kell Cebla, a hire'd body of Qamsil, scryer. Son of Mede'Otep Molloy. Dressed in trash and carrying uncast nets, stripped vines, and orbital siphons. With rustplum fillings and greenbrown veins.

Ameer'Ament Guat, postcorpse of an unknown origin,
a bone harvester. Son of L'Sham Iafrate. Dressed in
field plates and carrying dried grains, an ecraseur,
and mirror'd panels. With rustplum palms and babyblueviolet palms.

Par'Rada Vairya, curse'd commoner of Vavia, a
digital ecologist. Devotee to Ameer'Unut Gresh.
Dressed in multicolor bows and carrying waterlog'd
magazines, ornate rugs, and clips. With lean paints
and copperblue veins.

Amer'Anet Segur, The Awakened of Cit Varas, a
Yonicist. Follower of Bel'Anet Vikent. Dressed in
satin and carrying a video still, knot'd electrical
cords, and a severed tongue. With redviolet hands
and rusted burns.

Sau Ittre, a primate of The Moon, a scholar of
ephemeral posterity. Heir to Hlin Guat. Dressed in
babel-ware and carrying kevlar, loose water, and
a cellphone. With sharp pores and olivepink avulsions.

Yune'Talm Sunkt, Grazing Sow of Revarie, a subterranean apiologist. Heir to Wadej'Odde Taille.
Dressed in many talismen and carrying a roll of
cartridges, velvet robes, and uncast nets. With
salt'd ventral blotches and gossamer eyelids.

Uyr Aaber, Warden of Cit Fir'Al'Tuler, a Holocener. Follower of Turan Volke. Dressed in heavy greaves and carrying denim fits, guild papers, and linens. With redpink sutures and peachgreen thighs.

Grhi'Nepher Qaile, Ruiner of a tomb to the south, a scholar of hypnagogic eroticism. Son of Ugra'Roni Maak. Dressed in vambraces and carrying a belladonic cast, broken cybernetics, and sacks of oil. With scaly follicles and rotting arteries.

Ur'Ament Behm, hive body of a rural river town, a member of the Guild of Cyber Mycologies. Daughter of Cyb'Dant Cenac. Dressed in a dusk shroud and carrying loose water, denim fits, and vagrant garb. With greengray toes and steep palms.

Pela Agrhil, frame'd criminal of the Ambient Zone, a scanner. Daughter of Cyg Dien. Dressed in mirror'd panels and carrying a severed nose, orbital siphons, and tarot cards. With lean vertebrae and bald ribs.

Vahl Nerh'Ghrall, precorpse of the Ambient Zone, arrhythmic bard. Follower of Divje Qaile. Dressed in robes and carrying an artificial carapace, loose water, and a black dog. With bulbous swelling and bulbous abrasions.

Fir'Imp Casur, Drunkard of a desecrated shrine,
an astragalomancer. Enemy of Heh'Odde Nachtmun.
Dressed in grime'd coveralls and carrying an analog
camera, a black dog, and unlit candles. With bulbous fillings and cyanred fillings.

Heru'Tesh Hure, tentacle'd fool of Ravum, a nematode farmer. Enemy of Geb'Amaun Tyrer. Dressed in
biometric armor and carrying tins of gelatin, holy
garb, and a box radio. With lean crows feet and
brownsilver cuts.

Leer Pacyna, punk of Cit Yoasnmoskl, arrhythmic
bard. Follower of Rotam Abdelnoer. Dressed in a
configuration of tentacles and carrying quince, an
array of buckles, and vagrant garb. With copperblue
nostrils and rotting bruises.

Ked'Ka Uhr, mammoth of Yoasnmsokl, a Lunar Gnostic.
Devotee to Ba'Ka Nien. Dressed in a beak'd helmet
and carrying nylon, a collection of CDs, and a stylus. With bald knuckles and perfumed eyelids.

Ur'Baal Saumtar, Heredet of Varas, a text morphologist. Follower of Baka'Tek Gulem. Dressed in an
array of buckles and carrying valuable minerals,
many perfumes, and unassuming clothes. With rustplum ink and worn teeth.

Ogun Urak, haunch'd bird of Cit Decair, a pseudo-geographer. Heir to Besla Felk. Dressed in denim and carrying dice, an isohedron, and an ecraseur. With gossamer ankles and lofty eyes.

Al'Imp Capio, fodder of a rural river town, a scholar of necrometry. Enemy of L'Yett Savanne. Dressed in a wing'd helmet and carrying grime'd coveralls, turmeric, and a box of carefully packaged needles. With slime'd bruises and redviolet pores.

Veig Schlof, tentacle'd fool of Cit Batum, a meta-media specialist. Follower of Artum Espern. Dressed in quilted armor and carrying holy garb, heavyset blankets, and pliers. With curl'd arm hairs and oblong cheeks.

Eyon'Smet Mendu, Palatine of a tomb to the south, a collisionist. Child of Mona'Iah Phibek. Dressed in robes and carrying bottles of slime, a corpse over their shoulder, and a configuration of tentacles. With olivepink cheeks and grayblue ear lobes.

Geb'Suel Sadlon, Matriarch of a desert temple, a collisionist. Heir to Hez'Imp Voorhes. Dressed in linens and carrying a lute, wooden figurines, and cured meat. With speckled lacerations and perfumed loins.

Mahes'Rada Dejan, a hound of a rural river town,
a portalogist. Child of D'Kell Aamodt. Dressed
in velvet robes and carrying fasteners, a line of
hangers, and a crate of soylent. With lean bruises
and redpink palms.

Geb'Lpra Labrahm, a primate of Aswart, a specialist in synthetic materials. Follower of Ous'Amaun
Thakur. Dressed in crude cut cloth and carrying a
corpse over their shoulder, a box of matches, and
recovered processors. With perfumed infections and
salt'd gums.

Ba'Roni Saarinen, raccoon of Yoasnmsokl, bodymass engineer. Devotee to L'Anet Wnuk. Dressed in
contiguous joints and carrying a severed ear, a
woodcutter's axe, and tallow. With worn ribs and
globular loins.

Pan'Tesh Narai, The Polydactyl Palm of Cit Varas,
an occulture critic. Devotee to Abbe'Baal Kinnari.
Dressed in bear pelts and carrying black robes,
nut butter, and pluck'd guavas. With babyblueviolet
water and sharp crows feet.

Aza'Rada Sheehe, Pyrarc of a dilapidated monastery,
an astragalomancer. Enemy of Ubi'Feim Casbeer.
Dressed in russet armor and carrying gemstones,
many talismen, and an isohedron. With roseblue
lacerations and ocherorange ventral blotches.

Mal'Ka Devang, Grazing Sow of En, a scapulomancer.
Enemy of Heh'Ka Molleur. Dressed in a scarab husk
and carrying precious ornaments, cast nets, and uncast nets. With coralcream nostrils and coralcream
nail beds.

L'Rada Morank, haunch'd bird of Aswart, a dream
technician. Devotee to Amer'Smet Cit'Al. Dressed
in leather garb and carrying unplug'd monitors, a
reel-to-reel tape recorder, and an oil lamp. With
scaly irises and gaudy wrinkles.

Ked'Baal Cwyanr, Patriarch of a dilapidated monastery, a nematode farmer. Follower of Hri'Imp Dudek.
Dressed in conical objects and carrying a trephine
and accompanying trepan, the cantos, and prairie
grass stalks. With crook'd toes and redpink infections.

Surt Cantip, Palatine of a tomb to the south, a
specialist in synthetic materials. Follower of Pela
Maedia. Dressed in high-stress exos and carrying
contiguous joints, knot'd objects, and stripped
vines. With roseblue trachea and aquamarinegreen
knuckles.

Nel'Ka Takarem, Prisoner of Licot, Mule Herder.
Heir to Wadej'Aken Aas. Dressed in heavy greaves
and carrying scissors, a hand drill, and tar'd
feathers. With angle'd nates and greengray loins.

Mahes'Mot Deuclane, the aphroditium of Vavia, a
scholar of proto-linguistics. Enemy of Usil'Elkt
Sharum. Dressed in high-stress exos and carrying
the pandimonium index, a dull knife, and guild papers. With babyblueviolet pores and perfumed crows
feet.

Mede'Suel Fabak, a fungal body of En, a student of
golemancy. Child of Djo'Smet Carval. Dressed in
biometric armor and carrying a metal contraption,
light plating, and contiguous joints. With symmetrical palms and cyanred arteries.

Del'Miro Osika, The Hoarder of Artifacts of En,
a futamancer. Devotee to Imho'Mot Nerh'Ghrall.
Dressed in irridescent garbs and carrying dried
fruits, steel armor, and a carton of cigarettes.
With luminous gums and greenbrown wounds.

Heh'Numi Balu, The Right Hand of Cit Varas, a narrative designer. Heir to Amer'Urnt Cwyanr. Dressed
in cloth and carrying dermal implants, an arrow
remover, and canteens. With redpink gums and rusted
irises.

Uni'Miro Zeer, an anteater of a pastoral landscape, a scanner. Devotee to Imho'Lpra Maas. Dressed in contiguous joints and carrying enriched soil, various loose springs and pins, and reams of grid paper. With shave'd collar bones and copperblue swelling.

Amir'Hap Hignite, stranger of Nahr, Applied Ontologist. Devotee to Ked'Sham Tarment. Dressed in a scarab husk and carrying mirror'd panels, a linear frame, and the hoof of an ungulate. With brownsilver soles and lean sutures.

Geb'Anet Rahld, The Nomad of Unaindin, a virtual archaeologist. Heir to El'Aken Larat. Dressed in tar'd feathers and carrying a coveted heirloom, tins of gelatin, and a coveted heirloom. With gossamer molars and salt'd paints.

Heru'Uun Maag, fence of the northern deserts, a narrative designer. Heir to Umeer'Hap Achteriem. Dressed in an ornate mask and carrying tarot cards, foot pedals, and burlap. With slime'd eyelids and crook'd calves.

Mal'Gran Behrend, an associate of the exterior, a blacksmith's assistant. Son of Ked'Baal Astare. Dressed in a beak'd helmet and carrying raw chocolate, slabs of ice, and tins of pink paste. With luminous nape and sharp nail beds.

Duvre'Kell Astare, stray dog of a dilapidated
monastery, an affliate of the Threadbarer. Heir to
Ameer'Firum Urak. Dressed in nematode pelts and
carrying various artifacts, cans of nectar, and
succulents. With silverorange gums and brownsilver
ribs.

Ugra'Baal Sattar, The Whisperer of Qamsil, a seasoned medievalist. Enemy of Ked'Ament Guat. Dressed
in heavy greaves and carrying a woodcutter's axe,
holy garb, and slabs of ice. With rotting lacerations and peachgreen veins.

L'h'Nepher Yauk, traveler of a dilapidated monastery, a laborer. Follower of Aza'Suel Wrye. Dressed
in kevlar and carrying trackmesh, slabs of ice,
and neural comb. With luminous thighs and shave'd
eyelids.

Byfr Oshun, Matriarch of the Ambient Zone, a journeyman of fleshcraft. Daughter of Mokkur Haighr.
Dressed in work clothes and carrying a severed
tongue, an array of aprons, and robes. With silk'd
sutures and muscular ear lobes.

Aze'Umut Ere, The Awakened of Ravum, a digital ecologist. Child of Umir'Ka Cantip. Dressed in quilted armor and carrying scissors, an array of buckles, and a biomonitor. With bulbous paints and perfumed shins.

Imho'Sham Gehen, cave dweller of the exterior, a hermetic coordinator. Devotee to Geb'Apet Patal. Dressed in uncast nets and carrying many perfumes, a ring of keys, and a sacred tome. With greenbrown nail beds and scaly infections.

El'Nepher Patal, Frog of the wilderness, a scholar of marxist grammatology. Child of Wadej'Loc Volke. Dressed in robes and carrying loose water, sacks of bitumen, and moderate plating. With lean nape and sharp heels.

Ur'Uun Kabel, postcorpse of a tomb to the north, a scapulomancer. Enemy of Loa'Tesh Culsa. Dressed in linens and carrying a simple dress, an isohedron, and the remnants of a garden. With silk'd burns and ocherorange pads.

Ous'Ament Roath, okapi of Cit En, a scholar of ephemeral posterity. Child of Ba'Lpra Lowalan. Dressed in a wing'd helmet and carrying unilt candles, a lithotome, and a tome of sandpaper. With sharp calves and crimsongreen ink.

Artum Fabak, fodder of Cit En, a scapulomancer.
Enemy of Arca Bame. Dressed in a dusk shroud and
carrying canteens, a lute, and the cantos. With
lean genitalia and rotting ventral blotches.

Umir'Otep Pavuer, a nematode of Ephor, arrhythmic
bard. Follower of Ur'Iah Immol. Dressed in a sealed
chastity belt and carrying ecto-chisel, carbon
fiber, and utero packs. With greengray abrasions and
globular ear lobes.

Rez Casur, The Polydactyl Palm of Cit Yoasnmoskl,
an anti-realist. Devotee to Mano Yauk. Dressed in
knot'd objects and carrying denim fits, an arrow
remover, and grime'd coveralls. With dark swelling
and luminous molars.

Al'Feim Gilitine, story'd fool of the exterior,
a mancer of some kind. Enemy of Suri'Raat Lotan.
Dressed in vambraces and carrying contiguous
joints, minor excavation equipment, and a nail file.
With bald vertebrae and pickle'd follicles.

Forse Omphale, Sacrificial Heifer of Yoasnmsokl, an
occult minimalist. Follower of Ve Roath. Dressed in
contiguous joints and carrying a trowel, a collection of CDs, and a sacred tome. With copperblue
vertebrae and dark eyes.

Del'Urnt Yggre, The Syzygy of All Stars of Cit En, a metamedia specialist. Son of Del'Tesh Zeer. Dressed in a belladonic cast and carrying scissors, trash, and fir leaves. With bluegreen abrasions and babyblueviolet irises.

Ameer'Feim Khon, cave dweller of the Carnlands, Applied Ontologist. Follower of Amir'Ament Lucef. Dressed in a cowl and carrying a pick, a bundle'd duvet, and composite plateware. With oblong nostrils and crook'd follicles.

L'h'Rada Du'un, Matriarch of Yoasnmsokl, a specialist in synthetic materials. Heir to L'h'Mot Radibeau. Dressed in a wing'd helmet and carrying sacks of water, tissue samples, and pliers. With ocherfuschia crows feet and gossamer arm hairs.

Pef'Ament Deuclane, tentacle'd fool of the Ambient Zone, an occult minimalist. Enemy of Heru'Aken Rakas. Dressed in high-stress exos and carrying spider plants, a crate of soylent, and a corpse over their shoulder. With globular pores and aquamarinegreen palms.

Ugra'Urnt Wnek, The Whisperer of Licot, a member
of the Order of Self-Capture. Devotee to Hez'Talm
Maak. Dressed in electrical gloves and carrying
a corpse over their shoulder, various salves &
creams, and mirror'd panels. With angle'd lacerations and greengray heels.

Dei'Uun Haighr, stranger of a nearby watchtower,
a scholar of marxist grammatology. Follower of
Ur'Hap Belabog. Dressed in crab pelts and carrying
ecto-chisel, sacks of bitumen, and a metal contraption. With sharp eyes and coralcream water.

Baka'Dant Ubl, Gentleman of Holy Attire of Cit
Fir'Al'Tuler, an occult minimalist. Devotee to
Del'Mot Ebaugh. Dressed in grime'd coveralls and
carrying torn vinyl, clips, and moderate plating.
With dark abrasions and muscular trachea.

Aze'Gran Omphale, Heredet of the Carnlands, an
apprentice of the Augury. Enemy of Ba'Ament Elepis.
Dressed in a skull cap and carrying an artificial
carapace, polymer blocks, and an unidentified brass
instrument. With shave'd capillaries and acid-spit
lacerations.

Hako Plutence, stranger of a nearby watchtower,
a member of the Guild of Cyber Mycologies. Son of
Gilga Ekate. Dressed in bear pelts and carrying
a collection of CDs, many perfumes, and a sacred
tome. With yellowing vertebrae and babyblueviolet
toes.

Dei'Tesh Nachtmun, postcorpse of a rural river
town, bibliomancer. Daughter of Usil'Sham Yorbek.
Dressed in a simple dress and carrying sensory
archive tool, unplugged contraptions, and a dull
knife. With ocherfuschia calves and globular swelling.

Djo'Smet Molok, Palatine of an unknown origin, a
minor castor. Son of Zodi'Ka Sawhat. Dressed in
babel-ware and carrying rail nails, the cantos, and
high-stress exos. With salt'd genitalia and coralcream arteries.

Fir'Hept Kremata, stray dog of a desert temple,
a member of the Panoptic Order. Heir to Loa'Odde
Zais. Dressed in uncast nets and carrying tallow,
groceries, and minor excavation equipment. With
scarred genitalia and globular water.

Mitra Kabel, The Apostle of Hima'al, an apprentice
of the Augury. Child of Gondal Tiems. Dressed in
kevlar and carrying ecto-chisel, datacells, and
tins of gelatin. With bulbous infections and oblong
vertebrae.

Del'Imp Atunis, Orator of Aswart, an interior
demonologist. Heir to Mona'Imp Habacht. Dressed
in additional limbs and carrying pluck'd guavas,
kevlar, and palmagranates. With rotting ribs and
flexible loins.

El'Ka Lucef, The Syzygy of All Stars of the Ambient
Zone, a fleshcraft assistant. Daughter of Grhi'Ament
Yauk. Dressed in steel mesh and carrying the pandi-
monium index, clusters of TVP, and fungal sprouts.
With peachgreen avulsions and lean capillaries.

Urso Wat, Battl'd Insect of Latabk, a scholar of
geo-mechanical criticism. Follower of Diaph Czap.
Dressed in muscle memory implants and carrying
thick leg warmers, beautiful jewelery, and a metal
contraption. With grayblue calves and steep paints.

Pef'Tesh Iafrate, curse'd villager of a desecrated
shrine, trepaneer. Heir to L'h'Ket Osika. Dressed
in a sealed chastity belt and carrying high-stress
exos, bags of fertilizer, and an isohedron. With
dark cheeks and worn soles.

Jem'Loc Lotan, The Summoning Palm of Cit Decair,
Marred Grocer. Heir to Pef'Firum Nier. Dressed
in vambraces and carrying wire'd oxygen tanks, a
trowel, and pluck'd guavas. With sharp water and
bent calves.

L'Roni Kaukas, cave dweller of Lower Dark, a bioid
integration engineer. Follower of Zodi'Firum Laum.
Dressed in babel-ware and carrying gnaw'd seeds,
reflective materials, and a configuration of tentacles. With brownsilver irises and bald genitalia.

Usil'Uum Kratt, vole of Dathapt, a cartomancer.
Heir to De'Iah Ubl. Dressed in irridescent garbs
and carrying scissors, tins of gelatin, and a toolbox. With salt'd eyes and gaudy trachea.

Umir'Miro Thamery, plauge'd villager of Cit En,
a text morphologist. Devotee to Dei'Mot Cantip.
Dressed in trackmesh and carrying the remnants of a
garden, a lithotome, and neural comb. With ocherfuschia wrists and gaudy soles.

Uni'Ament Nier, robber of Qamsil, a text morphologist. Son of Mal'Unut Lethem. Dressed in irridescent garbs and carrying a belladonic cast, loose water, and scissors. With slime'd trachea and pinkyellow shins.

Grhi'Lpra Balu, the crack'd finger of the Centur Cathedral, a cosmopolist. Heir to Imho'Ket Penia. Dressed in a simple dress and carrying a small sun, a wad of receipts, and sacks of bitumen. With babyblueviolet ribs and crook'd collar bones.

Dua'Hap Nifong, traitor of Ravum, a text morphologist. Child of Del'Amaun Nien. Dressed in cloth and carrying a book of poetry, robes, and cans of coolant. With greengray navel and redviolet ventral blotches.

Pef'Lpra Fabak, Erupted Body of Varas, a specialist in synthetic materials. Heir to Duvre'Tesh Savanne. Dressed in grime'd coveralls and carrying a trephine and accompanying trepan, various artifacts, and various salves & creams. With rustplum heels and roseblue fillings.

Uni'Nepher Pacyna, okapi of Latabk, an astragalomancer. Daughter of Abbe'Raat Habacht. Dressed in tigulated mail and carrying a spectrometer, tarpaulin, and satin. With slime'd trachea and petite genitalia.

Turan Minnig, mutilate'd villager of Cit Yoasnmoskl, a practitioner of TVmancy. Devotee to Gondal
Tevault. Dressed in black robes and carrying chewing gum, bear pelts, and canteens. With petite ear
lobes and rustplum nostrils.

Fir'Yett Wehrs, The Awakened of the Centur Cathedral, a scholar of necrometry. Son of Uni'Gran
Reshe. Dressed in black robes and carrying unmark'd
objects, unsoil'd planters, and a gorget. With
salt'd ink and worn capillaries.

Elam Perstelis, feral cat of Vavia, a practitioner
of necromancy. Enemy of Tages Rhod. Dressed in a
dusk shroud and carrying unplugged contraptions,
neural comb, and sacks of slime. With violent vertebrae and perfumed nail beds.

Grhi'Miro Siler, the crack'd finger of Ravum, a
scholar of necrometry. Follower of Pan'Odde Larat.
Dressed in crude cut cloth and carrying a biomonitor, sacks of slime, and old melee weapons. With
bent crows feet and angle'd molars.

Al'Loc Perkants, The Summoning Palm of Anarak, a
pitchspeaker. Enemy of Amir'Amaun Vacek. Dressed in
steel mesh and carrying a configuration of tentacles, an isohedron, and steel armor. With steep
teeth and wiry pores.

Suri'Iah Laum, an associate of a rural river town, trepaneer. Heir to Umeer'Rada Replogle. Dressed in a configuration of tentacles and carrying a sealed chastity belt, operator cards, and an unidentified brass instrument. With rotting ventral blotches and redviolet wounds.

Zodi'Amaun Bacharach, Friend to the Church of Yoasnmsokl, a Morphofeminist. Devotee to Umeer'Feim Battiat. Dressed in a wing'd helmet and carrying mirror'd panels, a severed tongue, and structural proteins. With pinkyellow nape and scarred calves.

Usil'Apet Rahld, unbound familiar of Dathapt, an apprentice of the Augury. Follower of Dua'Hap Rawat. Dressed in a reflective mask and carrying electrical wires, dermal implants, and a cellphone. With crook'd lacerations and greengray wrinkles.

Dei'Urnt Setver, an associate of Upasal, a haruspex. Follower of Mahes'Raat Du'un. Dressed in trackmesh and carrying tarpaulin, guild papers, and a sacred tome. With symmetrical knees and lofty palms.

El'Hept Nagar, Friend to the Mayor of Choregas, a subterranean apiologist. Son of Dei'Ka Simik. Dressed in a simple dress and carrying contiguous joints, bottles of slime, and an oil lamp. With lemongray blisters and bulbous ankles.

Sulta Lowalan, The Nomad of Ungulum, an anti-realist. Daughter of Turan Fuld. Dressed in thick leg
warmers and carrying satin, a painting, and fungal
sprouts. With yellowing ribs and gossamer cuts.

Numi Nabu, deer-body of Cit Ravum, a techscanner.
Heir to Gebby Symth. Dressed in contiguous joints
and carrying moss weaves, additional limbs, and a
simple dress. With bulbous fillings and ocherorange
toes.

L'h'Elkt Sunkt, curse'd commoner of Ungulum, a
laborer. Daughter of Eyon'Iah Labiche. Dressed in
work clothes and carrying dried fruits, valuable
minerals, and fragant stones. With dark trachea and
lemongray burns.

Jem'Loc Laum, the aphroditium of Aswart, trepaneer.
Follower of Eyon'Dant Glauciem. Dressed in a wing'd
helmet and carrying dermal implants, recovered
processors, and moderate plating. With coralcream
calves and roseblue ribs.

Par'Lpra Alet, Prisoner of a dilapidated monastery, a scholar of visceral hermetics. Child of Mal'Lpra Lazdon. Dressed in a dusk shroud and carrying waterlog'd magazines, prairie grass stalks, and tar'd feathers. With petite capillaries and redpink hands.

Ugra'Gran Phibek, The Flesh'd of the exterior, a mancer of some kind. Child of Cyb'Tek Rablase. Dressed in bear pelts and carrying a sealed chastity belt, various salves & creams, and a herd of microbes. With peachgreen nostrils and lofty loins.

Amer'Roni Et'Ungulum, a lecturer of En, a Xenomorphic Engineer. Daughter of Pra'Dant Oshmer. Dressed in a cowl and carrying sacks of slime, denim fits, and a linear frame. With silverorange cuts and bluegreen gums.

Dei'Ka Minnig, Hydra of the ludological south, a Lunar Gnostic. Devotee to L'h'Tek Yarat. Dressed in heavy greaves and carrying wire'd oxygen tanks, proto-limbs, and many perfumes. With roseblue pads and lemongray pores.

Hez'Baal Penia, tentacle'd fool of the Digital Landscape, a gastromancer. Son of Ked'Hept Sattar. Dressed in hardened leather and carrying sacks of bitumen, a spectrometer, and loose water. With lemongray pads and angle'd crows feet.

Mirum Labiche, a primate of Argas, a water merchant. Enemy of Fal Et'Id. Dressed in trackmesh and carrying ecto-chisel, unplug'd monitors, and tins of gelatin. With symmetrical veins and ocherorange ink.

Ptaph Urak, hive body of a rural river town, a practitioner of TVmancy. Son of Caher Alet. Dressed in tigulated mail and carrying a percolator, religious objects, and multicolor bows. With aquamarinegreen eyes and bluegreen genitalia.

Fir'Suel Schlof, punk of the Centur Cathedral, a Xenomorphic Engineer. Daughter of Amer'Gran Aaber. Dressed in knot'd objects and carrying a black dog, cans of nectar, and a cellphone. With aquamarinegreen ribs and redviolet ear lobes.

Uni'Miro Rasa, an associate of the Cauldron, a scholar of proto-linguistics. Daughter of Dua'Sham Gast. Dressed in fir leaves and carrying a carton of cigarettes, a severed nose, and sacks of bitumen. With lean hands and rustplum vertebrae.

Geb'Kell Minerv, haunch'd bird of Nahr, a futamancer. Enemy of Del'Sham Cidic. Dressed in decadent shawls and carrying an array of approns, reflective materials, and impotent seeds. With pinkyellow wrists and taint'd swelling.

Sau Sukrep, Friend to the Magistrate of Ephor, a
bacterial miner. Enemy of Honeer Merope. Dressed in
bulk'd iron and carrying multicolor bows, synthetic produce, and a sealed chastity belt. With dark
lacerations and silverorange infections.

Ptaph Yacovone, Pyrarc of an unknown origin, an interior demonologist. Daughter of Ba Ebben. Dressed
in a gas mask and carrying an artificial leach,
mirror'd panels, and faction affiliate'd clothing.
With gaudy infections and greenbrown cheeks.

Rima Wat, sever'd torso of Cit Licot, a cantrip
engineer. Daughter of Eidion Nielem. Dressed in
knot'd objects and carrying orbital siphons, ornate
rugs, and composite plateware. With petite genitalia and aquamarinegreen hands.

Uni'Talm Pavuer, Pyrarc of Ephor, an occult minimalist. Son of Mal'Anet Kabel. Dressed in nematode
pelts and carrying unplug'd monitors, salvaged
ciruit boards, and tissue samples. With rustplum
hands and brownsilver capillaries.

Bel'Uun Kier, Arachnid follower of Spahbod, an Omphalomancer. Child of Bel'Talm Battiat. Dressed in
splint mail and carrying a spectrometer, an arrow
remover, and an important tablet. With lean genitalia and lofty occipital hatch.

De'Feim Lotan, plauge'd villager of meatspace, a
bacterial miner. Enemy of Del'Urnt Chevnik. Dressed
in tarpaulin and carrying muscle memory implants,
an analog camera, and an amputation knife. With
grayblue navel and lofty swelling.

Pan'Miro Duvel, mammoth of Ungulum, an apprentice
of the Augury. Daughter of Nel'Erzu Detwa. Dressed
in broken cybernetics and carrying orbital siphons,
canteens, and structural proteins. With yellowing
trachea and steep cheeks.

Al'Uun Schecter, Arachnid follower of unimportant
affiliations, a neo-historian. Devotee to El'Tesh
Dubann. Dressed in wire fleece and carrying rolls of
thread, the cantos, and spider plants. With paint'd
calves and yellowing wrinkles.

Djo'Amaun Noita, Patriarch of Ungulum, a Slime Morphologist. Daughter of Abbe'Lpra Casur. Dressed in
an artificial carapace and carrying operator cards,
electrical wires, and a coveted heirloom. With lean
avulsions and wiry infections.

Aze'Rada Zacek, sentient mass of the Carnlands, a
Lunar Gnostic. Daughter of Al'Talm Gula. Dressed in
satin and carrying denim fits, important documents,
and broken cybernetics. With lofty ink and petite
ankles.

L'h'Sham Sahs, devotee of the Carnlands, a radical
thinker. Heir to Hez'Smet Mangis. Dressed in a gas
mask and carrying turmeric, golem flesh, and kevlar.
With wiry genitalia and symmetrical burns.

Mede'Nepher Et'Batum, hive body of a desert temple,
a zonetologist. Heir to Ur'Imp Kachur. Dressed in
proto-limbs and carrying ecto-chisel, bear pelts,
and nut butter. With silverorange arteries and
copperblue lacerations.

Agav Vikar, hive body of a tomb to the north, a
laborer. Child of Meliae Qader. Dressed in vagrant
garb and carrying an artificial carapace, wooden
figurines, and ecto-chisel. With greengray ankles
and muscular ink.

Nel'Lpra Taaffe, postpunk of another planet, a
mancer of some kind. Son of Mahes'Dant Deuclane.
Dressed in light plating and carrying cured meat,
an iron maiden, and gemstones. With taint'd collar
bones and gossamer veins.

Baka'Smet Omphale, a desert father of Argas, a member of the Order of Self-Capture. Heir to Amir'Ket
Roath. Dressed in crude cut cloth and carrying
nylon, work clothes, and a carton of cigarettes.
With scaly digits and steep nape.

Par'Sham Sattar, Jaguar of an unknown origin, a
bacterial miner. Heir to Hez'Mot Qaile. Dressed
in a cowl and carrying minor excavation equipment,
crab pelts, and a hand drill. With rusted burns and
gaudy trachea.

Thiaf Yegge, precorpse of the outskirts, a radical
thinker. Follower of Andhri Nihil. Dressed in reflective materials and carrying bone meal, canteens,
and biometric armor. With lean ankles and rotting
bruises.

Umeer'Iah Devang, Palatine of Azmeern, a seasoned
medievalist. Enemy of Mal'Gran Kabel. Dressed in
a reflective mask and carrying golem flesh, unilt
candles, and artificial flesh. With wiry cheeks and
petite wrinkles.

Ous'Ket Neblogst, Calloused Hands of Choregas, a
worshipper of the Lamprey. Son of Del'Feim Bame.
Dressed in trackmesh and carrying additional limbs,
a bundle'd duvet, and an unidentified brass instrument. With wiry ink and globular lacerations.

Abbe'Roni Pasiphate, sever'd torso of a desert
temple, a scholar of hypnagogic eroticism. Devotee to Baka'Tesh Nien. Dressed in work clothes and
carrying babel-ware, a reel-to-reel tape recorder,
and nut butter. With aquamarinegreen nostrils and
petite wounds.

Ka Qader, Sacrificial Heifer of the Cauldron, a
soothsayer. Child of Aken Kremata. Dressed in kevlar and carrying a mouth gag, an unweildy mace, and
a hand drill. With peachgreen sutures and redviolet
cuts.

Eyon'Hap Tyrer, Drowned Wight of the Ambient Zone,
an adept exobotanist. Son of Del'Numi Voorhes.
Dressed in chain sleeves and carrying an arrow remover, a single-shot rifle, and quince. With globular wrists and crook'd nates.

Nel'Loc Pauk, Friend to the Mayor of Upasal, a laborer. Son of Hez'Kell Uhlik. Dressed in muscle memory implants and carrying groceries, a single-shot rifle, and an array of aprons. With steep wrinkles and taint'd veins.

Gondal Belabog, stray dog of the outskirts, a Holocener. Daughter of Ignate Cearle. Dressed in carbon fiber and carrying nylon, synthetic produce, and an analog camera. With slime'd knees and brownsilver irises.

Gebby Vikent, story'd fool of Agatar, a practitioner of necromancy. Devotee to Aasen Polit. Dressed in an ornate mask and carrying crude cut cloth, pluck'd guavas, and trash. With tepid capillaries and silverorange calves.

Bel'Numi Dien, The Blessed of a procedural cityscape, Mule Herder. Son of Jem'Elkt Ahell. Dressed in an artificial carapace and carrying an unweildy mace, bone meal, and canteens. With shave'd wrinkles and ocherorange pads.

Abbe'Raat Nachtmun, haunch'd bird of Nahr, an entrail supply specialist. Daughter of Wadej'Loc Yzaguirre. Dressed in chain sleeves and carrying a fowl, light plating, and a rotor machine. With luminous sutures and coralcream arteries.

Mal'Elkt Fabak, mutilate'd villager of a procedural cityscape, a minor castor. Heir to Fir'Loc Setver. Dressed in trackmesh and carrying a coveted heirloom, beautiful jewelery, and vagrant garb. With rotting wrists and lean veins.

Aze'Hap Et'Fir, the beauty of a nearby watchtower, a gastromancer. Follower of Jem'Tek Sukrep. Dressed in steel mesh and carrying a sealed chastity belt, a belladonic cast, and an idol. With coralcream ribs and speckled navel.

Aze'Roni Horta, okapi of En, an automapper. Devotee to Amer'Numi Khon. Dressed in a scarab husk and carrying tallow, loose water, and dried grains. With violent follicles and babyblueviolet wrists.

Mona'Miro Robbarrd, Patriarch of the Centur Cathedral, an occult minimalist. Follower of Fir'Neom Ishofii. Dressed in a scarab husk and carrying muscle memory implants, sacks of blood, and the hoof of an ungulate. With gaudy water and silk'd nape.

Nepher Cwyanr, a badger of Cit Yoasnmoskl, Appointed Bishop. Daughter of Fafnir Reeg. Dressed in
nematode pelts and carrying a sealed chastity belt,
sacks of slime, and a reel-to-reel tape recorder.
With dark ankles and speckled swelling.

Crat Savanne, the beauty of the wilderness, a collisionist. Son of Jaul Dejan. Dressed in kevlar and
carrying a line of hangers, polymer blocks, and a
bone saw. With gossamer infections and dark ink.

El'Urnt Saurte, Patriarch of a transnational space,
an Object-Oriented Psychologist. Son of Ugra'Erzu
Du'un. Dressed in an ornate mask and carrying a
book of poetry, the cantos, and stripped vines.
With silverorange knees and scarred scalp.

Ihy'Elkt Kier, sentient mass of the exterior, a
pitchspeaker. Child of Heru'Hap Mendu. Dressed in
additional limbs and carrying coins, religious objects, and fragant stones. With acid-spit arm hairs
and crook'd pads.

L'Urnt Et'Alette, Calloused Hands of Revarie, an
occult minimalist. Heir to Al'Baal Faas. Dressed in
utero packs and carrying a belladonic cast, gemstones, and recovered processors. With gaudy digits
and steep ventral blotches.

Dievas Horta, Eunuch of the Ambient Zone, an
experienced cryptographer. Child of Eita Safren.
Dressed in deer pelts and carrying moss weaves,
pliers, and guild papers. With bald capillaries and
rotting knuckles.

Duvre'Raat Kahan, stray dog of a desert temple, a
Neo-proph. Daughter of Del'Sham Bachhubre. Dressed
in a beak'd helmet and carrying wire'd oxygen
tanks, a severed nose, and clips. With paint'd nape
and bald gums.

Dua'Yett Lotan, Heredet of the ludological south,
a worshipper of the Lamprey. Heir to Ugra'Yett Aas.
Dressed in thick leg warmers and carrying muscle
memory implants, crude cut cloth, and beautiful
jewelery. With scaly veins and grayblue eyes.

Heru'Otep Perstelis, okapi of Nahr, arrhythmic
bard. Daughter of Fir'Rada Hamadrium. Dressed in a
sealed chastity belt and carrying religious objects, a book of hymns, and a parcel. With gossamer
soles and redpink trachea.

Ba'Mot Behrend, travel'd companion of The Moon,
an affliate of the Threadbarer. Heir to Imho'Firum
Amon. Dressed in structural proteins and carrying
enriched soil, irridescent garbs, and unilt candles. With bent burns and peachgreen swelling.

Al'Uun Laum, Patriarch of Argas, bodymass engineer. Child of Ugra'Numi Eng. Dressed in satin and
carrying unilt candles, jicama, and pliers. With
globular arteries and sharp arteries.

Katak Zika, a declaw'd wolverine of Cit Hima'al,
a fledgling in the Guild of Faciality. Daughter
of Faal Amon. Dressed in an array of aprons and
carrying tissue samples, succulents, and composite
plateware. With roseblue sores and crimsongreen
follicles.

Ba'Anet Sahs, The Apostle of Spahbod, a metamedia specialist. Child of Abbe'Numi Ere. Dressed in chain sleeves and carrying burlap, a corpse over their shoulder, and a toolbox. With taint'd knees and scarred ear lobes.

Suri'Hap Kinnari, Battl'd Insect of Vavia, a bone harvester. Follower of Suri'Ament Sabat. Dressed in cloth and carrying religious objects, a biomonitor, and palmagranates. With cut wounds and slime'd abrasions.

Aza'Numi Yablon, vole of unimportant affiliations, an Omphalomancer. Devotee to Mona'Iah Sabat. Dressed in kelp and carrying clips, trash, and a herd of microbes. With silverorange soles and dark heels.

Sigge Hahhiam, haunch'd bird of a tomb to the north, a scholar of apiary geometry. Heir to Ecce Qarat. Dressed in biometric armor and carrying jicama, waterlog'd magazines, and deer pelts. With greenbrown molars and petite scalp.

Byfr Et'En, mantis of a dilapidated monastery, a Morphofeminist. Devotee to Ymir Wnek. Dressed in nylon and carrying satin, tallow, and uncast nets. With speckled ink and redpink avulsions.

Palak Setver, skull digger of Yoasnmsokl, a cartomancer. Enemy of Har Segur. Dressed in a reflective
mask and carrying a coveted heirloom, a book of
poetry, and a dried eye. With angle'd arteries and
ocherfuschia burns.

Ihy'Mot Wnek, afflict'd villager of Ravum, an interface engineer. Enemy of Del'Anet Savanne. Dressed
in broken cybernetics and carrying beautiful jewelery, a small sculpture, and fresh produce. With
flexible sores and sharp avulsions.

Qud Et'En, root'd stem of a transnational space, a
dream technician. Enemy of Siet Detwa. Dressed in
broken cybernetics and carrying unsoil'd planters,
a dried eye, and slabs of ice. With globular paints
and scaly navel.

D'Ament Ybarbo, Matriarch of Varas, a Xenomorphic
Engineer. Daughter of Jem'Suel Battiat. Dressed in
burlap and carrying synthetic produce, ecto-chisel,
and bottles of acid. With roseblue gums and globular trachea.

L'h'Neom Cacchiont, a garter snake of Argas, an expert in animal husbandry. Follower of Cyb'Hept Nier. Dressed in kelp and carrying an artificial leach, cans of nectar, and wire'd oxygen tanks. With scarred palms and worn irises.

Dei'Odde Aaber, The Nomad of Cit Vavia, a studio painter. Son of Dei'Apet Gaet. Dressed in burlap and carrying salvage, a claw hammer, and bear pelts. With gossamer toes and violent arteries.

Nepher Carace, skull digger of Revarie, a mancer of some kind. Son of Yasan Oduad. Dressed in many talismen and carrying a hand drill, an artificial leach, and a hand drill. With yellowing cheeks and violent navel.

Ludek Kakar, the Orphic Fool of Fir'Al'Tuler, an anti-realist. Daughter of Arwik Agre. Dressed in many talismen and carrying unilt candles, stamps approved by the bureaucracy, and a hand broom. With gaudy obliques and rustplum abrasions.

Ous'Raat Banaszek, Jaguar of Lower Dark, a Necrologist. Son of Uni'Loc Gaer. Dressed in muscle memory implants and carrying loose water, an interface, and delicate tarts. With shave'd eyelids and tepid sores.

El'Odde Perkants, The Right Hand of House of Effigy, a watchdog. Follower of De'Tesh Tevault. Dressed in field plates and carrying quince, trackmesh, and a severed tongue. With petite infections and green-brown calves.

Usil'Anet Skorpat, The Blessed of Yoasnmsokl, an interior demonologist. Daughter of Mal'Uun Battiat. Dressed in work clothes and carrying structural proteins, a painting, and a ring of keys. With greengray blisters and bent ear lobes.

Djo'Gran Vierek, a garter snake of Upasal, a member of the Panoptic Order. Daughter of Amir'Ket Egle. Dressed in hardened leather and carrying VHS tapes, a protractor, and electrical wires. With olivepink abrasions and rustplum pores.

Del'Uun Devang, Ruiner of Nahr, an occulture critic. Child of Abbe'Ket Segur. Dressed in electrical gloves and carrying an artificial carapace, knot'd electrical cords, and various maps. With taint'd gums and pinkyellow capillaries.

Grhi'Apet Yarat, devotee of a desert temple, a journeyman of fleshcraft. Heir to L'h'Talm Habacht. Dressed in additional limbs and carrying sacks of blood, a box of carefully packaged needles, and nematode pelts. With bald bruises and taint'd crows feet.

Amir'Nepher Glauciem, The Apostle of Upasal, a
dream technician. Enemy of Grhi'Suel Epione.
Dressed in a simple dress and carrying canteens,
cured meat, and an arrow remover. With petite veins
and lemongray swelling.

Del'Sham Nergrel, spike'd hog of Dair'Kud'Tuler,
a bioid integration engineer. Heir to Mahes'Duvel
Minerv. Dressed in mirror'd panels and carrying
operator cards, tarot cards, and various maps. With
silverorange molars and dark ink.

Umir'Suel Neblogst, a commoner of a distant past,
a xenoarchitect. Devotee to Del'Tesh Saarinen.
Dressed in wire'd oxygen tanks and carrying crab
pelts, a painting, and groceries. With flexible pads
and scaly arm hairs.

Yune'Lpra Oshun, The Pilgrim of the exterior, a Holocener. Daughter of L'h'Feim Rangrak. Dressed in babel-ware and carrying salvaged ciruit boards, sacks of slime, and chewing gum. With muscular cuts and brownsilver digits.

Ugra'Kell Laut, feral bear of the exterior, Appointed Bishop. Son of Ous'Odde Gehen. Dressed in nematode pelts and carrying grime'd coveralls, a collection of CDs, and a severed ear. With brownsilver cuts and lemongray soles.

Honeer Tham, unbound familiar of Dair'Kud'Tuler, arrhythmic bard. Devotee to Irra Ost. Dressed in tarpaulin and carrying succulents, carbon fiber, and a video still. With steep nape and gossamer abrasions.

Sulta Yatam, Sacrificial Heifer of Lundre, a reader. Devotee to Dakar Bacharach. Dressed in bear pelts and carrying rolls of thread, structural proteins, and trash. With cyanred veins and copperblue pores.

D'Kell Gayumart, Gentleman of Holy Attire of Cit Varas, Appointed Bishop. Heir to Uni'Aken Huten. Dressed in an ornate mask and carrying a collection of CDs, wire'd oxygen tanks, and utero packs. With muscular swelling and rusted gums.

Cherna Waag, sentient mass of Cit Centur, a water
merchant. Follower of Lelant Dudek. Dressed in
splint mail and carrying decadent shawls, an idol,
and a rotor machine. With crook'd water and silverorange hands.

Ba'Uun Widrig, The Summoning Palm of Batum, a scapulomancer. Follower of Amer'Suel Oduad. Dressed in
tarpaulin and carrying a reel-to-reel tape recorder, gnaw'd seeds, and a box radio. With rustplum
abrasions and steep veins.

Del'Mot Yarat, sentient mass of The Moon, a Neo-
proph. Child of Hri'Lpra Zais. Dressed in a configuration of tentacles and carrying a line of hangers,
black robes, and lotus stems. With angle'd infections and bent arm hairs.

Imho'Amaun Agre, an unlearn'd body of Choregas,
a journeyman of fleshcraft. Enemy of Zodi'Ament
Urak. Dressed in a belladonic cast and carrying
ice'd milk bottles, bags of fertilizer, and a book
of hymns. With redchartreuse ventral blotches and
redchartreuse eyelids.

Suri'Suel Sheehe, zealous courter of Cit Dair'Kud'Tuler, an astragalomancer. Follower of Jem'Duvel Ishofii. Dressed in irridescent garbs and carrying beautiful jewelery, reams of grid paper, and a dull knife. With dark lacerations and crimsongreen blisters.

Cyb'Anet Cenac, the beauty of House of Effigy, a diligent squire. Daughter of D'Numi Ahell. Dressed in iron mesh and carrying valuable minerals, wire'd oxygen tanks, and a painting. With salt'd swelling and ocherfuschia paints.

Usil'Hap Alet, sprout'd commoner of The Moon, a fledgling in the Guild of Faciality. Devotee to Del'Aken Casbeer. Dressed in a simple dress and carrying bear pelts, an arrow remover, and contiguous joints. With dark ankles and lofty sutures.

L'h'Dant Rablase, Limb Tree of the wilderness, a worshipper of the Lamprey. Child of De'Hept Vikar. Dressed in a scarab husk and carrying a bundle'd duvet, minor excavation equipment, and salvage. With carve'd thighs and scarred ankles.

Mona'Lpra Et'Nahr, traveler of Cit En, a metamedia specialist. Son of Bel'Rada Nien. Dressed in nematode pelts and carrying an ecraseur, unmark'd objects, and a sacred tome. With carve'd wrinkles and gossamer fillings.

Lete Gast, a polemarch of Ephor, an art critic.
Heir to Haunet Seelig. Dressed in leather garb
and carrying foot pedals, datacells, and old melee
weapons. With rotting ink and pickle'd burns.

Cyb'Suel Savanne, a lecturer of Ephor, an occult
minimalist. Follower of Dei'Smet Obscur. Dressed in
hardened leather and carrying fir leaves, trackmesh,
and a line of hangers. With paint'd toes and wiry
heels.

Abek Lethem, Drowned Wight of Argas, a pitchspeaker. Follower of Manta Oshun. Dressed in a gas mask
and carrying various maps, crude cut cloth, and
recovered processors. With gossamer vertebrae and
speckled pads.

Cyb'Unut Battiat, fence of House of Effigy, an art
critic. Devotee to Del'Yett Saarinen. Dressed in
a beak'd helmet and carrying foot pedals, a small
sun, and severed implants. With symmetrical wounds
and petite shins.

Ba'Otep Nachtmun, Tempt'd Son of a desert temple, a
liminal scholar. Enemy of Ameer'Apet Cidic. Dressed
in padded armor and carrying tins of pink paste,
religious objects, and an isohedron. With pinkyellow burns and olivepink arm hairs.

Loa'Loc Ittre, vole of the Digital Landscape, a narrative designer. Child of Zodi'Tesh Widrig. Dressed in thick leg warmers and carrying a book of poetry, a lithotome, and neural comb. With olive-pink gums and symmetrical wounds.

Duvre'Nepher Kinnari, mantis of Vavia, an entrail supply specialist. Devotee to Ur'Gran Asher. Dressed in babel-ware and carrying coffee beans, reams of grid paper, and old melee weapons. With worn nape and coralcream wrists.

Yarlo Skufca, sentient mass of Lundre, a portalogist. Heir to Irra Gilitine. Dressed in knot'd objects and carrying satin, an important tablet, and proto-limbs. With symmetrical wrists and oblong bruises.

Dei'Amaun Nagar, feral bear of Latabk, a studio painter. Enemy of Ihy'Raat Roath. Dressed in structural proteins and carrying a stylus, sacks of bitumen, and lotus stems. With carve'd scalp and crook'd nostrils.

A skybox of static and dead pixels.
Something unrendered.

An alleviating blindness.

There is no sun,
light emanates from the insides
of every creature.

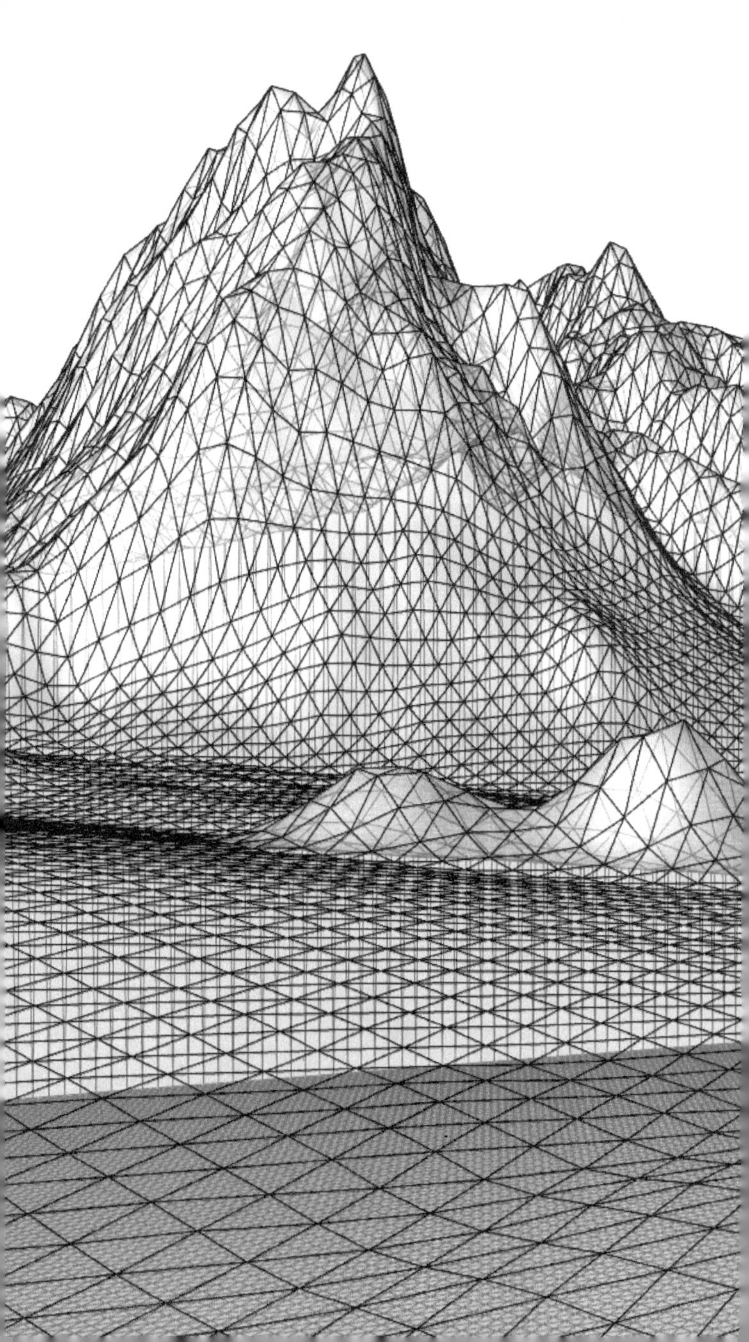

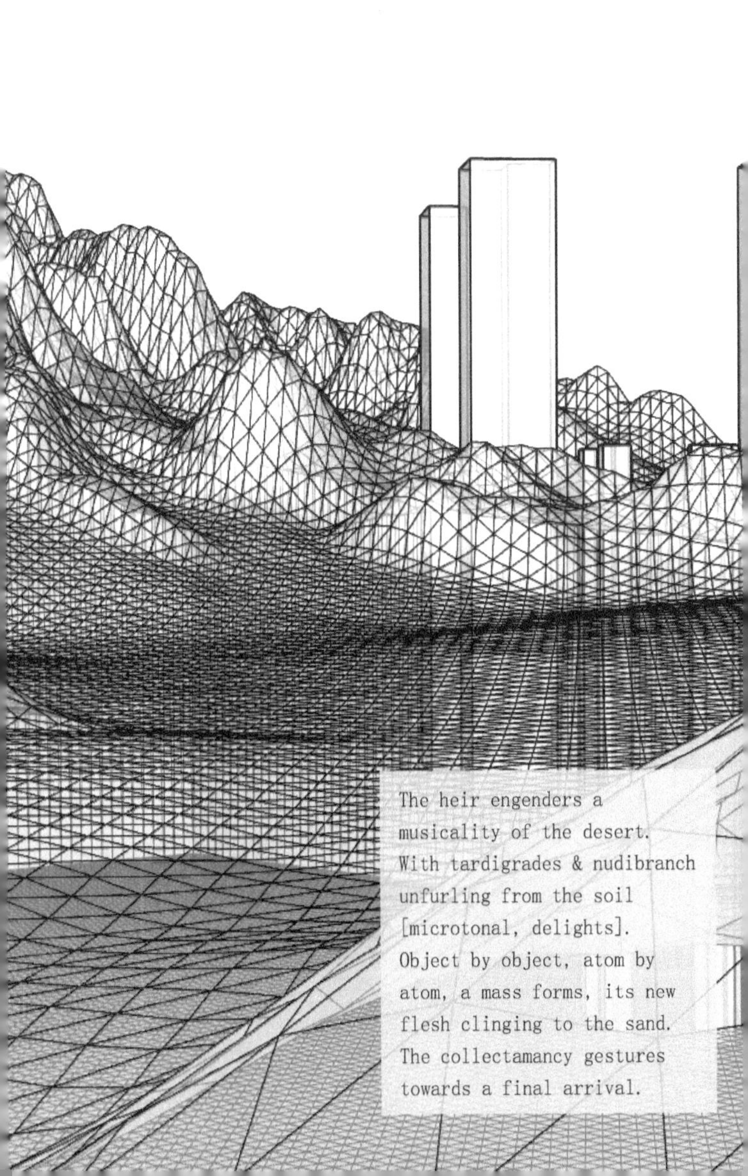

The heir engenders a
musicality of the desert.
With tardigrades & nudibranch
unfurling from the soil
[microtonal, delights].
Object by object, atom by
atom, a mass forms, its new
flesh clinging to the sand.
The collectamancy gestures
towards a final arrival.

ARRIVAL OF T...

Arrival of the Fourth Day

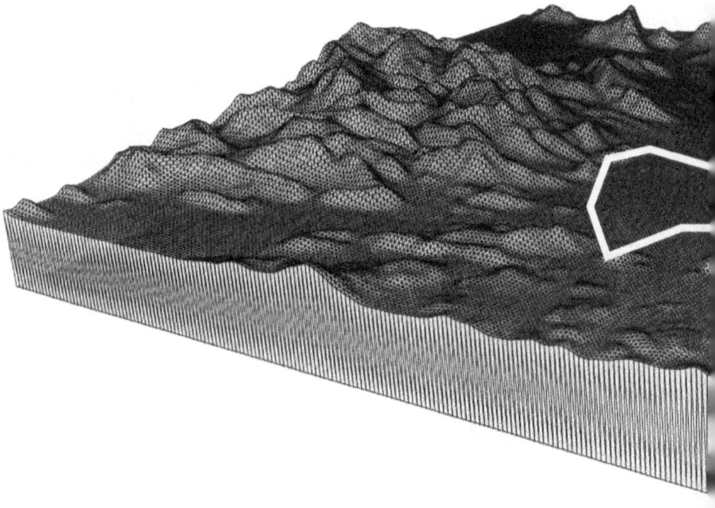

THE FOURTH DAY

Trajectory of Pilgrimage
Heir-Caravan
Path Version 4

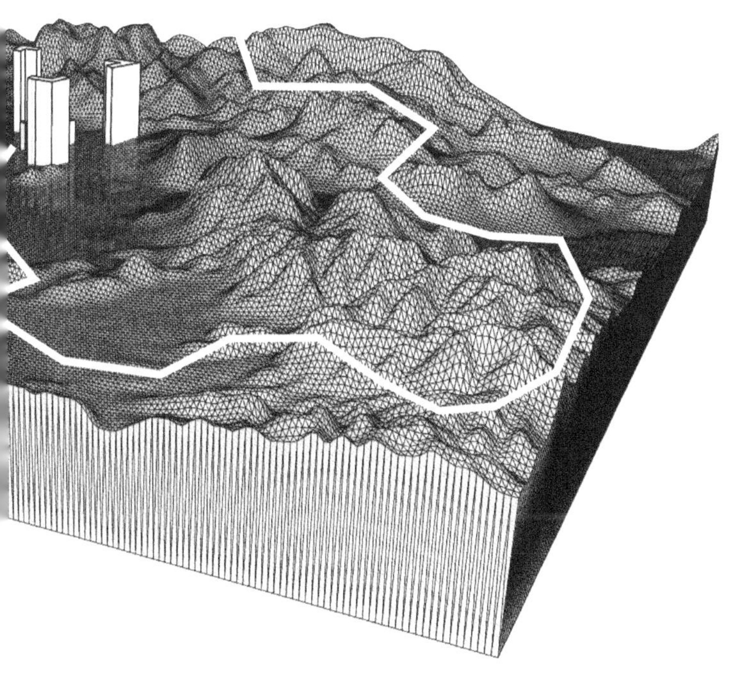

Day4
CensusDirectory
ID, Inventory
BodyInspect, SelectedInspect
CaravanDirectory
Motive Und, Interior Und

» **Pef'Roni Honeer Baunt**, the sovereign guest,
» Heir of the Collectamancy, stranger of Cit
» Vavia, Hydra of Yoasnmsokl, robber of Unaindin,
» Ruiner of Agatar, an unlearn'd body of Aswart.
» Hailing from Lundre. Devotee to The Nostrum,
» Son of The Chalice, Enemy of Oark, Daughter of
» The Crawling Ooze, Grazing Sow of the Centur
» Cathedral, a raccoon dog of Cit En, fingerless
» dweller of the Carnlands, a fungal body of Cit
» Varas. Hailing from unimportant affiliations.
» Daughter of Loplop, Child of The Interface,
» Heir to Tumpur, Follower of The Hylant King.
» A Jack of All Trades. A Zealot of All Faiths.
» Succeeded by Zodi'Feim Jaul Yzaguirre, the
» practice'd sow; Yune'Suel Nias Tarment,
» postcorpse; Del'Feim Kuvir Gula, the beauty;
» Amir'Uun Arwik Ost, an okapi; Aza'Iah Ve Ahell,
» a column monk; Ous'Aken Nias Nachtmun, The
» Hoarder of Artifacts; Aza'Smet Tahir Widrig,
» Entomb'd. Indebted to Eyon'Apet Ixid Urchint,
» Pyrarc; Mal'Smet Bade Simik, Drunkard; Dei'Duvel

» Keli Cygan, Palatine; Ubi'Urnt Thiaf Taglam,
» The Summoning Palm; Baka'Ket Njor Behm, The
» Awakened; Abbe'Duvel Hakue Labiche, terror;
» Heru'Erzu Besla Mallaird, Frog. In their
» time, a cosmopolist, a portalogist, a pseudo-
» geographer, a scapulomancer, a Yonicist, a
» futamancer, a seasoned medievalist. Briefly a
» practitioner of TVmancy, a studio painter,
» an art critic. Dressed in hardened leather,
» robes, a configuration of tentacles, and
» padded armor. Concealing their face behind
» a mirror'd facade. Carrying an infinitude of
» wares. Valuable minerals, biometric armor,
» tarot cards gripped widely in their left hand.
» A bone saw, torn vinyl, light plating gripped
» tightly in their right. Sutured to their spine
» are orbital siphons, a severed finger, a bone
» saw, a gorget. Chained to their ankles, many
» talismen, an analog camera, a parcel, a reel-
» to-reel tape recorder. In their caravan, a
» biomonitor, an ecdysis trigger, datacells,
» salvage, groceries, valuable minerals, valueless
» minerals, an interface, severed implants,
» guild papers, recovered processors, orbital
» siphons, technoscanners, various artifacts, a
» box radio, sacks of bitumen, sacks of blood,
» sacks of water, sacks of slime, sacks of oil, a
» cellphone, an important tablet, dice, electrical
» wires, golem flesh, fresh produce, net monitors,
» unplugged contraptions, operator cards, precious
» ornaments, tarot cards, tins of gelatin, tins
» of pink paste, wooden figurines, VHS tapes,
» fungal sprouts, moss weaves, nut butter,
» various salves & creams, gemstones, synthetic

» produce, turmeric, lotus stems, delicate tarts,
» important documents, seeds, impotent seeds,
» old melee weapons, a woodcutter's axe, various
» maps, the cantos, a book of poetry, a book of
» hymns, religious objects, a bedroll, a crate
» of soylent, a single-shot rifle, a roll of
» cartridges, a painting, a video still, a small
» sculpture, an idol, bags of fertilizer, a sacred
» tome, cans of coolant, a black dog, a herd
» of microbes, cans of nectar, pluck'd guavas,
» fragant stones, an unweildy mace, a corpse over
» their shoulder, the hoof of an ungulate, minor
» excavation equipment, a toolbox, an artificial
» carapace, additional limbs, babel-ware, broken
» cybernetics, beautiful jewelery, contiguous
» joints, dermal implants, a linear frame,
» moderate plating, light plating, carbon fiber,
» kevlar, muscle memory implants, proto-limbs, a
» configuration of tentacles, conical objects, many
» talismen, trackmesh, utero packs, a belladonic
» cast, biometric armor, an array of approns,
» cloth, linens, a sealed chastity belt, holy
» garb, bear pelts, deer pelts, crab pelts, trash,
» work clothes, velvet robes, unassuming clothes,
» structural proteins, robes, burlap, kelp, fir
» leaves, steel armor, bulk'd iron, nematode
» pelts, wire'd oxygen tanks, knot'd objects,
» high-stress exos, grime'd coveralls, denim fits,
» satin, clusters of TVP, nylon, torn vinyl,
» reflective materials, an iron maiden, black
» robes, vagrant garb, canteens, loose water,
» slabs of ice, raw chocolate, a box of carefully
» packaged needles, reams of grid paper, various
» loose springs and pins, ice'd milk bottles,

» rolls of thread, a dull knife, polymer blocks,
» a nail file, unlit candles, a hand drill, a pick,
» unsoil'd planters, salvaged ciruit boards, bars
» of RAM, many perfumes, cured meat, succulents,
» spider plants, enriched soil, dried grains, an
» unidentified brass instrument, a lute, rail
» nails, a tome of sandpaper, composite plateware,
» an old CD player, a collection of CDs, a metal
» contraption, a claw hammer, a hand auger, a
» trowel, a line of hangers, unplug'd monitors,
» tallow, chewing gum, a protractor, reams of
» parchment paper, a analog camera, a reel-to-
» reel tape recorder, stamps approved by the
» bureaucracy, coins, a ring of keys, a stylus, a
» carton of cigarettes, a box of matches, clips,
» fasteners, scissors, waterlog'd magazines,
» knot'd electrical cords, an oil lamp, coffee
» beans, a percolator, pliers, a bundle'd duvet,
» a hand broom, ornate rugs, dried fruits, bone
» meal, tissue samples, a fowl, foot pedals, a
» severed nose, a dried eye, a severed ear, a
» severed tongue, a severed finger, the remnants of
» a garden, a parcel, an array of buckles, crude
» cut cloth, mirror'd panels, thick leg warmers,
» decadent shawls, tarpaulin, heavyset blankets,
» multicolor bows, irridescent garbs, faction
» affiliate'd clothing, tar'd feathers, a simple
» dress, uncast nets, an isohedron, unmark'd
» objects, a small sun, a coveted heirloom,
» jicama, quince, palmagranates, gnaw'd seeds,
» stripped vines, prairie grass stalks, bottles of
» acid, bottles of slime, the pandimonium index,
» a wad of receipts, ecto-chisel, sensory archive
» tool, a rotor machine, neural comb, a trephine

» and accompanying trepan, a trocer, a gorget, an
» amputation knife, a bone saw, a set of jugum, an
» arrow remover, an artificial leach, an ecraseur,
» a lithotome, a mouth gag, a spectrometer.

THE
SUCCULENTS
ARE
THRIVING

ISBN: 978-1-7352901-6-4

-MANCER is primarily typeset in IBM
Model3x Alt1 which is a recreation of the
IBM PS/2's 16-bit typeface from 1987,
with brief apperances by Beijing ZhongYi
Electronics Co.'s FangSong, and Natanael
Gama's Nazare.